PRAIS… AN…

"Groe brings both … city known to the Vikings as Miklagard to life through her strong characters. Readers will watch for Groe's next historical romance."

—*Booklist*

"From Scandinavia to the Byzantine slave markets, this steamy love story calls to mind the great mistresses of the genre: Small, Henley and Mason. Filled with forbidden love, betrayal, redemption and hope, Groe's strong start will leave readers eager for more."

—*Romantic Times*

"Ms. Groe is a fresh new voice in romance. Dramatic and stirring, *Maidensong* will leave you clamoring for more of Diana Groe's work."

—Connie Mason, *New York Times* Bestselling Author of *A Taste of Paradise*

"This story is fast-paced and extremely enjoyable. If you enjoy a passionate tale told across the tapestry of a well-woven historical backdrop, then you must pick up this book!"

—*Historical Romance Writers*

"*Maidensong* is a beautifully written epic tale of love, honor, and sacrifice…."

—… Reviews Today

"*Maid*… …urney…. Diana Groe's … amount of storytelling … ney—you'll be glad yo…

—Fresh Fiction

"The novel is very refreshing…unique."

—All About Romance

A VIKING BY ANY OTHER NAME...

"Is that all I am in your eyes? Just a Northman?" When Brenna tried to pull away, he tugged her in close and cupped her chin. "Can you not say my true name? Not even once?"

He leaned toward her, his deep eyes dark in the moonlight. His mouth was so close, one corner turned slightly up. Brenna gulped, wondering what that mouth might taste like.

"Jorand," she said softly.

The name was nearly swallowed up as his lips covered hers in a kiss both sudden and inevitable. Her first impulse was to pull away, but his mouth beguiled her. It was not the kind of kiss she expected from a man like him.

His mouth was warm and sure, pressing against hers just enough to let her know she'd been kissed before he pulled back. It was as sweet a kiss as she could imagine. A kiss that wanted to give, not take. A kiss that left no bitterness in its wake.

"There now, that wasn't so terrible, was it?" he asked.

"Saying your name or letting you kiss me?"

"Both."

Her lips twitched in a suppressed smile. "It was tolerable."

"Just tolerable?" He grinned. "I can do better than that."

Other *Leisure* books by Diana Groe:

MAIDENSONG

ERINSONG

DIANA GROE

LEISURE BOOKS NEW YORK CITY

A LEISURE BOOK®

November 2006

Published by

Dorchester Publishing Co., Inc.
200 Madison Avenue
New York, NY 10016

ISBN 0-8439-5789-1

Printed in the United States of America.

ERINSONG

CHAPTER ONE

A shriek rent the air.

Brenna dropped the bucket of mussels and ran toward the sound. She shouldn't have let Moira wander away. If anything happened to her younger sister, their father would never forgive her.

She'd never forgive herself.

Fear made her wing-footed. When she rounded the outcropping of dark basalt, she found Moira cautiously circling a body on the sand. It was a man curled on his side, one long arm draped over a wooden cask.

Brenna breathed out a sigh. God be praised, Moira was unhurt.

"Is he dead, do ye think?" her sister asked.

"Seems to be." Brenna used the butt of her walking stick to push the man's shoulder and roll him onto his back. He flopped over as lifelessly as a beached porpoise. Dark blood crusted at his hairline where he'd obviously taken a blow.

"Oh, he's a fine strong lad. Look at the arms on him, Brenna."

The stranger was even more heavily muscled than the local smith, and though he wasn't stretched out to full length, Brenna could see that if he were standing upright, he would be far taller than any man in her father's keep. His pale hair was a tangled mess, but even dusted with brine and sand, the man's face reminded Brenna of the fierce warlike angels painted on the scriptorium walls at Clonmacnoise Abbey—stern and forbidding, but heart-stoppingly beautiful.

Brenna's gaze fell on the runic symbols carved into the hilt of the knife at the man's waist. Her lip curled with loathing. "One of the *Normanni.*"

"A Northman?" Moira leaned closer to him. "Mother used to frighten us with stories of Northmen when we were little, but even though they've raided near us, I've never seen one in all me living life." She cocked a questioning brow at Brenna. "Do ye mean to tell me ye have?"

"Aye, though I wish I had not." Brenna's voice was flat and she raised the pointed end of her staff toward the still figure.

"Are all Northmen so fair, then?"

"No, not all," Brenna said through clenched jaw.

"This one surely is. He's so pretty. 'Tis a pity he's dead." Moira reached down to smooth a damp lock of hair from the man's cheek.

Suddenly his eyelids flew open, and he grabbed Moira's wrist. She screamed and tried to pull away, but the stranger's grip was firm.

No, not this time, Brenna thought.

White-hot rage surged through her and a low growl erupted from the back of her throat. The *Ostman* heathen dared put his filthy hand on her sister. Almost in reflex, she jabbed his thigh with her staff, burying the sharp point into his flesh. Her stomach lurched at the way the shaft stuck, embedded in the man's heavy muscle. Brenna jerked backward on it, but couldn't pull it free for another stab.

The good nuns at Clonmacnoise had admonished her that anger, or any other strong passion for that matter, was a sin. But Brenna knew if she were able, she'd pound the man into raw meat before the fury inside her was quelled.

Eyes wide with surprise, the stranger howled and released Moira.

"Run!" Brenna ordered. Her younger sister fled, disappearing around the rocks, fleet-footed as a hind.

The man wrapped his long fingers around Brenna's makeshift spear and yanked it from his leg with a grunt and a spurt of blood. Then he jerked the other end of the staff from her grasp.

Despite his injury, the man rose to his feet, blood spreading on the dun-colored leggings and streaking toward his knee. He tossed her stick into the gorse bushes. Then he turned to face her, his handsome features marred by a black frown.

For one paralyzing moment, Brenna couldn't breathe. The lapping of the waves played over in her head like a half-remembered song. A gull screamed and she was sharply aware of the fishy reek of the sea. The Northman blocked her way.

She feinted to throw him off balance, then turned and raced down the beach in the opposite direction Moira had fled. She heard the man's footfalls pounding behind her and lengthened her stride. He shouted something to her in an evil-sounding language, and though his tone wasn't threatening, she wouldn't be tricked by the likes of him.

Surely she could outrun a half-drowned man with a hole in his leg. Surely she could—

She felt a blow to her lower back as the man lunged, wrapping his arms around her waist. Brenna pitched headlong into the gritty sand. They rolled together, over and over, Brenna scrambling to get away, the man grasping at her to keep her with him. When they finally came to a stop, Brenna was pinned beneath the big man's body.

"Get off me, ye *Finn-Gall* demon!" Brenna pummeled his chest with her fists till the man caught up her hands and pressed them into the sand above her head. She flailed her feet trying to kick him, but he wrapped his long legs around hers, binding her fast.

All she had left were words, and she spewed out the most hateful curses she'd ever heard. She invoked every plague imaginable to rain down on the stranger's golden head and offered his immortal soul to Beelzebub with all the venom she could muster.

The man didn't blink an eyelash, his impossibly blue eyes going darker by the moment. His face hovered over hers, his expression unreadable. He let her rant until she was utterly spent and gasping.

"That's the best string of insults I've ever heard," he said calmly. The corners of his mouth turned up in a wry smile despite the furrow between his dark brows.

Brenna felt the blood rush from her face.

"Ye understand me?"

"Let me see. You seem to think I'm something called a succubus from the Netherworld and you invited the Prince of Darkness, whoever he is, to feast on my liver. *Ja*, girl, I think I understand you."

Brenna felt his belly quiver as if he suppressed a

laugh. In spite of the way his brows knit together, he seemed genuinely amused, Devil take him.

"How is it ye speak our tongue?"

The smile faded and the man's frown deepened. "I . . . don't know."

He continued to study her face as if the answer might be found there. Though his body felt heavy on hers, he lay perfectly still, making no threatening movements.

That wouldn't last long, Brenna suspected.

If she could keep the man talking, distract him a bit, maybe she'd be able to get away. Surely Moira had arrived back at the keep by now. Da and the men would be grabbing their bows and sprinting toward the beach to her rescue. She drew a shaky breath, taking heart at the thought that the fighting men of Erin might pop over the hillock at any moment. "Where will ye be coming from?"

A grimace creased the Northman's face, and his eyes flitted back and forth in their reddened sockets. He'd spent quite some time in the sea, Brenna realized.

"I don't know." His voice was a hoarse whisper.

"Don't know? Many's the man who's lost his way and doesn't know where he is, but sure and ye are the first I've seen who couldn't say where he'd been."

The warm stickiness of the man's blood seeped through the fabric of her tunic. Maybe blood loss accounted for the panic flickering across the man's features. She must have jabbed him deeper than she thought.

"How did ye find yourself in the sea?" she asked.

His eyes rolled again, as though searching for the answer. His grip loosened, but she still couldn't escape. At least he hadn't tried to slobber on her or ruck up her skirt. Though his body pressed hers into the sand, he showed little interest in her. He seemed to be more confused than anything else.

"Ye don't know much, do ye?" She arched a brow at him. "Maybe ye'll be telling me your name, then?"

"My name," he repeated woodenly.

"Aye, 'tis not a hard thing, surely." She managed to slide her hands out of his grasp, but he didn't seem to notice. "All God's creatures have names. Even Northmen, I'd wager."

The man pressed his hands against her cheeks, holding her head immobile, and stared into Brenna's eyes. His chest heaved and she silently cursed herself for baiting him.

Then to her surprise, he rolled off her and sat up. She crabbed backward, scuttling away from him, and scrambled to her feet.

Brenna had every intention of dashing over the small rise of sand and into the hills, but the Northman was behaving so strangely, taking no notice of her at all. And besides, if she stayed to keep an eye on him, Da would be proud she hadn't let him get away. It wasn't much, but if she showed a bit of courage now, maybe Da would begin to forgive her for her cowardice at Clonmacnoise.

It was worth the risk.

Brenna watched in morbid fascination as the Northman sat holding his head, rocking forth and back, making small groans in time with the movement. His moans grew louder until finally he threw his head back in frustration and roared wordlessly to the sky.

The bone-chilling sound sent Brenna's heart to her toes.

Saints above, a madman! She froze like a hare in the thicket who knows a fox is sniffing nearby.

CHAPTER TWO

He thumped his head with the heel of his palm, but no clear memory would form. It was as though he had winked into existence the moment he woke on the beach. For a brief flicker, he caught the vague outline of a face in his mind, but as soon as he focused on it, the image wavered and faded like morning mist.

What was wrong with him? Thoughts flitted through his brain like a school of cod, darting about and disappearing into the depths before he could get a net around one.

At the edge of his vision the girl was still there, shifting her weight from one foot to the other as if she wasn't sure what to do. It had been a mistake to vent his frustration in that insane howl. All it accomplished was to terrorize the one person who might be able to help him. He must bridle himself.

Why doesn't she run off? he wondered. The way his leg was beginning to throb, he doubted he could catch her again.

He turned his head to look at her. Her curly brown

hair billowed out like a banner in the breeze. The girl's gray eyes were wide with a combination of fear and fascination. The even features on her oval face were strained. She reminded him of a small squirrel caught in the paralyzing gaze of an adder. With a pang he realized that made him the snake.

"Be easy, girl. I'll not harm you."

"Me Da says Northmen go mad and scream like that before battle." She took a half step toward him, eyeing the wound on his thigh. "Are ye truly mad then?"

He snorted. "A true madman wouldn't be likely to know, would he, now? You think I'm a Northman?"

"Aye." Her face screwed into a frown.

"What makes you so sure?"

"The symbols on your knife sheath. I've seen runic writing before. Besides, ye've the look of a Northman," she said briskly. "And I heard ye speaking their savage tongue."

A blinding white light shot through his brain, followed by images of a dragonheaded ship, the dim hall of a longhouse filled with feasting warriors, and great gray swells of the sea. *Ja,* he was a Northman. The language and lore careening through his mind confirmed it.

But no name, no sense of himself came.

"I can't give you my name, but I'd like to know yours." He suspected any movement toward her would make her bolt, so he kept still. "How are you called?"

She glanced over her shoulder.

Looking for a rescue party, no doubt, he thought. He was unarmed save for his knife and knew he was in no shape to defend himself against more than a handful of men. If he didn't befriend her before they arrived, he'd be in a tight spot.

"As you said before, 'tis a simple thing." He tried flashing a smile at her, but her frown only deepened. "Where's the harm in giving me a name to call you?"

She fisted her hands at her waist and heaved a sigh. "Brenna," she said through clenched teeth. "I'm Brenna, daughter of Brian Ui Niall, the Donegal."

"The Donegal?"

"King of Donegal, if you like," she said with dignity, drawing herself up to her full height.

Which wasn't saying much, he thought. She was a little slip of a thing, even though she'd fought him like a cornered badger.

"Well, Your Highness, if I'd known I'd been stabbed by a princess, I'd have tried to bleed more importantly."

Brenna made a small growling noise in the back of her throat, then stooped and ripped a length of cloth from her undershift. She strode toward him with purpose. "Sit back then, Northman, and let me see about this."

He leaned back on his elbows and watched as she wrapped the length of cloth around his thigh and cinched it tight. The expression on her face was determined and workmanlike, with not a hint of tender concern. She didn't like him one bit.

"Do you always doctor the men you maim?" he asked as she tied off the knot. His tongue felt thick in his mouth, and he wished she had a waterskin dangling from the girdle at her trim waist.

"I'd hardly call it maiming." Brenna straightened and skittered back out of his reach. "That should stop the bleeding then. I've done what I can for ye. 'Pray for your enemies and do good to them,' Father Michael always says."

"And I'm your enemy?"

"Ye be a Northman. 'Tis enough." The fear he'd read earlier in her wild eyes was replaced by loathing. "Besides, ye put your hands on me sister. The wee poke of a stick is the very least ye might expect."

"That was your sister?"

Her lips pressed together in a firm line. "Aye, and if ye think to try it again, I'll fetch me staff and skewer ye good and proper next time. That'll teach ye to mishandle a daughter of the house of Ui Niall."

"I barely knew what I was doing when I grabbed your sister's wrist." He fixed her with an intent look. "What do you intend to do with me now that I've rolled a 'daughter of the house' in the sand?"

She flushed deep scarlet.

He cocked his head at her. She looked fetching enough to roll again, despite the throbbing in his leg.

"I... I'll not do anything with ye," she stammered, edging away from him.

"That's a pity," he said, wincing as he rose to his feet. "Tell me. Are all the women of this land cursed with a foul temper and a heavy hand with a sharp stick?"

When she glared at him, he remembered he should try to befriend her. So far he'd not made a promising start.

He trudged back toward the spot where he'd wakened on the shore and was pleasantly surprised when he heard her light footfalls behind him, albeit at a safe distance.

"Since I don't know my name, perhaps you could

pick one for me, Brenna, Princess of Donegal," he called over his shoulder.

"Ye'll not live long enough to be needing a name."

That confirmed it. She was expecting help and soon. He turned to face her as he continued to walk backward toward the barrel he'd noticed in the sand. "All creatures have names. You said so yourself. If we're going to be friends, you'll need something to call me till I remember my proper one."

"I'm doubting we'll be friends," she said as she trailed after him.

"And I'm sure we will be."

"Call yourself what ye will," she said with exasperation. "I don't give names to the hens in the fowl yard, knowin' sooner or later they'll end up in me stewpot. Just 'Northman' will have to do for the likes of ye."

Despite her dour words, he decided he liked the musical lilt of her voice. "Tell me, what does Brenna mean?"

She was quiet for a moment. "I was expected to be a lad, and would have been named Brian. When I wasn't, me da just altered his name a bit and I was called Brenna, both for him and for me hair."

"Your hair?"

"Brenna means dark-haired." She made an unsuccessful attempt at smoothing her unruly tresses. "Mine was like jet when I was born."

"Named for your father, hmm? He must be very proud of you."

"I can assure ye, he's not," she muttered.

Her expression was so pained, a knot formed in his own chest. "Still, Brenna suits you. It's a fine name. I like the sound of it." He rolled her name over his tongue once more. "If you won't choose a name for me, I guess you'll have to introduce me to your father as Northman then."

"To me father?"

"*Ja,* he's on his way, I'll wager." He still wished he had a name to hang on himself. It would steady him. "Don't you think your sister went to fetch him? Or maybe she's not as quick of mind as you."

Brenna glanced up the deserted beach. "Da is on his way," she said with surety. "He'll be bringing a whole gang of men with him. And none of them with any love at all for Northmen."

"Hmph!" He knelt beside the weathered cask on the beach. "Is this mine?"

"Ye were wrapped around it when we found ye. I'm supposing 'tis yours."

He ran his fingers over the runes etched on the end of the barrel. The bung was intact. If the cask was well made, the contents should still be good.

"Is your father a drinking man?"

Brenna laughed out loud. "Sure, and ye have no idea where ye are, do ye, Northman?"

"Not even enough for a guess." He shook his head ruefully.

"So then, ye have washed up on Erin, where the High Kings have ruled from Tara for hundreds of years, and dear St. Patrick drove out both the snakes and the heathen from its twice-blessed shores." She jutted her chin upward in pride. "And on Erin, drink is mother's milk for every man over the age of six."

"Good," he said quietly. "Perhaps he'll favor a wager as well."

A buzzing rippled the air and he was startled to see an arrow quivering in the sand near his knee.

A row of heads appeared over the hillock. A sinewy,

dark-haired man climbed to the top, another arrow nocked on the string. Brian of Donegal leveled his aim at the Northman's chest with cool precision. The mantle of leadership rested easily on the Irishman's shoulders and the men with him followed suit.

"Release me daughter!"

The Northman shouldered the cask and rose to his feet. "Greetings, Brian, King of Donegal. I've done your daughter no hurt." He grimaced and added softly enough for only Brenna to hear, "Though she can't say the same for me."

Brenna crossed her arms over her chest and sidled away from him.

Brian and his men trotted across the sand and formed a ring around the Northman. The Donegal edged his daughter behind him, with a quick, assessing glance, taking note of Brenna's disheveled hair and sand-crusted tunic.

"Has he harmed ye, lass?" the king asked softly.

"No, Da." Brenna dropped her gaze to her feet and stepped back, meek as a lamb.

"Ye did well keeping an eye on the fiend," Brian said, gruff approval on his features. "But we'd have found him at any rate. Ye took an awful chance, daughter. Don't do the like again."

Brenna's lips tightened into a thin line.

The Northman was surprised by the change in the girl. Brenna had been firmly in charge since he opened his eyes, ordering her sister to safety, attacking him, and keeping her wits about her when he pinned her to the sand. She was even brave enough not to run off when she could have. To see her subdued now struck him as odd.

But he didn't have long to puzzle over it. Brian Ui

Niall hadn't lowered the point of his arrow one jot. The Donegal narrowed his eyes at the Northman.

"What business have ye here?" Ui Niall asked.

"I can't say."

"A Northman never travels alone. Like a pack of wolves from the sea, ye are. Where be the rest of your heathen crew?"

"I don't know." He frowned. Why did they hate him so?

"Ye'd best be telling me, and quickly now. My finger gets tired of holding back this arrow."

"He truly doesn't know, Da," Brenna explained, placing a restraining hand on her father's arm. "His wits are addled. The man doesn't even know his own name."

"Your daughter is right. I don't remember anything before I woke up on this beach."

Brian squinted at him, taking his measure. " 'Tis easy enough to trick a woman, but ye're daft if ye believe I'll be fooled by a Northman."

"Better we should just kill him, says I," one of Brian's men grumbled.

"Hold there, Connor," Brenna interrupted the king's bloodthirsty follower. "One Northman alone isn't likely to harm us. Alive, he may be useful. We know precious little about the *Finn-Gall*. I'll warrant he remembers more than he wants us to know. Or he will, if he's allowed to live. If he's dead, he can't tell us anything."

The king's gaze shifted to his daughter for a flicker as if considering her words. Even so, the Donegal raised the point of his arrow at the Northman again.

"Are you a betting man, Brian of Donegal?" the Northman asked, his voice surprisingly calm.

The tip of the arrow dipped just slightly. "What wager have ye in mind, *Ostman?*"

Northman thumped the cask with his knuckle. "This barrel came up out of the sea with me. It's either full of ale or salt water. Here's my wager: If the drink is good, I'm telling the truth about not remembering. You lose nothing by letting me live." He shrugged eloquently. "If the ale is foul, then you can kill me."

"We can kill ye at will, *Ostman,* and use the ale to toast your dead carcass." Nevertheless, Brian's keen dark gaze swept over the briny cask. Then he looked again at his daughter, an unspoken question in his narrowed eyes. Brenna sent him a silent entreaty, and the Northman's hopes rose. The Irish princess was pleading his case without a word.

Clever girl, he thought. Now if only the Irish king doted upon his offspring to heed her.

Brian eased the tension in his bow and replaced the arrow in the quiver slung over his back.

"Wager accepted, Northman," the king said. "Ye are either a fool or a brave lad. Come back to me keep and we'll raise a horn to prove which. No sense in drinking out here when we can do it in comfort. Aidan, take the cask. Connor, bind his hands."

The Northman's wrists were cinched together and the knot jerked tight. Then he was shoved into line with the Irishmen as they began plodding up a path leading into the hills. Brenna walked ahead of him and he allowed himself to enjoy the twitch of her hips as she climbed.

"Princess," he whispered to her.

She didn't answer him, but she turned her head to one side, so he knew she'd heard him.

"I thank you for your help."

"'Twas not for ye I spoke," she whispered back. "'Twas only sense. If you're no use to me father, he'll kill ye anyway."

The Northman expected no less. "Why didn't you introduce me properly?"

"How could I be doing that? There's nothing proper about ye, Northman," Brenna hissed at him.

"I'd like it better if you found something else to call me," he said. "Northman isn't a well-favored name around here."

She flashed a look back over her shoulder that should have reduced him to cinders.

They walked in silence for a while, the only sound the even thudding of leather-shod feet on the hard-packed path.

"I don't understand," he finally said. "Why do you all hate my kind so?"

Brenna whirled and planted her fists on her waist. "Look ye into yonder clearing and tell me what you see."

He peered through the spindly stand of trees. Blackened timber and the crumbling ruins of a round structure were surrounded by scorched grass. "Looks like there was a fire."

"Aye," Brenna said. "There was a fire, but before that there was a crofter's cottage where a man and his wife lived with their three bairns and one on the way. Liam and Colleen, they were, and they had nothing of value—nothing but each other. After the Northmen came, all we found were charred bones. And ye wonder that we hate ye."

"I'll not hold a grudge against women just because I was stabbed by one once," he said, favoring his good leg a bit more than necessary. "Even if I am a Northman as you say, I don't see how you can blame me for this."

"Can ye not?" The silver flecks in her gray eyes flashed at him. He recognized both controlled fury and lively intelligence in her level gaze. "Ye speak our tongue. That means 'tis not your first time on our island. For aught ye know, ye may have been the leader of that murderous raid. Can ye in good conscience tell me different?" She turned on her heel and marched up the path behind her father's men.

He stared after her, then back at the blackened ruins. Connor gave him another shove.

"Get on wi' ye!"

He stumbled forward, following Brenna's swaying skirt. The girl was right. He couldn't deny he might have led the raiders that killed those crofters. He really had no clue what sort of man he was. Was he capable of butchering a family—women and children—for no reason?

He had no way to know.

The thought made his head throb, and he raised his bound hands to feel the crust of matted hair at his temple. Why couldn't he remember? He strained to concentrate as he walked. Disjointed images, indistinct faces, and sudden flashes of sound split his brain, but nothing coherent came.

He must have slowed his pace because Connor pushed him forward again.

Better to concentrate on now, he decided. *Let the past trouble about itself.*

His present was trouble enough.

Chapter Three

Sunlight streamed in the open windows of the scriptorium, sending dust motes swirling. The call of a song thrush, sharp staccato blasts followed by a trill, floated on the breeze. The cool waters of the river Shannon called to Brenna, but she couldn't answer the summons. There was too much work to do. She sighed, dipped her stylus in the shimmering liquid, and turned back to the nearly transparent sheet of vellum.

The Gospel of Matthew lay on the table before her. She squinted, intent on the delicate interlace she inked in, rimming the page with layers of undulating chains. With deft strokes, she added crosshatching in gold over blue. As she worked, her gaze was drawn to the text.

In Ramah was there a voice heard, lamentation,
And weeping, and great mourning,
Rachael weeping for her children, and would not be comforted, because they are not.

An empty ache throbbed in her chest. She shook her head and focused on the ornamentation again. As she neared the lower corner of the page, the design wavered and writhed. Brenna squeezed her eyes shut and pinched the bridge of her nose. Father Michael warned her to take frequent breaks to protect her vision when she was illuminating a manuscript. She'd been at this close work too long.

She breathed deeply. The sharp scent of ink and the comfortable mustiness of books soothed her. But when she opened her eyes and looked down at the folio, her hand flew to her mouth. The chain pattern had grown a serpent's head and was slinking off the page and across the table. Blue and gold smeared on the dark oak.

Brenna leaped to her feet, sending her chair crashing to the stone floor behind her. From out in the courtyard, a scream pierced the air, pulling her to the open window. Clonmacnoise Abbey was overrun by hairy Northmen, their axes dripping red.

She turned to flee, but there was a small bundle on the table where the vellum had been. A tiny hand stretched out of the coarse blanket and reached toward her.

A babe! She snatched up the child and ran out of the scriptorium and down the corridor.

The clatter of footfalls behind her spurred her on. She felt someone's hot breath on her nape, and gorge rose in the back of her throat.

It was him. She knew it. She knew he'd be there. He was always there. Dread lay in her belly like a lump of underdone porridge. She tossed a glance over her shoulder.

But it wasn't him.

Instead it was the abbot, his usually pleasant, pudgy features distorted in rage. He whirled her around, snatched the child from her arms, and raised a booted foot to kick her in the gut.

Brenna lofted into the air as lightly as if she were a cankerwort seed. She seemed to watch herself from outside her own body as she sailed through the tall double doors of the abbey and landed with a thud in the dirt.

Brenna's whole body jerked. Her eyes flew open and she stared up at the underside of the thatched roof, the final wavering image from the nightmare leaving her confused for a moment. Beside her, Moira moaned softly and rolled over, taking most of the blankets with her. Brenna was safe in her own bed.

'Twas just a dream, she told herself. Her heart pounded against her ribs and she willed her breathing to slow. *Just a foolish dream.* It had no power to harm her. Still, her hand shook as she pushed back what little of the coverlet Moira had left her. Brenna eased out of bed without waking her sister.

She wouldn't dwell on the nightmare for one blink more, wouldn't let herself call up the half-remembered dewy fresh scent of the babe. She banished the dream from her mind. Anything else was the path to madness.

Brenna padded to the shuttered window and pushed it open to let in the dawn. The cock cried in the barnyard below. The guineas would need tending, and soon.

And so would the Northman.

Whatever had possessed Da?

Last evening when the rescue party arrived back at the keep, her father had trussed up the stranger in the round room occupying the main floor of the tower while the king and his war party feasted. Brenna felt a flutter of pity for the Northman when the conversation turned to inventive ways of killing him if the ale turned out to be bad.

"Drown the blackguard in a bog," Connor said, pounding his wooden drinking bowl on the table.

"A nice slow garroting would be none too good for

an *Ostman* demon, I'm thinkin'," Aidan said, a hard glint in his eyes. Worship of the old gods had mostly faded with the coming of St. Patrick and his Christ, but strangling a sacrificial victim was still deeply ingrained in some of Erin's sons.

Then the suggestions turned truly grim, each man trying to outdo the other in gore, clearly hoping to terrify the Northman.

But the stranger threw back his golden head and laughed.

He was addle-brained for sure, Brenna decided.

"If worse comes to worst, perhaps you'll fetch your bows and use me for target practice," the Northman said calmly. "If you've no better ideas for killing me than those, it's clear your wits are in need of sharpening. No doubt your aim could use it as well."

Silence blanketed the hall for the space of several heartbeats. Then Brian Ui Niall slammed his rough hand on the table and started to chuckle. Soon the rest of the warriors joined in and Brenna recognized the gleam of grudging respect on several hardened faces.

When her father pried the bung out of the ale cask with his long hunting knife, Brenna surprised herself. She actually hoped the ale was good.

To a man, they all leaned forward as the king sampled the first horn.

Brian drank deeply, ran his tongue over his lips and made his pronouncement. "Nectar."

Relief flooded warmly to Brenna's toes.

At least, she'd felt relieved at first. After her father decided she'd have the responsibility of seeing the Northman put to useful occupation, she began to wish the cask had been full of seawater. It was one thing not to want him dead. Being in charge of the

Northman, forced to bear him company, was another thing altogether.

Brenna pulled the shutters closed again, leaving just enough of a crack to let in the soft morning light. She shrugged her brown linen tunic over her head, then pulled on woolen socks, winding strips of cloth around her calves to keep them up. Lastly, she put on the old shoes she reserved for the barnyard.

Brenna slid out of the small cell she and Moira shared and climbed down successive ladders to the lowest level of the keep. The stone tower had been designed with a siege in mind, each of the successive floors accessible only by a single ladder that could be pulled up by defenders if necessary. Down in the main hall, a few of her father's warriors had been too far gone in their cups to make it home last night. She was careful not to wake them.

Padraigh was sprawled before the smoldering ash of the peat fire. Aidan and the largest of the wolfhounds were curled up like two spoons. Brenna stepped over the snoring figure of Connor McNaught on her way to the door. She wondered briefly who was minding his motherless bairns while he drank himself to oblivion in her father's hall.

"Men," she muttered with a curl of her lip. Brenna knotted a *brat* around her shoulders, letting the short cape drape over her frame, before she slipped out to face the Northman.

He'd given his word that he wouldn't run off, and Brian Ui Niall was willing to take it. In truth, there was nowhere for him to run. A Northman alone would be easy pickings for any hunting party in the wilds. Her father could set his great hounds after the stranger and they'd have him in no time. Since the man didn't even know who he was, he wasn't likely to know where his countrymen were and couldn't count on them for aid.

Last month, the traveling peddler had told Brenna a horde of the Norse heathens had set up an over-winter camp far to the south near the mouth of the river Liffey. The new settlement lasted through the damp Irish winter on the leeward side of Erin, and the heavenly green spring bid the intruders stay. The Northmen were probably still there, but her Northman would have no chance of finding them, on his own and afoot.

Brenna scattered grain for the hens scuttling around her hem. Then she lifted the latch on the cattle byre, where the Northman had been given leave to sleep. He was nowhere to be seen.

"Devil take the man!" she huffed. "It's daft we are to be trusting the likes of him."

"The likes of whom?"

Brenna nearly jumped out of her skin. Moira had slipped out of the keep behind her.

"Don't be sneaking up on me like that," Brenna said, rubbing her forearms. "Ye've given me gooseflesh."

Moira peered around her sister into the byre. "Where's your Northman?"

"How would I be knowing that? I'm not God Almighty, am I?" Her tone was sharper than she'd intended. Her stomach balled into a firm knot. Instead of feeling glad to be rid of him, she was upset the Northman was missing, and that made her feel even worse.

"Brennie, there's no cause for blasphemy," Moira said, lifting her chin. "Wonder where he's gone off to."

"Ah, so ye've taken to him already, have ye?"

" 'Tis no sin to use the eyes God gave me, is it? He's a handsome lad indeed." Moira sighed, then nudged Brenna with her elbow. "And here ye had me thinkin' ye've no time for noticing a fine man's face."

"And neither I do. 'Twas Da who saw fit to make me his keeper, not me. And speaking of fitting ..." Brenna stomped across the barnyard to see if the Northman was in the pigsty where he might as well belong. There was no sign of him. "I should have given him a name when he asked it of me. Beelzebub comes to mind."

" 'Tis so unfair Da gave him to ye."

"He didn't *give* him to me. Da only gave me charge of the man," Brenna explained. She didn't feel the need to add that Brian Ui Niall cautioned her to tell him straightaway if the Northman so much as looked cross-eyed at her. She also suspected the king had set one of the more reliable of his men to keep a surreptitious watch over her dealings with the stranger. Forcing her to spend time with *Ostman* was just her father's way of punishing her for interfering when the king had intended to kill the Northman outright on the beach. "May heaven bless him with a good clout to the head."

Moira raised a brow as though she wasn't sure whether her sister meant the Northman or their father.

"I don't see him anywhere, Brennie."

"Nor do I." Brenna gnawed at the inside of her cheek, wondering if she should rouse her father to look for the Northman. She decided against it. If he gave her father cause, the king might have him killed out of annoyance. "Come then. I planned for him to fetch the water this fine morning, but there's nothing for it. Ye can help me with it instead."

Brenna balanced the stout yoke across her sister's shoulders and hefted the two buckets herself. They'd have to struggle with the yoke together once the pails were full.

"Doesn't this make ye wish ye had a man of your own, Brennie? A married woman has no need to haul her own water." Moira started across the yard. "Heaven knows it's past time ye made a match."

"And what makes ye think a husband would be any more biddable than the Northman we can't seem to find? Stop fussing about me. Ye'll only be wasting your breath and tryin' me patience."

"But what of Connor McNaught? Did ye never think on him?" Moira asked, swinging the yoke wide as she turned to look back at Brenna. "He's not so hard on the eyes and he's got that darling farm. And him being a widower and needing a woman to care for his bairns and all. Do ye not think he'd make a fine husband?"

"No, Moira." Brenna struggled to keep her voice even. "I've no great liking for him."

"Ye've no likin' for any man."

"That's God's truth," Brenna muttered as she hefted the buckets and slogged behind Moira. "Nor need for one, either."

"But I have." Moira pulled a mock tragic face. "Sometimes I feel as if I'll burst out of me own skin for lack of havin' a fine man to hold me. And ye know Da will not hear of me takin' a husband till ye are married good and proper."

Married good and proper. As if it were possible now.

Brenna pulled her lips into a hard line, then felt the corners twitch in spite of herself. It was impossible to feel gloomy for long when her sister was around.

Moira was like sunshine with feet. Brenna couldn't help but smile.

Back when Brenna cared about such things, she sometimes silently bemoaned the fact that Moira had been the only one in the family blessed with fiery good looks. She felt dowdy as a sparrow beside the fine plumage of her younger sister. What lad could be expected to spare Brenna a sideways glance when Moira fluttered into the keep?

But now Brenna was thankful for her mousy brown hair and general plainness. The last thing she wanted was to catch a man's eye.

"I missed ye when ye were gone." Moira sighed. "The year seemed a lifetime."

"Aye, so it did." Brenna's voice cracked. *Certainly another life.*

"And in some ways, I think ye've yet to come back to us, Brennie," Moira said. "Stormy as a raincloud ye are more than half the time and I haven't heard ye sing once these long weeks past. I'm glad ye decided not to take the veil. Never did think it suited ye, all that obeying and repenting, and no opportunity to sin at all—"

"Moira!"

"I'd be mad in a month."

"Ye probably would." Brenna smiled at the unlikely image of her pretty sister in a plain habit, shut off from her crowd of admirers. No, the Church wouldn't do for the likes of Moira, but for Brenna, it had seemed the answer. Especially since Sinead was going too.

"Now, our Sinead, I'm sure she's taken to the religious life with all the fervor of an angel," Moira said. "We always knew she was marked for sainthood."

"Aye," Brenna said softly, her older sister's mild face flickering in her mind. "She's an angel, in truth."

"Fair Sinead never seemed to know the meaning of sin, but ye! I thought to meself when ye left with her for Clonmacnoise that ye were cut from a different bolt of cloth." Moira grinned wickedly at her. "I don't mean it badly, but ye must admit someone who conspired to put slow dye in the soap and turn all the hands in the keep bright yellow is not destined for a life of contemplation."

Brenna chuckled at the memory. "It did take a bit for Da to figure that one out."

Moira laughed. "No doubt ye'd have bedeviled the abbess with more of the same if ye'd taken the vows." Her smile faded. "Yet now ye've come back, ye're still betwixt and between. I've a feeling ye haven't quite decided to live amongst us. Whatever happened to ye at Clonmacnoise?"

Brenna bit her bottom lip. She and Moira had born each other's secrets since Moira was old enough to put two words together. Yet looking into her sister's fresh, innocent eyes, Brenna couldn't bring herself to tell her. Better to let her stay ignorant, even if she pouted. It was bad enough Da knew. She didn't think she could bear it if Moira looked at her with the same reproach she saw in her father's eyes.

"Never ye mind," Brenna said briskly. "We've enough to do this day without stirring up the past."

Moira shrugged and chattered happily as they chugged down the path to the stream. She invited Brenna to admire her newly crimsoned nails and wondered aloud if she could talk their father into buying that darling little silver cross the peddler had shown her last month. She wanted to wear it for next

St. Brigid's feast day, she said. Moira fervently hoped the old man who traveled about hawking his wares didn't sell it before he made his way back to Donegal.

Brenna loved her sister dearly, but she had learned early on to detach her ears when Moira was on a prattle.

As they neared the stream, she heard a sound she couldn't identify. Brenna froze.

"Hush ye now," she ordered Moira.

The sound came from the water, a snarling fierce sound that made her wonder if they'd stumbled onto a wolf pack. She eased the buckets down and stole over to the edge of the embankment to peer at the water below.

She caught a glimpse of fair hair. The growling noise came from the Northman, and from the regular rhythm of the sound, Brenna could only guess that he was trying to sing. She parted the bracken to sneak a better look.

He was standing hip-deep in midstream, naked as Adam in all his glory.

No, Brenna thought as she sucked in her breath. *Not Adam.* With dawn burnishing his hair gold, this man was surely more like Lucifer the Fallen. An angel of light designed to pull the unwary into outer darkness.

Water slid from his broad shoulders and down his chest. When he stretched languidly, the muscles in his arms and torso rippled in perfection. In the soft light, the fine hairs on his flat abdomen glistened like the fur on a bee's belly. He plunged himself under the water and came up shaking his head, like one of the wolfhounds, splattering droplets in every direction. Then he started to wade out of the stream.

From behind her, Brenna heard Moira's breath hiss over her teeth.

"Oh, Brennie, would ye look at his—"

Brenna wheeled around, dragging her sister away from the ledge.

"Get ye back to the keep this instant, I tell ye, and guard the innocence of your eyes!" Brenna whispered furiously, giving Moira a fierce shake.

"And what of your eyes?"

"Don't ye be bothering your head about that," Brenna said crossly. "Mind me now or I'll tell Da and he'll lock ye in the keep till ye're wrinkled as a winter apple and twice as sour."

A flicker of concern flitted across Moira's face. "But is it safe for ye? To be here alone, I mean?"

" 'Twill be fine," she said with more confidence than she felt. "Get ye gone now and I'll be along directly."

Brenna watched as Moira skittered up the path. Then she edged over to the embankment and leaned against a tree, facing away from the water. She was determined not to look at him again. Once was definitely enough.

"Northman!" she called out.

"Is that you, Princess?" He chuckled, a low seductive rumble. "I thought it might be."

"What do ye mean by that?" Brenna felt blood rush into her cheeks. The infernal man thought she'd been spying on him.

"Just that you'd be the only one up this early," His tone was without guile. "It appears I'm going to live long enough to need a name after all. Have you thought of one for me?"

"Perhaps I'll pick a name so vile, ye'll jump back into the sea and swim away."

"I'll risk it."

"How about Conway?" The tiniest hint of mischief crept into her voice.

"And what does Conway mean?"

"Yellow hound," Brenna admitted.

"I'm flattered," he said. "Is that the best you can do?"

"Perhaps ye'd like to be called Doran—"

"Which no doubt means Norse slug-worm."

She stifled a laugh with her hand. "No, though Doran is a name that suits ye. It means 'wandering stranger.' Ye can't argue with that."

"No, but I want you to choose a name you'll be happy calling me." More splashing sounds traveled up to her. "When you look at me, what's the first name that comes to your mind?"

"I'm not looking at ye," she insisted, fighting the urge to do just that.

His rumbling laugh taunted her. "A name, Princess. That's all I ask."

"Keefe Murphy," she said quickly, then clamped her lips tight. She hadn't meant to let the words slip out.

"Keefe Murphy." He tried it on for size. "Sounds decent. Why do you think it should be my name for the time being?"

"Murphy means 'sea warrior,' and ye've no doubt come from the sea."

"And Keefe?"

Handsome. She couldn't admit she found him fair to look upon. Her cheeks heated with fresh color. "I cannot say, but it suits ye. Ye must trust me for that."

"You're the only one I can trust right now. Good enough, Brenna. Keefe it is, then," he said. "The king of Donegal's hall was filled with heroes last night. I'll wager some of them are still there, the worse for their heroics. That ale was potent."

"And lucky for you 'twas in a well-made cask." Brenna made the mistake of turning around to talk to him and caught him tugging up his leggings.

Well made indeed, she admitted grudgingly. Before she could avert her eyes, he looked up and met her gaze directly. The man's smile would have melted the Stone of Tara.

"I've already had my bath, Brenna. But I could be coaxed back into the water if you join me."

The heat in his blue eyes made them go dark. Brenna's insides squirmed. It was one thing to admire the fine line of a man's frame. To see him openly admire her in return set her quaking like a stand of aspen in a gale. But she'd be damned if she'd let him see her fear. Brenna took refuge in rage.

A low noise of disgust erupted from her lips as she hurled the buckets down at him.

"Curse ye for a misbegotten son of Satan!" she spewed. "The only water I'd join ye in would be bog water, so I could get a closer look while me Da drowns ye! Don't ye be daring to look at me that way ever, ever again. Fill the buckets and fetch them back to the keep. And be quick about it, or I'll set the hounds on ye."

Brenna hoisted her tunic, baring her legs to the knee, and ran up the path. She swiped angrily at the tear spilling down her cheek.

So much for her vow that a Northman would never make her cry again.

Chapter Four

Keefe crested the rise. He barely noticed the weight of the full buckets dangling from the yoke settled across his shoulders, but the wound in his thigh slowed his pace. His gaze swept over the home of Brian Ui Niall. There was the sagging cattle byre, a chicken coop listing to the south, and a half dozen circular thatch-roofed huts clustered around the stone tower of the keep.

A jagged streak of light seared across his vision and he suddenly seemed to see a sturdy longhouse with smoke rising from evenly spaced holes in the roof. Laughter rolled out of the open door. Then a swirl of color splashed before his eyes and he caught a glimpse of very different image—a glittering alabaster palace and a high-domed structure too celestial to have been made by human hands.

He lowered the buckets to the ground, swaying dizzily. Was that a memory? Had he actually seen such magnificence or was he gifted with an active imagination?

The image wavered and dissolved, and he found himself gazing once more at the motley collection of buildings that made up the king of Donegal's stronghold. No moat, no defense except a waist-high stone wall broken in so many places it wouldn't keep out a determined cow.

Why did he notice that? Was he a warrior? A raider? Did he have a family to protect and support? His head ached when he tried to force a memory. So far all he'd gleaned of his former life was a few disjointed images and a snippet of a song.

Surely more would come.

Keefe turned in a slow circle. No other habitation was visible from the king's hilltop, but curls of smoke rising above the trees betrayed the presence of several crofters' cottages within a day's walk of the keep.

Keefe shouldered his burden and carried the water to Brenna at the far end of the courtyard. She was busy adding woad to a large cauldron near the entrance to an anteroom attached to the keep. Through the open door, Keefe saw several standing looms, piles of wool to be carded, spindles and distaff. It was a homey room, rich with the scent of lanolin and alive with vibrant colored cloth, obviously the exclusive haunt of women in the keep.

"Where is your village from here?" Keefe asked, pouring water into the waiting cauldron. Maybe the name of a settlement would jar loose a memory.

"Me what?"

"The nearest town," he said. The grimace on her face told him she still didn't understand the question. "You know. A town, a place where people live close together?"

"And why would we be wanting to do that?"

"For trade, for protection." He felt his way, threading through unfamiliar corridors in his mind searching for the right path. Something about the way the Irish farmsteads sprawled over the hills and dales with no visible connection, no sense of a settlement, didn't seem right to him, but he couldn't say why. "A town is where merchants and craftsmen set up shop to sell their wares."

"Ye mean a fair, surely." Brenna stirred the water and seemed satisfied when it turned a rich blue color. "Of course we have a fair on both Samhain and Beltane. Everyone comes, the young and the old. 'Tis merry enough, but I wouldn't want to be living there."

"Why not?"

"After the contests, the men are drunk for days. If we lived every day as we do at fair time, we'd get no work from them at all."

"So you have no village. This is all there is to your father's kingdom?" Keefe swept his hand in a wide arc to indicate the decaying compound. "Seems to me any Irishman in possession of a high spot can call himself a king if he likes."

Brenna bristled, her gray eyes frosting over. "Me father is head of the Donegal clan with three hundred men at his call. He settles disputes and passes judgment." A spurt of indignation colored her cheeks with flame. "Many's the blood feud he's put a stop to, and it's a wise man as can do that. Brian Ui Niall is king of far more than this keep. I'll thank ye not to speak lightly of me father and him sparin' your neck only last evening. None but a fool berates what he doesn't understand."

He cocked his head at her. Brenna was loyal, he had to give her that, but she was so prickly. "Are you always so easily irritated?"

"Only by an irritating man." She turned her attention back to the vat of dye and stirred it furiously. Blue liquid surged over the sides and splashed onto the flagstones. Color rose in her face, making the sprinkling of freckles across her nose less noticeable. "Fetch me some peat and help me get the fire going hotter. There's a stack behind the cattle byre."

"As you wish, Princess." He gave her a mock bow. Except for the deep line etched between her brows, Keefe decided she was prettier when she was angry.

As he rounded the corner of the byre, he noticed some wood piled in a jumble near the midden heap. The dark burled grain caught his eye. It was the remains of a chair. The graceful back was intricately carved but had been shattered into two pieces and one of the legs was broken off, leaving a jagged stump.

Something about the chair jarred his mind. The smell of sawdust rose in his nostrils. He remembered hefting the weight of an adze and the smooth feel of polished, fine-grained wood under his palms. He flexed his fingers and suddenly knew he could fix that chair.

Keefe gathered up the pieces of wood and carried them along with the peat back to Brenna.

"No!" she said. "We'll not be burning that."

"Of course not." Keefe set down the armful of pieces and held up the sections of the back, fitting them together and judging the best way to reunite them. "Why burn what I can repair?"

Brenna stopped mixing the brew with her long

wooden paddle and looked at him intently. "Can ye truly?"

"I think so." His mind worked feverishly, traveling down a new, yet strangely familiar, road. Choosing and preparing the wood, the tools, the carefully honed craft that was both art and science—knowledge poured back into him with a rush that left him light-headed.

He was a carpenter. That much he could be certain of. But what manner of carpenter washed up on a beach with naught but a keg of ale? Questions and self-doubt assaulted him afresh, but he shoved them aside.

"Where can I find some woodworking tools?"

Brenna pointed toward a lean-to. "What tools there be ye'll find in the smith's shed." The hopeful expression on her face faded. "I'm doubting there's aught ye can do for the chair. Our cooper told me 'twas hopeless, but after ye've broken your fast, I give ye leave to try."

Brenna pinned up the last of the light blue linen to flap dry in the slanting sunlight. Wool took color easily, darkening to the shade of twilight just before the sky turns inky black, but flax caught the hue of the heavens on a fine summer morn.

"There's a good day's work," she said approvingly as she eyed the bolts of saffron, deep green, and soft gray undulating in the breeze.

The scent of a rich stew wafted out of the keep. Moira had been busy as well.

Brenna brushed a strand of curling hair out of her eyes and tucked it behind her ear. As she worked through the morning, Keefe crisscrossed the yard several times, fetching different items he needed to attempt the repair of the chair. She hadn't seen the Northman since she checked on him at midday.

She knew he was still there, though. From time to time, she'd catch snatches of the rhythmic noise she guessed was a song. It wasn't the most pleasant of sounds, but she recognized it as the same tune he'd been trying to sing when she'd happened upon him at his ablutions.

The sound invoked the memory of seeing him in splendid nakedness, the cool stream lapping at his hips. The smoothness of skin pulled taut over his muscles, the water tickling over his chest, the soft fuzz of fine hairs on his belly—

Brenna shook herself to ward off the vision. What was wrong with her? She knew what men were. Especially Northmen. She'd seen the flicker of lust in his eye when he tried to lure her into the water with him. Brian Ui Niall's daughter would be no man's fool, nor his plaything, either.

She squared her shoulders and marched across the yard to the smith's shed.

"The man lolls in the shade all day, singing his heathen songs and playing at work while the rest of us toil under God's sun," she muttered under her breath. "He'll be singing a different tune when I'm through with him, and no mistake."

Keefe seemed not to hear her when she rounded the corner. He was squatting down, hands busy, tongue firmly clamped between his teeth in concentration. The rapt expression on his face told Brenna he was deeply engrossed in his work, and for a moment, she allowed herself to admire his golden hair, fine features, and darkly even brows.

Keefe Murpy must be a snare sent from Satan himself, Brenna decided. It wasn't natural for a man to be so . . . beautiful. She forced herself to look at the chair.

"Oh!" Brenna skittered over and knelt beside him. She ran a finger reverently over the carved back, now neatly pegged together with a new section wedged in where it had previously been shattered. "Ye've done it."

His smile nearly made her forget the chair.

"It's not finished yet," he said. "I plan to carve the new section to match the old. The pattern ran true all the way across, didn't it?"

"Aye," Brenna said. "I can't believe ye've made it whole again."

"But that's just the start." Keefe's enthusiasm was infectious as he pointed to the newly turned leg. "I had to use a different type of wood. The chair was made of something that doesn't seem to grow around here."

"That's right," Brenna said. "It came from the south, from me mother's people."

"I wondered. I couldn't match the wood to anything nearby, but I should be able to make a stain that will bring it closer to the rest of the chair in appearance." He ran a hand over the leg. "Once I'm done you'll have to look closely to tell which one is the replacement."

Brenna sighed. "It'll never be the same, though."

"No," he admitted. "When something is broken, you can't make it new, however hard you try."

When he turned to look at her, Brenna suspected he saw beneath her face to her scarred soul.

"It'll never be the same," he admitted.

Brenna's shoulders slumped. *Of course not. Once things are done, they can't be undone.*

"It won't be the same, but it can be better," he said, turning the chair on end. "Look here. I've reinforced the seat and the back so it's much stronger than before. But it's repaired in a way that doesn't add any bulk or destroy the line of the chair."

Brenna smiled. "That's cleverly done."

"Why, princess," he said, "is that a kind word?"

When she lowered her brows at him and scowled, he raised his hands in mock surrender.

"Forget I said that." Then he leaned toward her. "I can tell this means something to you, though. Why is this chair so important?"

Brenna traced a fingertip over the carving, worn smooth in places from countless backs. " 'Tis old beyond reckoning. I was told it came to the family so many generations ago me people believe 'twas made by the Tuatha De Danaan." The ancient tribe of Erin was held in such high regard they'd been elevated to godlike status among the more superstitious. "As such, it was priceless. It belonged to me mother."

"Ah, I thought as much. A delicate chair for a delicate lady. It suits her."

"Aye," Brenna said. "She's always been fair. Moira takes her looks from the Connacht side of the family. I favor me father's people."

"She's very quiet, your mother."

"That's putting it mildly. She hasn't said a word since the chair was broken." Brenna thought for a moment about her distant mother, Una, a fragile beauty with a figure too waiflike to ever be considered matronly. "A few weeks ago, some of me father's men were drunk and things got a bit lively. By the time the scuffle was over, the chair was in pieces and Mother stopped talking."

"She stopped talking because of a chair?" Keefe picked up a small chisel and began to carve the entwined pattern, taking care to match the new to the old.

" 'Twas not for its value, though 'tis hard to put that aside. The chair itself was special to her," Brenna said. " 'Twas sent to her when me brother was born. She nursed him, dandled him on her knee, and weaned him on that chair."

"So you have a brother." Keefe looked up at her briefly. "Which one of the men is he?"

Brenna sighed and settled onto the hard-packed dirt floor beside him. "I *had* a brother."

CHAPTER FIVE

Brenna bit her lip and her whole body stiffened. Why had the words slipped out? This man had no right to her family's private grief. When he didn't press her for more, but returned to carving the wood and humming under his breath, she relaxed.

He turned the chair on its side to get closer to his work and started chanting unintelligible words.

"What is that noise ye're making?" she finally asked.

He tossed her an indignant look. "That *noise* is a song. It popped into my head this morning and so far it's about the only thing I can remember. I'm hoping if I sing it, more will follow."

He sang a few more growling phrases, then stopped.

"Have you remembered aught more?" she asked.

"No," he admitted. "I seem to be stuck on one verse."

"What is the song about?"

"It's about sailing the wide world," he said, his blue eyes trained on a distant point.

For the first time, Brenna wondered what it must be like to ride the heaving breast of the sea. When Keefe frowned, she felt a stab of sympathy for him. Not to know himself; the man must feel truly adrift.

"And the song is about going home," he added.

Home. Did he have people who missed him? A lover? Perhaps a whole string of women. Looking at his fine profile, she realized he must. How could he not?

The rhythmic chantey began again, haltingly this time, as he translated for her.

Slice the gray waves of the sea
Lay the Hammer-fist down
To kettle and hearth with treasure I'll flee
To find my true Treasures grown.

He brushed away some of the flaking wood with a rough fingertip. "I'm not exactly sure what it means."

"True treasures," Brenna repeated. "What could that be to a Northman but the wealth from someone else's labor?"

He met her gaze directly. "I was thinking true treasure might mean a family."

Brenna gulped. Everyone knew Northmen didn't show any more care to their women and offspring than a stray dog gave to the bitch he'd covered. At least that was what she'd always heard, but something in this Northman's expression told her he would care.

"By those lights, your song is about a man finding his bairns changed in his absence." Brenna was at a loss to explain her sudden shortness of breath. "Do ye suppose it means ye have a family that this verse has come to ye?"

Keefe laughed. "No matter what happened to him, somehow I think a man would have a hard time forgetting that."

He hummed the disjointed tune again.

A hard fist knotted in her stomach. Why should it matter to her if he did have a woman somewhere? Still, the song grated on Brenna like strong spirits on an open wound.

"Must ye keep making that racket?"

"A song helps me concentrate," he said. "If you don't like mine, maybe you could sing me one of yours."

"I'm not a minstrel girl to warble at your beck and call," Brenna snapped.

"It's just a song, princess." He seemed undaunted by her frown. "Surely even the Irish know a song or two."

"Aye, so we do."

"Then where's the harm in sharing one with me as I work?" His lopsided smile would melt a harder heart than hers.

" 'Tis plain I'll have no peace till I do. Very well then." She folded her hands in her lap and searched her repertoire for the right song for the occasion. "Ah! Just the thing. 'Tis a song that explains why we Irish enjoy foul weather."

Brenna's sweet soprano rose pure and clear despite the minor twist in the tune.

Bitter blows the wind this night
Toss up the ocean's hair so white
Merciless men I need not fear
Who cross from Lothland on ocean clear.

When the last melancholy note died, the corners of Keefe's mouth turned down. She could tell he felt the jab at his Norse heritage, then.

"Are all the Irish songs so sad?"

"If they are, 'tis only because our lives are often sad," Brenna said defensively.

He worked in silence for a moment, then turned to look at her. "Was your brother killed by a Northman?"

"No," she said softly.

"Good." He directed his attention back to his carving. "I'm glad to know I'm not responsible for all your woe."

The simple statement stung Brenna. Perhaps she was wrong to blame Keefe for what happened at Clonmacnoise. Still, he was a Northman. Sometimes she thought holding on to her hatred was all that kept her sane.

"A sorrow shared is a sorrow halved," he whispered. "What happened to your brother?"

Brenna wasn't sure why, but it seemed right, seemed safe to tell him. "Sean was killed by the Ulaid, a neighboring clan."

"And your mother took it hard."

"She was fair wild with grief." Brenna was only a child when her tall, strong brother died. Una, Queen of Donegal, had wailed like a banshee when Sean's arrow-pierced body was carried into the keep. Her usually mild features contorted into a snarling mask as she demanded Brenna's father launch a blood feud against the offenders. Looking back, Brenna barely recognized the frenzied harridan with her mother's voice.

"Sean's death was an accident. Some men of Ulaid, led by their king's son, Ennis, were hunting and strayed into Donegal. They mistook Sean for game in the thicket. It was a foolish waste, but it could have made the rivers run red. Me father settled the matter without a war."

"How did he do that?" Keefe wondered. Killing a noble heir was a heinous offense, never mind that it was accidental.

"He marched to the Ulaid's stronghold with the whole of the Ui Niall clan at his back, demanding the life of the Ulaid's son in exchange," Brenna explained. "Me father convinced their king, Domhnall, that none would be served by a blood feud. Better that one should die for peace between the clans, said he, than dot the land with widows and grieving mothers on all sides over an accident. This way, loss was divided with an even hand. Me father is a wise man. The Ard Ri in Tara could not have brought us a fairer solution."

"Then honor was satisfied." Keefe nodded his approval.

"Aye," she said. "The Ulaid's son Ennis went willingly to his death a hero. The arrangement suited everyone but me mother. The blood of Domhnall's firstborn wasn't enough. She's never forgiven me da for not avenging Sean properly."

By finger widths, Brenna watched her mother retreat into herself till she was little more than a shell of the woman she'd been. Desperate to replace her lost son, Brian Ui Niall's wife produced a string of stillborn infants at yearly intervals. Then she stopped bearing even those pitiful bundles of malformed flesh. Brenna's mother pulled away from her husband and eventually from her daughters as well.

Only the chair captured her attention and anchored

her wandering mind in this world. An unnatural preoccupation at best, the queen polished and shined it daily till the wood gleamed. All she cared for was that chair. When it was broken during a late-night carouse in the keep, Una of the clan Connacht stopped caring altogether.

"Every Feast of Imbolc, I half expect Da to leave her and be done with the marriage." Brenna clamped her hand over her mouth. She hadn't intended to voice that fear, especially not to this strange man. What was it about his calm silence that invited her confidence?

"What's the Feast of Imbolc?" Keefe didn't even look up from his carving. He seemed to accept her startling confession without a qualm.

"'Tis the first of February, the day on which all marriages are renewed or dissolved," Brenna explained. "Either party may leave and no discredit will come to them if they do. 'Tis a sensible custom, whatever Father Michael may have to say about it. Da says it's saved many a soul from the sin of murder."

Keefe chuckled. "Your father *is* a wise man, princess."

"Aye," she said, knotting her fingers together. "But not even a wise man can mend a broken heart."

Keefe stopped working long enough to fix her with a steady gaze. "Some things that are broken must be dealt with quickly and not be allowed to get worse. Take this chair, for instance. It's a good thing I came upon it when I did. If it had been left in the weather much longer, the wood would have dried out and warped beyond my ability to repair it."

The Northman's eyes were like deep forest pools.

Brenna felt herself in real danger of falling into them. He seemed to see right into her heart and glimpse her secret shame.

"If something gets brittle, no amount of care will restore it." He ran a calloused hand over the chair. "But we caught this in time. As you said, it'll never be the same. But in some ways it will be better. Stronger. Even more beautiful for its imperfections."

She was certain he wasn't talking about the chair anymore. Brenna's heart thudded against her ribs. Surely he must hear it.

"Most men seem to want perfection," she said softly.

"And there are those who find perfection boring." He leaned toward her ever so slightly, as if daring her to shove him away. "The important thing is not to let the damage stand, not to harden with the passage of time." His voice lowered to a husky rumble. "You've suffered, Brenna. I see it. It's in your eyes every time you look at me."

Slowly, as if he were afraid she might startle and bolt away, he reached over to cup her cheek in his palm. His hand was warm, but Brenna was sure the heat blooming in her face would scorch him.

"Let me help you, princess."

His mouth was so close to hers. All she need do was turn her head and she knew his lips would cover hers. She'd already seen his hands work a miracle in wood. Could this man somehow take her guilty heart and make it right again?

"There ye are!" Moira's voice interrupted her thoughts and Brenna jerked herself away from the Northman.

"I've sounded the dinner bell three times. Have ye

not heard it? Oh, look!" Moira's eyes fairly danced with delight. "Ye've mended Mother's chair. What a fine clever man ye are, Keefe Murphy!"

When Moira stepped lightly into the shed to inspect his work, Keefe beamed under her praise. Brenna could hardly blame him for turning his attention to her pretty sister.

"Come to supper then, when ye've a mind to," Brenna snapped as she skittered out of the shed. All men were idiots, she decided.

" 'Tis plain to see how boring he finds perfection," she muttered, going on to denigrate the man's heritage back several generations. But she saved her most damning imprecations for herself.

What a fool she was! Thank the saints above Moira arrived when she did. Brenna had almost let a man lure her into lowering her guard with his honeyed words and deep-as-the-ocean eyes.

Now she knew Keefe Murphy was indeed a "fine clever man." Next time, she'd be doubly wary.

Chapter Six

The chair was finally finished.

Brenna insisted he keep the work out of sight lest her mother stumble upon it in progress and be dismayed, so Keefe kept it covered in the shed when he wasn't working on it. He stained the new pieces to match the old as closely as he could. Then he rubbed the whole chair with oil till the wood gleamed. The repair turned out even better than he'd hoped.

The princess kept him hopping during the day, fetching water, mucking out stables, and generally serving as her beast of burden. With a start, he realized he didn't mind. Even when Brenna's tone turned caustic, he found himself listening for her voice, wondering where she was when she wasn't directing his labor.

Brenna was a puzzle. Keefe was sure she'd been drawn to him. He'd certainly felt the attraction between them. It was strong as a riptide, but she fought against it like a swimmer caught between the shore and the deep. His Irish princess was no shallow shoal.

As he worked the wood, snippets of memory came back to him—places he was sure he'd seen. He remembered a seemingly bottomless lake whose surface shone like glass on calm days. It was in the Pictish lands, that wild country populated by fierce tribes who paint themselves blue before battle. In the dark depths of that lake, a terrible monster was rumored to live, a beast so horrible as to defy description.

Brenna was like that lake. Somewhere in her past, there lurked a monster. It would be worth his time, he decided, to sound her depths and uncover it. Whatever beast plagued her, Keefe was determined to slay it and free her from its power.

If she'd let him . . .

"Are ye sure 'tis finished?" Her voice roused him from his thoughts.

"It's as good as I can make it," he said as he hoisted the chair onto his shoulders.

"Come, then." Brenna led the way, carefully avoiding getting too close to him, he noticed. Ever since he tried to kiss her, she'd been skittish around him, like some wild young creature desperately needing the crumb he might offer, but fearful of the touch of his hand.

Keefe smiled as he trailed her to the keep. There'd be another chance. He'd make sure of it. And this time he wouldn't let her get away without feeling the softness of her lips under his.

It seemed the round hall of Brian Ui Niall was always full of retainers. As far as Keefe knew, these men all had farmsteads nearby, but they managed to find their way to the keep for a meal and a horn of ale on a regular basis. Keefe surmised their food and drink was the price of the Donegal's kingship.

His queen, Una of Connacht, didn't exactly preside as hostess at these nightly feasts. It was more as though she haunted them. Dutifully, she took her place beside her husband and picked at her food. Her dark-ringed eyes sent a message of silent reproach to the king at every glance.

Since Brenna had explained to him how simple divorce was on this island, Keefe wondered why the king didn't leave his somber queen. Then he saw the way Brian Ui Niall looked at his wife. The king loved her—or at least loved the shadow of the woman she'd been—too much to let her go.

The rowdy conversation in the hall ceased when Keefe strode to the center of the room with his burden. He gently placed the chair before Brenna's mother.

"I believe this belongs to you," he said, dropping to one knee before the queen of Donegal. Then he rose and stepped back.

Una looked up from her lap and stared at the chair. A light kindled behind her eyes and Keefe caught a glimpse of the beauty she'd been. As though the queen was finally aware of her surroundings, she swept the room with her gaze until her pale eyes met the king's anxious steel-gray ones. Her mouth curved into a trembling smile. She stood, walked slowly to the center of the room, and laid a quivering hand on the repaired back.

"I thank ye," she said in a hoarse whisper.

Keefe's mouth lifted in a smile. When he turned to look at Brenna, he saw her wide eyes glisten with tears. Her soul shined through those gray orbs, bare to the world. And it was a beautiful soul, full of kindness for all her bluster, and all the more lovely for the secret pain she bore.

He'd overheard several of the Irishmen praising the charms of the coppery-haired Moira, but if they could see Brenna as he did, they'd easily dismiss Moira's delicate allure. Brenna's beauty went clear to the bone.

"Northman, it's in your debt I find meself." Brian Ui Niall laid a hand on Keefe's shoulder. "When ye came to us with naught but a brave heart and a keg of fine ale, I didn't spare your life out of charity. I hoped to learn something of an enemy that's caused us no end of woe. And I wanted to use that new knowledge to harm ye and your countrymen if I could." The king's voice crackled with emotion as he watched his wife settle happily into her precious chair. "And now ye do me this great kindness."

"It was nothing," Keefe said. "You gave me a chance at life when many would have taken it away, whatever your motives."

"I'd give ye a boon, Keefe Murphy," the king went on. "I still hold ye to your word not to leave us, but short of that, I'd grant ye a request."

Keefe glanced at Brenna. For a moment, he considered asking for a kiss from the eldest daughter of the house, but thought better of it. He was pretty sure the king's hospitality stopped well short of his daughter's favors. And besides, given half a chance, he intended to entice Brenna into kissing him willingly, and soon.

"I remembered more while I worked on the queen's chair."

"Then ye know your true name?"

"No," Keefe said with a frown. "It was more like remembering how to do things. Mostly that I seem to have some experience with wood. I'd like to do some more carpentry."

"Sure and if that isn't the easiest request I've ever granted," the king said.

"I've seen the little coracles you and your men use for fishing," Keefe said. The hide-covered crafts were adequate, nothing more.

"What of them?"

"I can make them better," Keefe said. "They need a keel, a sort of backbone, running down the center. It'll make all the difference. If you give me leave, I'll build a little boat that will sail circles around your skin-covered hulls."

"Aye and he'll be sailing away at the first chance." Connor McNaught jumped into the conversation. "Now that he knows the lay of our land, the next full moon, we'll see a whole great boatload of the *Ostman* demons landing on our beach."

Murmurs of assent greeted this pronouncement. The support seemed to embolden Connor further and he strutted over to glare up at Keefe. If the difference in their heights troubled Connor, he gave no sign.

"I've given the king my word," Keefe said. A muscle ticked in his left cheek. He stifled the urge to knock the mocking expression off the Irishman's pugnacious face. "Brian Ui Niall has no reason to mistrust me."

"None but the accident of your birth, Northman." Connor swiped his mouth with the back of his hand. His pale eyes were already glassy from too many pints. "I still say ye cannot rely on a man who doesn't even know himself."

"I may not remember my name," Keefe said, flexing his fingers and balling them into fists, "but I know well enough my word is sacred."

"Sacred! And what might a heathen Ostman know of things sacred?" Connor spat back at him.

"Connor McNaught, ye're a fine one to talk." Brenna stepped between them, poking a finger into the center of Connor's chest. "Ye promised me only last week ye'd see the harness for the mare mended, but 'tis still in tatters."

Connor frowned and stepped back a pace.

"Keefe Murphy may be a heathen *Ostman*, as ye say, yet he's not promised but what he's delivered." Brenna's eyes flashed as she sent a scalding look toward Connor. "So just ye mind your tongue."

Keefe resisted the urge to laugh out loud. The princess was actually defending him, but he knew it would be unwise to point it out to her.

Connor looked to the king for support. "Ye surely aren't going to let him build a twice-cursed dragonship, are ye?"

Brian Ui Niall dragged a hand over his face. "I offered the man a boon. Shall it be said the word of Donegal is taken back just because 'tis inconvenient?" He caught Keefe with his steady gaze. "I'll be having your word ye'll not use the ship to sail away without me favor."

"You have it," Keefe said.

"Then I grant ye leave to build it."

Keefe nodded. "Fair enough. And so there's no misunderstanding, let me build her in that little sheltered cove. I can test her there for seaworthiness, but the reef will keep me from venturing farther. She'll have to be hauled overland to the beach before she can be fully tried. When I'm ready to do that, Connor can come with me, if he's up to it."

"Handsomer than that a man couldn't wish," the king said, clapping him on the back. "Brenna, me darlin', I leave it to ye to see our Keefe Murphy has what stores he needs for the building of this boat, this ... what was it ye said it wanted? A keel, was it?" He raised a questioning brow at Keefe. "Ah, it makes no never mind. Build it with me blessing."

"It would please me if you'd name the boat when it's finished," Keefe said to the king. "A good-omened name protects all who sail in the craft. I'll build a vessel worthy of a fine name."

"Why, name it for me, boy-o!" Brian suggested with smile.

"I can't do that," Keefe explained. "It needs to be a woman's name because a ship is like a woman. Reliable and treacherous in turns, but hard for a man to do without."

"Aye, that's a woman." Brian Ui Niall laughed in agreement and motioned to Brenna. "Bring a horn for the thirsty men, daughter. There's a good lass."

Brenna nodded and fetched a horn of ale for both the king and Keefe.

The Northman reached out to touch her arm as she passed him.

"Thank you for taking my side this night, Brenna."

Her lips tightened. "Don't be thinking more highly of yourself than ye ought, Keefe Murphy. Against the likes of Connor McNaught, I'd side with the Devil himself."

Chapter Seven

Brenna hugged herself against the stiff wind. From her perch on the rocky promontory, she watched the restless sea, scalloped with whitecaps. Clouds raced across the sky like a herd of long-maned white mares. Her view stretched to the distant horizon where water and sky merged in a smudge of gray.

She tried to focus on that distant point, but her gaze was drawn downward to the man working in the sheltered cove below. The bare skeleton of a miniature dragonship was taking shape, the curving strakes molded in sinuous contours. The symmetry, the clean, even lines of the craft, proclaimed it the work of a master. Keefe was undoubtedly a shipwright of great talent.

Even from this distance, Brenna sensed his satisfaction from the set of his shoulders. In the short time he'd been there, she'd learned to read his moods from his posture. When he was frustrated with a problem, the muscles between his shoulder blades gathered into a hard knot. When the work was going well, as it was now, his limbs were loose and relaxed.

She wouldn't admit it, even to herself, but she never tired of watching him. Covertly, of course. She'd die of shame if anyone noted and remarked on her interest in the man.

His attempt at song floated up to her. She was even getting used to hearing the soft, guttural chant he claimed he was singing.

He hadn't made any more advances toward her. But from time to time, she felt his eyes on her, hot and knowing. It irritated her that this Northman, this stranger, could lay her bare with just his gaze.

You've suffered, Brenna, he'd said. *I see it in your eyes every time you look at me.*

How had he been able to divine so much about her cut and bleeding soul?

"For someone with no use for men, ye seem to have no trouble keeping track of this one." Moira's voice pulled her out of her reverie as she came alongside Brenna.

"Are ye forgetting Da made me his keeper?"

"A truly onerous duty, that," her sister said dryly.

"Mayhap ye'd like the job." Brenna frowned at her. "Say the word and 'tis yours."

"No indeed. I'll be having far more fun teasing him away from the work ye've set for him. No doubt he'll be needing someone to soothe him when ye scold. Ye are a terrible taskmistress, ye know."

"Keefe sets his own pace," Brenna explained. "He drives himself to finish his other chores so he can hie himself here to work on that infernal boat of his."

"Infernal boat," Moria repeated, her presumptuous

smile raising the hackles on Brenna's neck. "Ah! So ye are afeard he'll leave as well."

"I fear no such thing," she denied. "If Da gives him leave to go, then good riddance says I, and not a moment too soon."

"Then you'll not be minding if I go down and take him these tarts fresh from the baking," Moira said. "Even a fine braw lad like our Keefe needs something to keep up his strength with all the work ye put him to."

"Do as ye please," Brenna said, trying to ignore the sinking feeling in her gut. Moira looked especially fetching today in her new green tunic and *brat*.

"Come with me, Brennie," Moira suggested. "We can gather mussels on the beach on the way back."

It was tempting, but Brenna shook her head. She didn't want Moira to know how rattled she felt around the stranger. Her sister could be a terrible tease.

"Not this time, but do ye go on. Only mind yourself," Brenna urged. "Remember who ye are and comport yourself as a daughter of the house should."

Moira laughed and turned lightly on her heel to start down the switchbacked path to the shore below. The foot-worn track led to the far edge of the beach. From there, she'd have to walk back up the rocky coast and round the point to join Keefe in the cove.

"I wish ye would come, and I'd lay silver Keefe would wish it, too," Moira called back over her shoulder. "Given the choice, your Northman would rather see ye than food, I'm thinking."

Brenna felt heat creep up her neck and flood her cheeks. So Moira had seen the way Keefe ogled her. Who else had noticed and tittered at her in secret?

And might they also have wondered if she'd done anything to encourage Keefe to strip her with his gaze as if she were a light-heeled wanton?

She wished she could sink into the very earth. Instead, Brenna grasped her skirts and broke into a trot back toward the keep.

"Steady, now," Kolgrim said. The dragonship rounded the southern point and made steadily for a long strand of beach. "We don't want anyone raising an alarm till we're in and out and on our way with whatever comes to hand."

"These little farmsteads are poor sport," one of his men grumbled.

"We aren't after loot now," Kolgrim reminded them. "We only need to stock up the larder before we raid the juicier prize."

"Already had more than we needed." Kolgrim overheard a few of the crewmen grumbling among themselves. They no longer bothered to mask their lack of trust in their captain.

It all started the night of that storm. They'd been heavily loaded with spoils from their last raid. Kolgrim remembered each detail with the hideous crispness terror brings to a man's memory. He'd stood in the prow of his ship, one arm wrapped around the long neck of the dragonhead while his second in command, Jorand, strained against the steering oar, muscling the *Sea Wolf,* dragonhead first, into the oncoming waves. Kolgrim held his breath and squinted against the briny spray.

"She won't hold!" he'd bellowed to be heard over the slashing wind.

The longship's timbers groaned as her prow tilted over the crest and plummeted down the wall of water into a deep trough. Gray swells rose above them, threatening to swamp the dragonship. A few of the sailors wailed in terror.

"She's breaking up."

"No, she's not." Jorand gripped the side of the *Sea Wolf* so hard his fingernails bit into the wood, as if he could hold her together by the force of his will. He dragged a bucket through the water at his ankles and dumped it over the side.

"Keep bailing," he yelled back to Kolgrim. "You've overloaded her. Toss some of the cargo. We have to lighten the ship."

The *Sea Wolf* held a dragon's hoard of silver and fine pilfered goods. Kolgrim wasn't about to start dumping it. The longship shuddered, bowing and flexing with each swell.

"Unless you want to swim back to Dublin, it's time to cut our losses!" Jorand shipped the steering oar and struggled to his feet. He clambered over the rest of the crew to the shallow cargo hold near the base of the mast. He drew out his knife and sliced the ropes that bound a stack of ale kegs. They rolled one after another into the dark sea. The *Sea Wolf* lifted, riding lighter, but Jorand didn't stop. He bent down to grapple with a heavy, locked chest.

"I'll lighten the ship," Kolgrim growled. He grabbed an oar and swung toward his onetime partner. The flat blade connected with Jorand's skull at the temple. Jorand reeled, lost his balance, and tumbled into the sea after the ale kegs, never to be seen again.

The worst of it was that Jorand had been right. In the end, they'd dumped all the cargo and barely managed to ride out the storm without further loss among the crew. But since then, the men had been sullen and spiritless.

It was all Jorand's fault, really.

"There's a monastery on the island down the coast. You all saw it as we sailed by last night. Inishmurray, they call it." Kolgrim's lip curled in derision. "Christians! Their coffers are always filled with silver and fineries and they trust naked hope to defend them. All we're likely to meet on that piece of rock are toothless old monks and ball-less young ones. From what I've heard, Inishmurray is ripe for the plucking."

"*Ja,* so you say." The other sailor spat into the waves. "But a man can't be at his fighting best when his stomach's knocking on his backbone."

"You've got the right of it, Einar," Kolgrim agreed, narrowing his eyes at the lone figure ambling along the rocky beach. The wind was at their backs and the *Sea Wolf* closed the distance with the same silence and stealth as the predator for which she was named.

The person on the beach meandered along, pausing here and there to pick up oddly shaped driftwood that made its way to the coast, obviously unaware of the raiders' approach. The captain of the longship recognized the sway of a skirt.

A woman.

"By Loki's hairy arse, it looks like there'll be plenty of sport at this stop." Kolgrim's voice sank to a rasping grunt. The woman's golden-red hair flashed in a shaft of sunlight that split the heavens and bathed her in its glow.

Kolgrim felt himself fully engorge. He favored redheads. "These little Irish wenches always put up a grand tussle."

Kolgrim guided the craft in close, no farther than the length of two longships away from her. The woman didn't hear them coming until the *Sea Wolf*'s hull scraped into the gritty sand.

She turned at the sound. The girl was younger than he'd expected, and pretty, her heart-shaped face white as moonstone. Kolgrim could've sworn it went whiter still when she saw them. She was afraid.

Good.

He leaped over the side of the ship, leaving Einar and the others to tie up the craft. The woman hoisted her skirt, showing a nicely turned pair of calves.

The promise of more to follow, he thought. She wheeled and ran, screaming at the top of her lungs.

"Keefe!" she yelled. Her piercing wail echoed off the rocky cliffs that rose from the shore. "Keefe Murphy!"

"So much for not raising an alarm," Kolgrim grumbled under this breath.

He didn't mind when a woman fought back. In fact, he preferred it that way. But he'd hoped to loot a farmstead or two without attracting any of the local rabble. If the girl kept caterwauling she'd bring the whole countryside down on them. Once roused, the Irish were fair fighters.

"The little skirt better be worth the trouble," Einar, his new second in command, called after him.

Kolgrim caught up with her in a few long strides and threw her to the ground. Not too hard, of course. If he knocked her out and she lay there unconscious, it would take all the fun out of it. He didn't fancy rutting a corpse.

But this quarry was far from docile. Her arms and legs windmilled at him. She hissed and spat like a cornered lynx. When her nails raked his cheek, he roared with laughter.

"Einar, hurry up and come hold her for me," Kolgrim said. "The little hussy wants to play, but I don't want her messing up my pretty face."

Einar sprinted to them. Then he dropped to his knees in the sand and forced a length of cloth between the girl's teeth. He jerked it tight and knotted it behind her slender neck.

"That should shut her up," Einar said. Then he caught her flailing hands and pinned them above her head.

Two other crewmen grabbed her legs, spreading them wide, and straddled her ankles. The other sailors crowded around, leering down at the girl wolfishly.

"Hurry up, Cap'n," one of them said. "There's an even dozen of us waiting."

Kolgrim rucked up the girl's tunic, exposing her delicate pale flesh and a neat triangle of coppery curls. He smiled in satisfaction. She was definitely worth the trouble. The terror in her wide green eyes was just an added treat.

He fumbled with the drawstring at the waist of his trews.

"A damned knot."

He drew out his long knife and sliced the string. But before he could lower his leggings, a sound split the air around them.

It was an enraged bellow, too full of wrath to be an

animal, too feral to be fully human. The roar bounded off the cliff face and repeated itself in a ghostly echo.

Kolgrim looked up to see a warrior rounding the point, charging toward them. The man's fair hair streamed behind him, his face distorted with fury, and in his upraised fist, he brandished the tool of a shipwright, a sharp-edged adze.

"It's Jorand!" one of the sailors cried.

"Or his shade," another voice quavered. "He's come up from Hel to drag us back down with him."

"Captain never should have tossed him overboard," said the first. "Bad luck, said I."

"I'll not fight a ghost!" More than half of Kolgrim's crew turned and fled back to the longship.

Jorand roared again as he closed the distance. Einar was slow to scrabble to his feet and never quite managed it. The phantom warrior buried his adze in the base of Einar's skull, nearly decapitating him with one stroke.

Then Jorand's shade wrenched the weapon free and sliced its wicked edge across another crewman's gut. The sailor screamed, clutching at his vitals as they spilled from his body in stinking gore.

"Jorand," Kolgrim said woodenly, his feet frozen to the spot.

It couldn't be. The shipbuilder had drowned. By now, Jorand's body must surely have been picked clean by the denizens of the deep and his soul consigned to icy Niflheim, the bleakest corner of Hel.

Yet Jorand's ghost stood before him, furious and quivering in a black *berserkr* rage. The phantom's heavily muscled right arm swung the adze again. This time one of Kolgrim's crew took the killing stroke right across his throat. Blood spurted like a fountain, painting a red streak across Jorand's face and heaving chest.

Kolgrim's erection shriveled and his bowels threatened to loosen on the spot. There was no sense in fighting a ghost. The dead had nothing to lose.

He held tightly to the waist of his trews and fled, terror giving him wings.

Before he shoved his vessel into the surf and bounded over the side, he turned to see another wounded raider sinking with finality onto the beach.

The ghost of Jorand stood over the splayed body of the girl, defending her against all comers. It roared at Kolgrim, slashing the deadly adze over its head.

"Row!" Kolgrim bellowed to what was left of his crew. "Row, damn you, or I'll kill you myself!"

Chapter Eight

He bellowed once more at the retreating raiders. The unholy sound poured from him as he expelled all the air in his lungs. It seemed to release both a power and a rage he'd never suspected was there. If only he could have laid his hands on that leader with the russet beard. He'd have squeezed the life out of the man with such joy, he trembled at the mere thought.

Blood pounded in his ears, roaring louder than the dash of surf against the rocky beach. He felt as though he might burst out of his own skin.

He took a shuddering breath. The red haze clouding his vision began to recede and he suddenly recognized what had happened to him. Battle lust. It was the power of *berserkr,* the trancelike state that came upon warriors. It made them cut themselves and feel no pain. A man who worked himself into the darkness of *berserkr* might gnash his own shield in his frenzy to fight. A warrior in the throes of the madness could charge naked into a melee and survive unscathed. A *berserkr* ceased to be human. He became a killing machine.

He looked around at the carnage on the beach. Had he actually slain four men? All he could remember were snatches of color and the screams of the dying. He stared at the adze in his hand. Ribbons of red snaked down the length of the handle and over his wrist. The smell of blood was eerily familiar to him.

He'd puzzled so hard these past weeks over *who* he was. Now, with a sickening lurch in his stomach, he wondered *what* he was.

A soft whimper pulled him out of himself.

"Moira," he said, turning and kneeling beside her. "Have they done you hurt?"

She had pulled her tunic down over her bare legs and wrenched the gag out of her mouth. But when he reached to help her up, she sidled away from him, wild eyed. With shock, he realized she was afraid of him.

Perhaps she was right to be.

Brenna's sister made several attempts to rise, but yelped in pain and sank back onto the sand. One of her ankles was visibly swollen.

"Be easy, now," he said, forcing himself to breathe slowly. "I'll not harm you."

Moira looked at the bodies of the dead raiders. All the color drained from her face. She rose to her knees and was promptly sick. When she finished emptying her stomach on the sand, she plopped down heavily and eyed him with suspicion.

"Keefe?" she said uncertainly.

"No, I don't think so," he said as he suddenly remembered the raiders seemed to know him and had used a name for him that rang true in his ears. "I'm called something else. It seems my real name is Jorand."

How did those men know him? Were they his comrades in his former life? That might explain why they hadn't fought back with any vigor. And if the gang of men who nearly ravished Moira were his companions, what did that say about him?

He felt as heavy and worn as a dull ax. He dropped the adze and sank to the sand.

"Jorand, is it?" Moira had stopped trembling and made an effort to smile at him. The color was returning to her face. "Then I'm after thanking ye, Jorand. God alone knows what would have happened if ye hadn't come when ye did." She turned her gaze away from the mangled bodies. "And did what ye did."

"We'd better get you back to the keep," Jorand said. "Can you stand?"

She tried to put weight on her foot and cried out in pain. "I don't think so. My ankle hurts like the very Devil himself is jabbing needles into it."

"Then I'll carry you."

"First, ye'd best be cleaning up." She waved a pale hand toward his face and chest. "Give yourself a good plunge in the sea. Otherwise, me da will think I'm being fetched home by a monster."

Jorand touched a palm to his cheek. It came away sticky with blood. He stumbled down to the shore and waded into the shallows.

The bracing, salty spray cleared his head. He wasn't sorry he'd killed those men. They deserved everything he gave them. But the ease with which he dispatched them, the burning in his veins as he hacked away, the jubilant triumph he felt... What had he been in his former life?

Perhaps he was a monster.

Chapter Nine

Brian Ui Niall didn't seem to think the Northman was a monster.

After the initial frenzy of their arrival at the keep, Moira explained how Keefe had rushed to her aid. Connor and Aidan ran to the beach before the tide rushed in and carried away the dead raiders, sweeping the coastline clean of any gore. Moira's story was confirmed.

Jorand, as Keefe Murphy was now known, was proclaimed a hero and a feast was declared in his honor. Brian Ui Niall sent out a call, summoning the whole Donegal clan to the keep for a celebration to be held on the night of the next full moon. The festivities promised to be grand.

One by one, the crofters sent back word of their acceptance. A tame Northman was novelty enough. The fact that the Donegal had trained one to attack his own kind was enough to send even the least inquisitive mind into flutters of curiosity.

Brenna buried herself in preparations. Since the

feast honored the man who fixed her precious chair, even Una bestirred herself enough to take an interest in the cleaning. The stone floor of the keep was swept, scrubbed, and freshly strewn with rushes.

"Maybe ye'll be making another batch of meat pasties, I'm thinking," Moira suggested. "If we hope to honor Jorand as he deserves, we don't want to be running out now, do we?"

After he rescued her sister, their father had released Jorand from all servitude and gave him free range over the region. Brenna was no longer bound to watch him or devise work to keep him occupied.

Jorand. The foreign name still lay heavily on Brenna's tongue. To her mind, the man would always be Keefe Murphy, her handsome sea warrior. Now that he no longer bore the name she'd given him, he seemed even less hers.

Brenna shook her head. What a fanciful notion! The stranger had never been hers, even when she first found him on the beach. And why on earth would she even want him if he was? Besides, it was too late for such fantasies. She'd never have a man of her own now.

On the appointed night of feasting, the king of Donegal's keep was jammed with people. Those who hadn't seen the tall, blond Northman before now crowded around Jorand, alternately suspicious and admiring, wanting to talk to him, to take the measure of this foreigner who'd saved a daughter of the house and earned the gratitude of their king.

Brenna never enjoyed crowds. Her craving for solitude had made her consider life as a novice at Clonmacnoise. With the peat fire smoking in the grate and the press of humanity all around her, Brenna had to escape the keep for some fresh air. She wrapped her *brat* around her shoulders and slipped into the darkness.

The soft summer evening gave way to a hazy night. From time to time the moon peeped from behind cloudbanks. As she wandered away from the keep, Brenna heard a few couplets of a crude drinking song followed by a burst of laughter. She kept walking till she could hear the singers no more and finally climbed atop the stone wall, settling down to enjoy the quiet. Far from the round stone tower, the only sounds she heard were the drone of insects and the occasional lonely hoot of an owl.

"It's a fair party, princess." Jorand stepped out of the shadows and leaned against the wall next to her.

She hadn't heard him approach and nearly toppled off her perch.

"I thought Northmen craved merrymaking just as well as the sons of Erin do," she said.

The moon chose that moment to slide from behind its feathery curtain and shine its full strength on Jorand's face. Brenna bit her lip. Her chest constricted just looking at him.

" 'Tis your celebration," she said. "Why are ye not after enjoying it then?"

"Maybe for the same reason you aren't."

"Too many people?"

"Or maybe not the right one." Jorand clasped his hands in front of him and leaned his elbows on the rock wall. Then he cocked his head at her and gave her a look that made her shiver.

Brenna was unable to meet his steady gaze. She scarcely breathed. The small hairs on his arm brushed against hers, but she couldn't bring herself to pull away. She was intensely aware of his scent, a hint of wood shavings and the tang of the sea over a warm, unmistakably masculine smell. Brenna cleared her throat in discomfort.

"I have not yet thanked ye, Northman."

"I noticed."

"'Tis not for lack of sentiment, I assure ye," she said quickly. "'Tis in your debt I am. 'Twas a blessing of God ye were there for me sister."

He dragged a hand over his face. "I don't know if the gods had much to do with it. I think it was more likely the handiwork of that devil you talk so much about."

"No, 'twas God," Brenna said, taking comfort in repeating what she'd heard from nearly everyone in Brian Ui Niall's keep. "Sure the Almighty strengthened your arm to defend Moira. Even Father Michael says so."

"And yet you sound doubtful."

How had he heard that in her voice? "No, not at all," she denied. "I was only wondering..."

"What, princess?"

If he divined her secrets so readily from the tone of her voice, what might he read in her face? She ducked her head to shield herself from his gaze. "Tis blasphemous to think it."

"You can tell me."

His smile should be counted as one of the seven deadly sins.

"I'm a heathen, remember," Jorand said. "I'm not likely to be shocked and I don't go to confession like you do, so who would I tell?"

Brenna knotted her fingers together. The temptation to talk to someone about her doubts was more than she could resist. Even if he didn't share her faith, Jorand's willingness to listen invited her confidence.

"'Tis only if the Lord God was there making sure ye were about to help Moira ... I'm wondering where the Almighty was when such things happened to ... to others."

"You mean like those crofters?"

When she frowned at him, he went on. "Remember? The burnt-out farmstead you showed me that first day. Northmen were there, you said."

"Aye, just so," she said, her heart hiccupping in her chest. "Why does misfortune come upon some and not others? Are they somehow deserving of their fate?" She chewed her bottom lip. "Are they unworthy?"

Jorand stared into the night sky where the starry Hunter strode through a break in the clouds. He was silent for so long, Brenna thought he must have misunderstood her dilemma or even forgotten she was there.

"No," he finally said. "It isn't a question of worthiness. It's just bad luck. As long as there are men in the world, there will be those who are determined to hurt others and there will be those who will be hurt. It doesn't mean they deserve it."

His words were like soothing balm on a burn. If Jorand was right, part of what happened at Clonmacnoise wasn't her fault, after all.

And it wasn't God's, either. Didn't Father Michael say He had no favorites, that He was no respecter of persons? Just because there were evil men in the world, that didn't mean God was any less good. But that wasn't the whole of her dilemma.

"Ye were quick to help me sister. What if ye hadn't?

I mean, suppose someone could have come to her aid and didn't?" The small muscles in her face strained as she fought to get the words out. "Suppose it was another person's fault she was even there in the first place?"

"You take too much on yourself," he said. "Your sister told me she'd seen you on the ridge before she came down to the beach. You couldn't have known Moira was going into danger. And even if you'd been there, you couldn't have helped her. You'd only have shared her fate."

Brenna sighed. He meant well, but he misunderstood her question and she wasn't prepared to enlighten him. She'd wrestled with these thoughts for months. Just when she'd begin to make peace with herself, something reopened the wound. Best to let it bleed. She wasn't ready to cauterize it in public.

"Brenna," Jorand said softly. "What happened to you?"

She felt as though he'd punched her in the gut. How was this man able to read her as though she was a freshly illuminated manuscript? It wouldn't do at all. The wall she erected around her heart had been breeched, but she quickly shored up her defenses.

"Devil if I know what ye mean," she said as she slid off the wall and started back to the keep.

He snatched up one of her hands.

"Oh, I think you do," he said as he pulled her toward him. "Whatever it is, you've got to let it out. It's like a worm eating you from the inside."

"There's a pleasant prospect." She glowered at him. "Thank ye for the lovely image ye've conjured for me, Northman."

"After all this time, that's all I still am in your sight.

Just a Northman." When she tried to pull away, he tugged her in close and cupped her chin. "Ah, Brenna. Can you not say my true name? Not even once?"

He leaned down toward her, his deep eyes dark in the moonlight. His mouth was so close, one corner turned slightly up. Brenna gulped, wondering what that mouth might taste like.

"Jorand," she said softly.

The name was nearly swallowed up as his lips covered hers in a kiss both sudden and inevitable. Her first impulse was to pull away, but his kiss beguiled her. It was not the kind of kiss she'd expected from a man like him.

His mouth was warm and sure. His lips pressed against hers just enough to let her know she'd been kissed before he pulled back. It was as sweet a kiss as she could imagine. A kiss that wanted to give, not take. A kiss that left no bitterness in its wake.

"There now, that wasn't so terrible, was it?" he asked.

"Do you mean saying your name or letting you kiss me?"

"Both."

Her lips twitched in a suppressed smile. "It was tolerable."

"Just tolerable?" He grinned. "I can do better than that."

Brenna stiffened as he pulled her closer. Fire danced along her body where it pressed against his. She fought against the urge to cry out.

The rising panic she felt must have shown on her face, even in the dim moonlight. "Hush now. Calm yourself, Brenna," he whispered. "I'll not hurt you. I'll never hurt you."

His mouth closed on hers once more, this time with more insistence. Brenna trembled under his lips, but felt warmth stole over her, as though she were being dipped into a hot bath. His mouth's gentle probing released a flood of new sensations in her belly. One by one, her locked muscles loosened and she relaxed into his strong body.

With hesitation, she let herself rest her palms on his shoulders, enjoying the feel of his muscles under the rough cloth of his tunic. Almost of their own volition, her hands crept up and draped around Jorand's neck, sliding under the thick blond hair that brushed past his shoulders. His bare skin was warm and smooth under her fingers.

One of his hands caressed her spine and then pressed her against him. Brenna felt the hardness in his groin and fear rushed back into her.

She shoved against his chest and he released her mouth.

"Never kiss me again, Northman," she spat between clenched teeth.

"Only if you can honestly tell me you didn't enjoy it," Jorand said, casting a knowing look.

Brenna made a growling noise in the back of her throat and yanked herself out of his arms. He didn't fight to keep her there. She stomped away toward the stone tower.

Halfway across the courtyard she met Moira.

"Where's Keefe—I mean Jorand?" her sister wanted to know. "Da is calling for him and I've looked everywhere."

"He's over there." Brenna pointed in the direction

of the rock wall. "Though I can't imagine what a body would want with the likes of him," she added sourly.

"I can." Moira's voice was as soft as newly churned butter.

"Fine then," Brenna said, at a loss to identify the new feeling swirling in her gut. "He's all yours, sister. Take him with me blessing."

As she stormed toward the keep, Brenna finally found a name for the sinking sensation inside her. It was fear. Fear that Moira would take her at her word.

And take her Northman.

CHAPTER TEN

The noise of laughter and roughhousing greeted her when Brenna opened the heavy oak door. Between the glaring torchlight and the swirl of colors on the tightly packed guests of the Donegal, she could scarcely keep her eyes open.

She hung her *brat* on the peg by the door and slid along the curving outer wall till she came to an arrow loop, a narrow cross-shaped opening in the stone. In case of attack, a defender could loose shafts in virtually any direction with very little risk to himself from an arrow loop. There was a narrow ledge before the slit wide enough for her to perch upon. She tucked her knees to her chin and her nose to the opening for fresh air.

Each time the keep door swung open, she looked over, expecting to see Jorand and her sister. Each time, her heart sank deeper with disappointment.

Was Moira in the Northman's arms in the moonlight now?

She balled the hem of skirt in her fists. *Why should I care?* she thought angrily, keeping her gaze cast to the floor lest anyone see her struggle to stay calm. A pair of scuffed shoes appeared in her line of sight. She looked up to see who was wearing them.

"Come, Brenna, give us a song," Connor McNaught demanded with a drunken slur in his voice.

"I don't feel inclined to sing," she said, willing him to go away.

"Then I'll have to do it meself." Connor clambered up on one of the stout tables and bellowed out a ribald song about the coronation of the king of the clan Conaill, a festive and crude ritual ending in the public copulation between the king and a white mare. It was an ancient custom and, as far as Brenna knew, still in practice. The crowd roared with laughter, but Brenna feared she might be ill.

Her gaze slid to the door against her volition. What was keeping her sister and the Northman?

"Ah, daughter!" Brian Ui Niall's voice rang out over the hall as he lifted her harp. "'Tis some time since we heard ye and this fine wee instrument. Give us a song, then."

Brenna's lips tightened into a line. She'd never felt less like singing in her life, but she couldn't refuse a direct request from her father, much less her king. She elbowed her way to Brian Ui Niall's side and took the harp from him. After tuning the cat-gut strings, she settled the instrument on her knee and waited for silence to fill the hall.

It had been a long time since she played her harp and her fingers were hesitant at first. But after a few feathery strokes, her hands remembered their business and released a delicate melody into the smoky air.

Then Brenna began to sing.

O'er the lonely hills I wander,
O'er cloud-wraithed mountain, by surging sea.
O whither have ye roamed, my dear one?
O will ye ne'er return to me?

As she started the last refrain, a slight stir in the air told her the keep door had opened. She looked up from the harp to see Jorand and her sister tumble in, all smiles, Moira's fluty laugh and Jorand's rumbling chuckle floating toward her. The sound pierced her heart like an arrow.

The Northman was head and shoulders taller than the other men in her father's keep, so it was no trouble to meet his gaze over the crowd. His smile faded as she continued to sing, but his eyes held the same fire that had burned in their depths just moments before he kissed her.

Brenna's voice caught in her throat, but she somehow managed to finish the song.

I sought my love in glens and dells
Where fairies haunt the darkling trees.
O whither have ye roamed, my dear one?
O will ye ne'er return to me?

When the last wisp of sound faded, the guests erupted in loud clapping and stomping till the floor of the keep trembled. Brian Ui Niall kissed Brenna on the cheek and silenced the crowd with upraised arms.

"'Tis good to know my little songbird hasn't forgotten how to warble," he said. "But pleasant as her songs are, that's not why I called all Donegal to the keep. We're here tonight to honor a stranger among us. Jorand, me lad, come up here."

The guests parted to make way for the big Northman.

When Jorand reached the king, Brian Ui Niall slapped both his hands on Jorand's shoulders and bid him to stand beside him and face the throng.

"In times past, I've hated your kind, Northman. They've been a scourge from the sea, the cause of endless woe to the people of Erin. I came to believe the raiders from Lothland were more beast than man."

The gathering nodded its assent.

"Since ye washed up on our shores, I've altered me thinking on that point somewhat. Now I'm after believing there's good and evil in all sorts of folk," the king said as he turned to Jorand. "Ye are one of the good ones."

The Northman studied the floor, as if embarrassed by her father's praise.

"For the way ye saved me daughter Moira, I'm deeply in your debt."

Brenna's heart lurched as Jorand looked over the heads of the gathered Irishmen toward Moira, who was leaning against the oak door.

"I'm glad I was there to help," Jorand said simply.

"So am I, lad," the king said. "And that's why I'm after joining my house to ye. Here before these witnesses, I'm offering ye me daughter's hand in marriage."

Jorand seemed struck dumb as he continued to

gaze at Moira. Brenna thought she might be sick on the spot.

"What say ye?" Brian demanded.

"The king does me honor but—"

"Good! 'Tis settled then. I'm pleased to announce the betrothal of me daughter to the Northman, Jorand," the king said. "We'll finalize the details of the agreement in private," he said softly, then bellowed out, "Father Michael, we'll be posting the banns on Sunday next."

Then, inexplicably, the king turned and took Brenna's hand. He led her to the Northman and placed her icy palm in Jorand's warm one. Then Brian held their joined hands aloft.

The crowd was silent for the space of a half dozen heartbeats, but then roused itself to offer a chorus of well-wishes and desultory cheers.

"God's grace on the pair of ye!" The king's blessing echoed off the stone walls. "And may your joining bring peace and an end to the ravages of Northmen on the people of Donegal."

Peace meant crops sown in season and full bellies all winter. Safety from Norse raiders was a sentiment the clan could endorse enthusiastically and the cheers were louder and more heartfelt this time.

Brenna hoped their marriage would bring peace to someone. Since she suspected her betrothed preferred her sister, the union wasn't likely to bring much peace to her.

Chapter Eleven

"Da, I cannot believe ye would make this match without so much as a by-your-leave from me!" Brenna's pent-up outrage nearly exploded when the last guests straggled out of the keep in the wee hours of the morning.

"Or me," Moira said coolly.

"Be easy, daughters," Brian Ui Niall said, raising his hands to silence them. "Moira, get ye to your bed this instant. Ye are not to trouble yourself further on this matter, and that's me final word."

Moira huffed her disappointment, but the king's dark scowl sent her stomping off to the ladder. A moment later, from the uppermost story, Brenna heard the door to their small room slam with vehemence.

Brian Ui Niall sighed. "Brenna, ye must trust me. 'Tis only your welfare I'm thinking of."

"Me welfare!" Her brows shot up. "To wed a stranger we know next to nothing of. And how can that possibly be conducive to me welfare?"

"He's hardly a stranger, Brenna. We may not know much of his past, but I'm thinking Jorand's shown us something of his true mettle in the short time he's been with us." The king tossed a glance at the Northman who sat, stony as the keep itself, by the smoldering peat fire. "Ye must admit we owe him for the way he saved your sister."

"But it doesn't mean ye owe him me!"

"Ye know as well as I that I cannot offer him Moira. It flies against all custom to marry off the younger before the elder is made a bride. If ye're not for the Church, ye need a husband, daughter." The king raked a hand through his dark hair. "Brenna, me heart, there's the other matter to consider."

Brenna felt herself blanch. How could her father broach that thorny subject now? "Surely ye don't still blame me for—"

"No, daughter," Brian cut her off quickly. "I only meant, as king, I have to weigh other things as well."

"Such as?"

"Domhnall of the clan Ulaid has heard of our Moira's beauty. He's asked for your sister for Fearghus, his remaining son," Brian said. "I cannot deny him."

Her father's words hit Brenna like stones tossed on a grave mound. When Brenna's brother was accidentally killed, Brian Ui Niall had forced Domhnall to sacrifice the life of his first born to keep peace between their clans. Now he could scarcely deny the Ulaid a bride of his choosing for his remaining heir. In a way, the request evened the score. Domhnall was depriving the Donegal of his cherished daughter just as Ui Niall had goaded him to offer up his son. Now Brian couldn't gainsay his neighbor. To do so would mean open war, and, given the opportunity, Brian Ui Niall was a man for peace.

Brenna had no more choice in the matter than her father. "Aye, Da, I understand."

"Ye must needs wed, daughter," Brian said simply. "Connor McNaught pressed me for ye—"

"I'd sooner marry a toad."

The king grinned. "I thought as much. That's why I offered ye to the Northman."

"And does the toad have any say in the matter?" Jorand asked dryly. He leaned back, massive arms crossed over his chest.

"Ah, no slight was intended, boy-o. Ye've missed me meaning," the king said hastily.

"No, I think I understand your situation pretty well. You have a daughter you can't place in the marriage market for some unnamed reason, and I'm available. If I accept, you've gained an ally against further raids from my countrymen, married off Brenna, and freed up Moira to seal the peace with your neighbor," Jorand said, his level gaze piercing Brenna to the bone. "If I decline, Brenna will end up marrying a man she detests even more than me and you'll have given your people one more reason to hate my kind. I think that about tallies it up, doesn't it, or have I missed something?"

Brenna felt the blood drain from her head. Her vision swam uncertainly. It was one thing for her to protest this match. For Jorand to refuse her now after he'd accepted her in public would disgrace her beyond bearing.

Brian narrowed his eyes at the Northman. "Does this mean ye'll not have me daughter?"

"Now you've missed my meaning," Jorand said.

"I just want everything clear and in the open. You said we'd agree to terms in private. So be it. Here are my terms. Once Brenna and I are wed, I'm free to go wherever and whenever I choose."

"Ye expect to wed a daughter of the house and make a sea widow of her in the selfsame day?" the king demanded.

"Not at all," Jorand said. "Brenna can come with me if she wishes. In fact, I hope she will. She told me some Northmen have set up a town on the river Liffey. Dublin, she called it. I mean to go to this Dublin to find out if I have kinsmen there." A frown spoiled the even line of Jorand's dark brows. "I know my true name now, but not my true self yet. I hope finding some familiar faces will bring back my memory."

"And what if your memory includes a wife elsewhere?" Brenna asked softly.

"No need to borrow trouble, daughter," the king said, then turned back to Jorand. "A wife must follow her husband if he wills it, but if me daughter wishes to stay here, ye must swear to allow it. Brenna has a home within me keep as long as I hold Donegal. Are we in accord?"

Jorand nodded.

"Is that all then?" Brian asked.

"No," the Northman answered. "I need to speak to Brenna in private before I give my final answer."

The king nodded and strode to the door. "Speak your piece then. I'll be back directly."

Brenna felt as though all her support had trailed Brian Ui Niall out of the keep. "No, ye'll not bargain me away like a heifer with a blemish! Surely there's some other way," she called after him. "Don't make me do this, Da."

Her legs went limp and she sank to the stone pavings in a small heap. To be haggled over instead of wooed, to have her future dicated to her without a choice—it was unbearable.

Her shoulders quaked in silent sobs. She covered her face with her hands and wept.

Then she felt a hand slide over the crown of her head, warm and gentle. Brenna opened her eyes and looked up.

"It's not so bad as that, princess." Jorand squatted beside her and offered her a small square of cloth. "I won't be such a bad husband. You've no need to fear. I'll not be harsh with you, I swear it."

Brenna gulped and wiped her eyes. Then she blew her nose like a trumpet.

"I'm not afraid of ye." Even to her own ears, her voice quaked uncertainly. "But it does me heart no favor to be wedding a man who thought he was agreeing to marry me sister."

"If that's what you think, you shouldn't worry," Jorand said. "If I were given my choice, believe me, Brenna, it would be you."

He was being polite, nothing more. She supposed she should be grateful. To start a marriage of convenience with courtesy was surely not a small thing.

Then why did her chest still ache?

He ran a hand through the length of her hair again and she trembled.

"You're sure you're not afraid?"

She shook her head. "Ye've given me no cause to fear ye."

Yet.

"Good," he said, still smoothing down her mass of

curls with his long-fingered hand. "That's a start, at least. But I need to know something."

"What?"

"What was it you almost said tonight? Something about your father not still blaming you for ... what?"

Brenna sat up straight and met his gaze directly. "Ye may as well know from the first, then." Her voice faltered but she forced herself to keep looking at him. "If ye marry me, ye'll not be wedding a giddy innocent. I know full well what passes between a man and a woman."

"That explains a thing or two." If he was surprised, he didn't show it. Brenna looked away. Did unholy knowledge leave a mark? A visible sign for all the world to read like too much sun left freckles?

"I can't say for sure," Jorand went on, "but if we marry, you might not be wedding a virgin either."

Saints and angels, he'd misunderstood her. Just because she knew what men were, he thought her unchaste.

If it were only that simple ...

The truth was too painful to explain. He'd learn soon enough. "That's different. Ye are a man and 'tis expected a man have ... experience."

"If I do, I have no memory of it. Answer me this, Brenna." His voice dropped to a low rumble. "Do you love this other man?"

"Ye don't understand." She balled the soiled kerchief in her fist. "When I think on him at all, I wish him dead."

She stared across the room, her eyes not focusing on anything in Brian Ui Niall's keep. Her sister Sinead's screams echoed in her mind.

"Ye've been given a gift, Jorand. Have ye never

thought that *not* remembering could be a boon? Blessed forgetfulness. I yearn for it with all me heart."

The tears erupted afresh and Jorand settled himself beside her on the pavings. He wrapped his arms around her, rocked her slowly, and let her cry.

"A man who can't remember and a woman who wants to forget," he said softly when her sobs subsided. "Aren't we a pair?"

"Aye." Brenna laughed in spite of herself and swiped at her eyes. "I guess we are."

"Then you'll have me for a husband?"

"Aye, if ye still wish to take me to wife," she said.

Jorand cupped her chin and forced her to meet his gaze. "More than anything."

"Then we'll marry," Brenna said, trying to control the strange quiver in her gut. "But I place on ye two conditions."

"Name them."

"One, ye take me to Clonmacnoise Abbey on the way to this Dublin ye seek. I have some ... doings there I must needs finish."

"Easily done. And the other?"

"Our marriage will be a handfast only." When he arched an inquiring brow, she explained. "We wed for a year and a day. At the end of that time, we may make the marriage permanent, or part company with no ill will."

"This handfast is a true marriage?"

"Aye," she said with a slight flutter in her chest. "A true marriage in all its parts, save only in its brevity."

"Why do you wish it so?"

"Ye don't know what ye'll find in Dublin. Da may be willing to dismiss it, but ye can't say for certain ye don't already have a wife and family waiting for ye. I need to remember that, and so do ye."

"True enough. It seems sensible to swear only to what we know we can keep," he agreed and held out a hand for her to clasp. "A handfast it will be."

"For a year and a day." Brenna gripped his palm and made the mistake of looking into his eyes. She knew she must guard her heart or else when he parted from her at the end of the appointed time, there'd be nothing left of it.

CHAPTER TWELVE

"Here now," Moira said as she swept back one of Brenna's curls and tucked it under the elaborate plait of braids crowning her head. Her sister slipped another sprig of flowers into the mass of hair above Brenna's left ear. "Much better. Ye are the most beautiful bride I've ever seen, Brennie, and that's God's truth."

"Wait till your own wedding a month hence," Brenna said. "I'll be a crow to your dove. Ye'll be made not only a bride, but a queen as well."

Moira's smile held an understandable lift of smugness. " 'Tis a good match Da has made for me, isn't it?"

"Fearghus of Ulaid has the best of the bargain, I'm thinking. Ye know nothing of him, sister. How can ye be so blithe about this marriage ye are pledged to?"

"And what do ye know of Jorand save that he has a pleasing form and a stout heart?"

Brenna shrugged. "Not much, I grant ye. His past is a closed book, even to himself."

"Then ye must write his future with your own fair hand," Moira said.

"For a year and a day, at least," Brenna said.

"And here is the crowning piece," Moira said. She fished in the pocket pinned to her tunic and drew out a shimmering silver chain. "Mother sends this to ye."

An ornate cross dangled before Brenna's eyes. It was the silver necklace her mother had worn for as long as she could remember. She'd always told her daughters it would go to the first bride among them. Of course, Brenna always expected Sinead would receive it, but her older sister set her heart on a religious life when she was a very little girl. The passage of years did nothing to dissuade her.

Brenna flushed with pleasure as she slipped the symbol of faith over her head. The silver chain was cool on her skin ad the cross nestled snugly in the hollow between her breasts. The necklace was the finest thing she'd ever owned. It felt like her mother's benediction and she was grateful for this tangible evidence of her distant mother's care. "Mother knows I'm to wed, then."

Moira's smile trembled. "She knows there's to be a wedding in the keep at least. Last evening when I helped her to bed, she took it off her neck and asked me to give it to the bride." Moira wrapped her arms around Brenna. "Oh, Brennie, she wouldn't know either of our names if her hope of heaven depended upon it."

"Then we must be grateful it doesn't," Brenna said.

Moira was unable to sustain melancholy for more than a handful of heartbeats. She grinned wickedly and leaned down to whisper in Brenna's ear. "Just think, this very night ye'll lie with a man, sister. Ye must tell me all after ye have been with your Northman. If it's left to Mother, I'll go ignorant to me bridal bed."

"As ye should," Brenna said primly, her face coloring with heat. She'd avoided thinking of that aspect of her impending marriage. But each time the vision of Jorand naked in the stream loomed up to haunt her. She felt her spine wilt.

Lord above, grant me courage to go through this ordeal and may I not hate the man hereafter, she prayed silently.

"Brenna, wipe that pained expression off your face," her sister scolded. "Honestly, ye'd think ye were destined for a bog instead of the arms of an exceedingly fair man. I'm not privy to all the particulars, but from the little I've heard, the marriage bed is not at all an unpleasant prospect."

Brenna was saved from making a reply by a soft rap on the door. Father Michael's gentle voice asked for admittance. Brenna scurried to let her old friend and teacher into the cramped cell.

The priest made signs of blessing over both the girls. Then Moira slipped out, with eyes rolling, to allow Brenna the privacy of the confessional.

"Since ye were a wee girl I dreamed of saying mass over your marriage. Then when ye went to Clonmacnoise to become a bride of Christ, I thought never to see ye wed. And now this." The thicket of wrinkles around Father Michael's eyes deepened with concern. "Ye are certain ye wish it thus, my child?"

"Aye, I do," Brenna said as she adjusted the enameled silver brooch holding the blue *brat* at her shoulder. She fumbled with the catch and pricked her finger. A bright red drop welled up and Brenna let a curse slip from her lips before she bound her fingertip with a small strip of cloth. "Forgive me, Father."

The priest made the sign of the cross in the air. "There are two kinds of folk I always absolve of unclean speech with no penance at all—women in labor and brides about to wed."

"I thank ye." Brenna grinned and hugged her mentor. "And thank ye for agreeing to the handfast. 'Tis best, believe me. But it does ease me heart to know ye'll be saying the blessing over us."

"Any girl set to marry a pagan Northman is in need of blessing."

"What a thing to say! Did ye not baptize Jorand yourself with your own hands?"

The Northman had become a nominal Christian at least. It was the only way Father Michael would consent to officiating, but the way her heart hammered against her ribs, Brenna couldn't say the old priest wasn't right. Jorand was so different from the men of Erin—larger, full of foreign eccentricities, and not quite safe. What was she thinking when she agreed to this match?

She took a deep breath. She could do this. She had to.

"Brenna, me love," Brian Ui Niall called up the ladder. " 'Tis time."

It seemed to Brenna that time expanded and contracted in a writhing pattern. She somehow managed to climb down the ladder and then the world rushed at her senses in a jumbled mass. She was aware of the fresh scent of the heather thrust into her hands, the rough brush of her father's lips on her temple, a blur of colors as she floated on Brian Ui Niall's arm through the throng to the waiting circle of stones and flower petals. The squeal of flutes suddenly hushed when she came to a stop before the big Northman.

Her husband. For a year and a day.

Her lover. Her vision tunneled at the thought. She couldn't dwell on that now.

Looking into Jorand's face, his features so damnably perfect, his eyes impossibly blue, his mouth slightly turned up at the corners as if he'd read her secret thoughts, Brenna feared she might faint dead away.

Breathe, she ordered herself.

Father Michael's prayer droned on in Latin, as if he was intent on Christianizing this rite as much as humanly possible. The heads of all the guests were bowed, and Brenna tried to follow their example, but she felt Jorand's eyes on her and had to look up again.

He flashed his teeth at her and winked.

"... of your own free will?"

Had someone said something? With a start, she realized she was expected to answer.

"Aye," Brenna said softly.

"And ye, Jorand." Brenna heard the slightest catch in Father Michael's voice. "Do ye come also into this circle of your own free will?"

"*Ja.*" His voice was deep and strong.

Father Michael presented a jewel-handled dagger to Brenna. She took it and, after a brief hesitation, punctured her palm with the sharp tip. Then she handed the weapon to Jorand. He closed his right fist around the blade and yanked it through with his other hand without so much as a flinch.

"Join hands," the priest ordered.

Brenna raised her hand and felt Jorand's palm against hers. Their fingers interlocked, blood mingling, as Father Michael bound a red cord around their wrists.

"With this binding I tie ye, heart to heart, together as one. With this knot, ye are joined in sacred union. May God smile upon thee, and bless thee with health and joy."

The priest pulled the knot tight. "Let the bride and groom recite the vow."

Brenna and Jorand had been given instruction on the proper wording, but now the rite suddenly flew right out of Brenna's mind. She couldn't think how to start.

"You are blood of my blood," Jorand began, triggering her memory.

"And bone of me bone," Brenna answered.

"I give ye me body, that we two might be one." She faltered a bit on that line, but Jorand's voice was strong enough for the two of them.

"Hand in hand, and blood in blood." Brenna even managed a tremulous smile.

"Let this green land witness our love," Jorand finished.

A tiny ribbon of red tickled down her wrist. Was it her blood or his? There was no way to tell.

Father Michael offered them Communion, placing a small bite of barley bread on their tongues. "Let this be your first meal as man and wife. May Christ bless this union and may ye never know hunger."

The priest raised a chalice of wine. "Let Christ's blood be your first drink as man and wife. May ye never know thirst."

Brenna sipped the stinging liquid, then handed it to Jorand, who drank while never taking his eyes from her. He was playing the role of devoted swain convincingly, she had to give him that. She blessed him for his thoughtfulness.

Father Michael handed the dagger to Jorand. "Let this be your first task as man and wife. Sever all ties with the past, cut off the bindings of the old, and sweep them away."

Jorand—now her husband, she realized with a start—sliced away the red cord, taking care not to nick her with the sharp blade. The binding fell to the earth, but he didn't release her hand immediately.

His other hand closed on her waist and he pulled her to him. Then his mouth met hers in a soft but not quite chaste kiss. When he released her, there was fire in his blue eyes only Brenna could see.

Flutes and pipes sounded and the crowd erupted in cheers. The eldest daughter of the house was made a wife and all Donegal rejoiced with its king.

The merrymaking that had started in the wee hours of the morning now began again in earnest.

Chapter Thirteen

Once the ceremony was finished, Brenna finally spared an eye for the decorations festooning the yard. Gay pennants embroidered with the Donegal crest—a sprig of heather on a bed of green—flapped overhead. Brenna recognized her sister's hand in the sprays of heather affixed to nearly every doorway, even over the lintel of the listing cattle byre. The air was perfumed with crushed petals stamped underfoot by all.

A small group of musicians—two flutes, a harp and a slightly out of tune sackbut—launched into a lively song. Every young heart lifted and a twirling dance started on the lush green grass. The elders drank their pints, looking on with indulgence and wry expressions tinged with a touch of envy for the sprightliness and high spirits of youth.

"I'm sorry, princess," Jorand said. "I don't think I know how to dance."

"Don't be troubling your head about it," she said. "I was never one for dancing much meself."

But even as she spoke the words, she was swept into the fray by Connor McNaught as he tripped past.

"Come, me Brenna," he said. She caught a strong whiff of whiskey on his breath as he leered toward her, flashing his yellowed teeth. "If that great Norse slug ye married hasn't the sense to dance with ye, allow me to do ye the honors."

He twirled her so violently, Brenna's world seemed to continue to swirl even once they'd begun a circular promenade with the other dancers.

"In fact, there's somewhat else I'd be happy to do for ye. Tip me the eye if your husband ruts ye no better than he dances." The hand on her waist crept up under one of her breasts, his thumb strafing her softness. "I've been a married man, as ye know, and can teach ye a trick or two. Just give the word, Brenna me dear, and I'll service ye with pleasure."

She struggled to free herself from his grasp, but Connor latched on to her with the tenacity of a wolfhound on the last bone. Then suddenly Connor's feet left the ground, forcing him to release Brenna.

Jorand had grabbed him by the scruff of the neck and lifted the smaller man till they were nearly nose to nose. Her husband bared his teeth at Connor. There was no mistaking Jorand's expression for a smile.

"This is Brenna's celebration, so I'll not mar it by thrashing you as you deserve." Jorand's voice was low, but the menace in the tone was so potent even Connor in his drunken stupor couldn't fail to mark it. "But by your Christ, if you ever lay so much as a finger on my wife again, I'll split you from gills to gullet in one stroke."

Jorand's strong fingers closed over Connor's throat. The Irishman's eyes bulged like a codfish flopping on the beach.

"Nod if you understand me," Jorand urged.

Connor's head bobbed with alacrity.

Jorand set him down, none too gently. "Now, you may beg my wife's forgiveness for the discourtesy you've shown her," he ordered. "And be careful to convince me you mean it."

Connor stammered out his apology and beat a hasty retreat through the crowd.

"Thank ye," Brenna said. No one, not even her father, had ever championed her so publicly.

"I can see defending you from other men will be a frequent chore," Jorand said. "I suppose it's just part of being the husband of so lovely a lady."

Warmth surged in her chest and spread downward, clear to her toes. The way he smiled at her made her feel lovely for the first time in her life.

"It's plain I need to dance with you, Brenna, whether I remember the steps or not."

"Perhaps ye know more than ye think. Just like the woodworking, it may come back to ye if we take a turn or two."

"I may tread on your toes," he warned.

" 'Tis a risk I'm prepared to take."

As they joined the ring of dancers, Brenna's heart was lighter than it had been in longer than she could remember.

The celebration flowed from dancing to feasting to drinking until torches were called for and, one by one, the pinpricks of stars showed on the black vault of the night sky.

"The garter!" someone cried out.

The chant was taken up by all the young men in the crowd. The bravest of the lot made to approach Brenna, making several ineffective snatches under her skirt. The lad intended only to reach under her hem and retrieve the coveted trophy, but the murderous look in Jorand's eye backed the youth up against the line of his companions.

"They mean no harm. Ye must give them me garters," Brenna whispered, turning her back to him and lifting her hem high enough to bare the delicate bands of blue tied in neat bows at the back of her knees. "Untie them and toss them to the lads."

Jorand knelt and tugged the ribbons free, his thumb brushing the crevice behind her knee. A shiver tingled up her thigh and Brenna thought her legs might buckle on the spot.

Her husband tossed the garters to the waiting crowd and was roundly cheered for his generosity.

'Tis nearly time. The realization spread panic through her veins. Brenna swayed on her feet.

"Are you well?" Jorand put an arm around her waist to steady her.

"Oh, aye," she answered, willing the shiver in her soul not to work its way out to her muscles. " 'Tis only now I cannot keep me stockings up."

"Then we'll have to remedy that by taking them off," Jorand said with a smile. Before she could protest, he scooped her off her feet and carried her toward the round hut that had been prepared for their use.

The bridal pair was hailed all around, and a small

procession of well-wishers dogged them on their way. Lewd suggestions and offers of lascivious assistance were shouted after them good-naturedly.

"If you would truly help a man in desperate straits, then open the door," Jorand bellowed. "As you can see, I've quite a handful here."

Approving laughter erupted from the crowd and Padraigh scurried to swing the portal wide.

"I'm in your debt," Jorand said to him as he carried Brenna into the waiting darkness. "See that you shut it behind us, friend."

Padraigh winked broadly and did as he was bid.

Chapter Fourteen

Once they were inside the wedding bower, Jorand stood holding her in his arms as if she were light as thistledown. Brenna scarcely breathed. He moved to kiss her but she turned her face away.

"Ye can put me down now."

He lowered Brenna to her feet and turned back to slide the heavy brace on the door. The noise of feasting went on beyond the opening, but it was muffled. The riot of merrymakers, her dear family, the priest who'd said the blessing over them—they were all shut off from her and she was alone with her handsome sea warrior, her Keefe Murphy.

Man and wife.

The short months since she'd found her Northman on the beach whirred through Brenna's mind in a blink. From hated stranger to wedded husband in less than the turning of a season. How was it possible it could have come to this?

Her gut churned with nervousness.

It was one thing to imagine being a wife. Even the

ceremony had a hazy, dreamlike quality, as though it had happened to someone else, not to Brenna herself. Now reality crashed into her with no mercy at all. Why had she ever agreed to such an arrangement? Brenna was suddenly aware that she could hear the pounding of her own heart.

Her gaze slid around the room as she fought off a rising panic. A small blaze danced in the central pit, an aromatic fire of freshly hewn pine. Smoke rose in undulating ribbons and disappeared through the hole in the roof. A swath of silver light from the half moon shafted in the same opening, illuminating a bed on the far side of the fire. Her bridal bed. She turned away quickly.

"Ye needn't have carried me, ye know," Brenna said. "I could easily have walked."

"No, that would never do." Jorand shook his head. "Do you not know it's bad luck for a bride to trip on the threshold? But if a bride is carried over, she has no chance to misstep."

" 'Tis a custom I've never heard."

"Hmm, must be one from my people."

"Mayhap ye know it because ye've carried a wife over your threshold before. Have ye remembered aught?"

He frowned and looked down, as if searching for a fresh memory. "No, Brenna. There's nothing more." A smile turned up the corners of his mouth. "And for the first time, I'm grateful. All I want to remember, all I want to think about tonight . . . is you."

He took her hand again, lacing his fingers with hers. When he lowered his head to kiss her, Brenna's chest constricted as she gulped a quick breath. True, he'd kissed her before, but never as husband, never with the right to follow the kiss with . . . She suddenly noticed the bandage on his hand, stiff with dried blood.

"Oh, I need to tend this or 'twill go bad." She tried to ignore the tiny thrill that shot through her when she touched him. Her body ran cold then hot so quickly, she was in danger of losing her balance. All business, Brenna unknotted the bandage and surveyed the long slice in his palm, making a tsking noise of disapproval with her tongue and teeth. "Did Father Michael not tell ye a mere drop of blood would do?"

There was no chair in the hut, so she led Jorand over to sit on the edge of the bed. Brenna reached beneath it and found the small bowl filled with a healing paste she knew Moira had prepared for this purpose. Brenna unwrapped her own hand and showed him the small triangular wound.

"Ye see?" She dabbed a bit of paste on the spot and wrapped it with a fresh strip of linen. "Once mine has healed, 'twill not even leave a scar."

He took the ends of the cloth and tied the knot for her across the back of her hand, running a thumb over her knuckles. Then he held out his palm for her ministrations. She fussed and clucked over the length of the cut while applying the medicine and tying a bandage.

"I cannot say the same for ye," she went on, realizing she was prattling as badly as Moira, but unable to stop her nervous tongue. "Ye'll bear a mark on that hand from now on, or I'm much mistook."

"That's what I wanted," Jorand said, as he settled both hands on each side of her waist. "A year and a day. That's all I can lay claim to you, princess. But by this cut, you've claimed me for the rest of my life. From this day forward, I'll carry a scar to remind me that you were mine and I was yours."

Brenna bit her lip. He feared he'd forget her as he had his former life. How difficult it must be not to be able to trust a body's own memory. Still, it pleased her that he wanted a remembrance of her. As she looked down into his eyes, she realized she'd need no token, no scar to remind her of him. Already, his fine features were burned into her soul.

"I've never seen this bed before," she said, trying to distract herself from the pull of those indigo eyes. "I wonder where Da got it."

"Does it please you, princess?" The low rumble of his voice made Brenna's knees wobble.

" 'Tis very fine," she said. Suddenly the reason for the bed, an image of her body twined with his, writhing and straining, popped into her head. Brenna was grateful he couldn't see her flush with color in the dim light.

"I made it myself. There wasn't time for much carving, but that can be mended later. I couldn't give you beauty, so I settled for stout." The heat in his gaze left no doubt he expected to need a sturdy bed before morning.

He reached up and cradled the back of her head in his palm, gently but insistently, lowering her mouth to his. When their lips finally met, the contact made Brenna startle and try to pull back, but he held her fast. A bewildering maelstrom of emotions swirled in her, curiosity at the new delight he'd awakened, and terror that at any moment could send her out the door, screaming.

His lips moved over hers, setting her senses reeling. When her mouth parted slightly, his tongue slid into her, tracing the curve of her teeth, seeking out her soft places. Warmth spread deep in her belly.

Brenna jerked back as if he'd scorched her with a hot iron. This time, he let her go.

"What's wrong, princess? You're as skittish as a yearling colt."

"Nothing," she lied. "I ... I just need to take down me hair for bed. If I sleep in these plaits, 'twill be a mass of tangles by morning."

"Let me help you," he offered.

Before she could protest, he stood behind her, working the sprigs of flowers from the intricately woven strands. He ran his fingers through her waist-length tresses, shaking loose the braids. When he was finished, he gathered a fistful of her hair and brought it to his lips. Jorand inhaled deeply.

"Your hair is a wonder, Brenna."

She laughed. There was nothing wonderful about her. Moira was the one who made men's eyes go slack-lidded with desire. Brenna hadn't lived a lifetime in the same keep with her fiery-haired sister without realizing a few truths about herself. She turned away from him.

"'Tis not. 'Tis wild and curly and the color of a mouse—"

"It smells fresh as grass on a summer day," he said, undeterred. "And I love the way it curls around my fingers. Can you not believe I find it fair?"

He pulled her hair to one side, then planted his lips on her neck below her ear. His mouth, that incredible blessed mouth, sent both tingles of pleasure and flashes of alarm dancing along the surface of her skin.

"I do find you fair, my princess. All fair." He untied the drawstring at the neck of her tunic and pulled the opening wider, baring her shoulders. "Your sweet voice, your wondrous hair, your soft skin . . ."

His voice grew thick with desire and Brenna felt his lips on her neck again, lower this time, following the line of her shoulder.

Her skin screamed for his touch and where his mouth traveled, the need was not abated, but rather increased. Without realizing she did so, she leaned back into him and he slid his hands around her to cup the softness of her breasts.

She'd been nauseated when Connor dared touch her so intimately. Now the tips of her breasts ached, straining against the cloth of her tunic. When he thrummed a broad thumb across them, she nearly cried out.

"Ah, Brenna," he said, burying his face in her mass of curls. "You please me so."

His hands worked at the tunic, tugging it off her shoulders, pinning her arms to her sides. His mouth traveled up the back of her neck in featherlight kisses. Jorand's broad, blunt fingertips danced over her collarbone, running from her shoulder to the base of her throat. Then his hand slid downward to caress the tops of her breasts where they bulged above her lowered tunic, pressing against the fabric.

Having her arms confined made Brenna feel helpless and short of breath. She struggled to free her hands and accidentally eased the tunic lower. Her breasts sprang free and the drawstring opening dropped to her hips.

Jorand put his hands on her shoulders and slowly turned her around. He met her eyes, and then his gaze traveled by finger-lengths downward, past her throat, over the hollow at its base where Brenna was sure he must see her pulse banging wildly, and then even lower to her bared breasts.

Her nipples hardened as he stared at them wordlessly. In the firelight, his expression was unreadable, but Brenna was aware his breathing had also changed. He extended a hand, stopping when Brenna shrank back, then advancing when she straightened her spine, determined to go forward with the full bargain. After all, she'd promised.

As he traced a lazy circle around each berry-colored areola, a nameless longing washed over her, warm as midsummer rain. She found herself leaning forward into his touch. Then he covered her aching breasts with his palms, pressing and gently kneading her soft flesh as his lips covered hers once more.

Brenna groaned into his mouth, startled by her response to the confusing sensations his hands sent swirling through her. She was not ignorant. She knew what to expect from a man. But nothing she knew of the way of a man with a maid had prepared her for his gentleness, for his intent to give, not take.

When he pulled her closer, she didn't resist. The coarse linen of his shirt rubbed against her sensitive nipples. One of his hands slid down her back to trail slow circles at the base of her spine.

His tongue filled her mouth and even as he thrust it in, Brenna was aware of a heaviness, a dull throbbing deep in her belly. The emptiness of her womb cried out in silent spasm. It was longing, she realized. Longing to be filled.

Brenna pulled back breathlessly. She'd had no

idea. Men were slaves to lust, of that she was sure. But no one ever told her a woman could want as well.

Jorand peeled off his shirt, baring his well-muscled chest and arms. In the flickering light of the fire, the small hairs on his chest and arms gleamed like filaments of gold, like the delicate strokes of liquid metal she used to illuminate pages of Holy Writ with cross-hatching and fantastic swirls. The body of her husband seemed no less a work of art.

And no less holy.

"Come to me, Brenna." When he spread his arms open in invitation, she went to him willingly.

The feel of his skin on hers was heaven itself and she pressed her hard-tipped breasts against him, resting her head on the solid expanse of his chest. His heart throbbed under her ear, and as he wrapped his arms around her, she heard the great muscle in his chest start to gallop. She inhaled deeply, taking in his masculine scent.

He held her tenderly, even though she felt a hard bulge against her belly. Since the time she'd caught him bathing in the stream, she knew he was gifted in his male part. But the reality of the size of his stiff phallus suddenly struck home as his hand cupped her buttocks and pressed her against him.

She shivered.

"Are you cold?"

"No." She took the opportunity to pull away from him.

"Good," he said smiling. "I'm inclined to see the rest of you, wife."

Before she could protest, he tugged the tunic down over her hips and dropped it in a pool at her feet.

His breath hissed over his teeth.

"By the gods, Brenna," he said softly. "You make me want to never sail again."

His gaze nearly scorched her. In reflex, she covered her sex with her hands.

"No, princess," he said, his voice husky. "Let me look at you. Let me ... touch you." He replaced her hands with his own large one, his fingers tangled in her soft, curling hair, caressing, probing, seeking out her deepest secrets. When he grazed a sensitive spot, a jolt of pleasure rippled through her whole body and Brenna gasped.

"Hmm." He'd made the same sound when he tasted one of Moira's tarts, a deep satisfied sigh. "It's time to try out that bed, I'm thinking."

Jorand scooped her up once more and carried her to the waiting bed. Brenna sank into the wool-stuffed mattress, the linens cool on her feverish skin. She watched, breathing uneasily, as he untied his trews and lowered them.

He was big. Very big.

Panic rose like bile in the back of her throat. *The rending, the tearing, the burning. Oh God, no ...* She pulled the blanket to her chin.

"Seems stout enough," he said, giving the bedstead a good shake before he slid in beside her.

When he reached for her, she stiffened. Why did pain have to follow the teasing pleasure he'd given her?

He kissed her again, this time with more urgency. The full length of his erect phallus brushed her thigh.

Merciful Mary, I'll be impaled.

Her breath came in short gasps. Her skin still shivered, yearning for his touch. The pleasure would be short-lived now, she suspected. Jorand was so much bigger than—Brenna wouldn't let herself even think of *him,* that *Other,* the nameless beast at Clonmacnoise. But a dark corner of her heart carried the terror of it. And soon the horror would start afresh, and this time Brenna herself would suffer the brutal, grinding rutting.

"NO!" She lashed out with her fists at him.

Jorand pulled back, stunned.

"What's wrong?"

"I can't do this." Brenna sat up, her knees under her chin with the blanket clutched tightly in her hands. "An' ye force me, I'll scream."

"A scream from you at this point is only likely to increase my reputation, princess." His chuckle faded as he realized she was in earnest. "What is this foolishness?"

" 'Tis not foolishness. 'Tis the way things are. I'll not bed you willingly, Northman, husband or no." When he started to reach for her, she straight-armed him. "If ye take me by force, ye'd best sleep lightly or ye'll wake with a dirk in your ribs. Before God Almighty, I swear it."

Even in the dim light, Brenna saw his eyes harden. A muscle twitched in his cheek.

"If I wouldn't let your sister be taken unwilling, what makes you think I'd do it to you?"

He was right. The injustice of her accusation stung, but she wouldn't back down.

"I've said me piece," Brenna said, fighting to keep her voice from trembling. Her insides roiled with fear and a nameless confusion. Surely this was what she wanted. "What's it to be?"

Wordlessly, he rolled off the bed and stepped into his leggings. Then her husband grabbed one of the blankets and jerked it off her.

"Enjoy your marriage bed, princess. I'll trouble you no more." His voice held the bitterness of rejection. He stomped to the far side of the fire and stretched out on the ground.

Brenna sighed. She slid down under the thin linens, now shivering with cold instead of fear. Her body rebelled, still clamoring for release.

The merrymaking outside their hut continued to blaze in raucous glory. Huddled in the bed, Brenna realized her first night as a wife would be long.

And lonely.

Chapter Fifteen

Brenna was surprised to find herself in the glade. She inhaled deeply, drinking in the moist green scent of the river Shannon. A light breeze soughed through the stand of aspen on the bank, the trees huddled like a trio of skinny spinsters dipping their toes in the water. Brenna stretched out on a flat, gray-speckled boulder and let her feet dangle in the rushing current. Sunlight filtered through the trees, kissing her cheeks with small patches of warmth. She closed her eyes and let the peace of this secluded place sink into her bones.

A jaunty whistled tune made her eyes pop open and she sat up, looking for the source of the sound.

It was only old Murtaugh, the abbey's sexton. With his stooped spine and leathery, wrinkled neck, he reminded Brenna of an ancient tortoise. Murtaugh was the only man within the walls of the cloister who hadn't taken a vow of celibacy, though at his advanced age, Brenna scarcely thought it worth the trouble.

"God be wi' ye, Sister," Murtaugh said, struggling under the weight of a coarse sack on his bent back.

Brenna tucked her bare feet up under her tunic, embarrassed to have been caught enjoying herself so freely. She was about to return his greeting with a pious sentiment of her own, when she noticed the sack rolling and bunching. Muffled cries reached Brenna's ears.

"What is it ye've got there?"

"Och, tis only a wee litter o' kittens born in the abbey last night. The tabby what whelped 'em crept out and left 'em mewlin' and starvin', pur things," he said with a shake of his grizzled head.

When he set the bag down and opened it, the kittens bleated their hungry lament all the louder. The old man reached in with a gnarled hand and stroked a little calico.

"There's naught to spare for 'em, so 'tis up to me to take care of 'em." Murtaugh's voice was throaty and rasping.

"And if there's naught to spare, how can ye do that?"

The old man closed up the sack and tied a strap around the opening, cinching it tight. "Why, the only way to ease their sufferin' is to drown 'em, o' course."

Murtaugh heaved up the sack, swung it over his head, and loosed it into the air.

Before the bag of kittens hit the water, Brenna heard a distinctively different sound escape from it. Another cry mingled with the terrified mewing. With a sharp pang in her chest, Brenna recognized the cry of a human baby.

"No!"

She staggered into the water, flailing after the disappearing sack. Her foot slipped and she fell headlong, water shooting up her nose. She fought to regain her footing, but suddenly felt a surprisingly strong grip on the base of her neck.

Murtaugh's bony, liver-spotted hands clasped around her throat. The old man's croaking voice carried down to her through the water, distorted and wavering.

"The only thing for it is to drown 'em," Murtaugh kept repeating as he forced her head deeper beneath the surface.

No, this was all wrong. Murtaugh was her friend. She writhed and struggled, her lungs threatening to burst out of her chest. The water was too full of sediment to see anything clearly. Her last precious breath exploded from her lips in a blur of bubbles. Pinpoints of light burst in her brain. The need to breathe was growing unbearable. She felt her mind spiraling, floating away with the current, leaving her body behind.

Brenna could stand no more. She inhaled.

The rush of oxygen into her lungs was sweeter than honeyed fruit. Brenna's body jerked as she woke. She breathed again, testing the air to make sure this wasn't more of the dream. A hint of smoke reached her nostrils as she eased into a sitting position.

The nightmares were getting worse. Brenna shook her head, trying to clear the hysteria of the dream from her mind. She clapped her hands over her ears. She could still hear the child's cry. Brenna closed her eyes and bit her lower lip till it throbbed.

When she opened her eyes and cautiously lowered her hands, all she heard was the steady drip of light rain through the smoke hole, pattering on the stones of the fire ring. A lark trilled.

During the night, the pinewood blaze had died and left only a whiff of fragrance as a reminder of its passing. Through the smoke hole, she could see the sky, a pearly gray expanse that betokened approaching dawn.

On the other side of the fire pit, she made out the sleeping form of her husband. Jorand was stretched out on his side, facing away from her, as though even looking at her by chance was distasteful to him.

She watched his back expand with each breath. Her chest ached, remembering the fierce look in his eyes. She knew he had a right to be angry, but she couldn't have done anything else. If she'd let him take her last night, the growing tenderness she felt for him would have been destroyed forever.

She wouldn't blame him if he hated her for her refusal. But she was willing to suffer his loathing if only she was not forced to hate him.

Brenna shivered, then slipped out of bed and put on her tunic. She tried to run a horn comb through her wild tresses, but soon gave it up as hopeless.

The cock crowed.

They'd be coming soon, the early morning well-wishers and nosy matrons intent on inspecting the marriage bed for signs of consummation. In a panic, she glanced back at her bridal bower. The blankets were neat, the linens barely disturbed. She'd slept huddled miserably on her side of the broad bed without venturing over the center line even once.

Brenna climbed back into the bed, pulling the linens from their tucked corners and balling the blankets at the foot. When she eased off and inspected this time, the bed gave the definite impression that a rousing tussle had taken place.

But the linens were clean. No virginal blood was shed. Her shame would become grist for the goodwives' wagging tongues and her new husband would be sniggered at and despised by all for a cuckold.

Her Northman made no sign of waking while she rustled around. Perhaps she could settle the problem without his knowledge.

She searched Jorand's pile of discarded clothing for the horn-handled dagger he always carried and breathed a sigh of relief when she found it. She climbed into the bed again and smoothed back the sheets. Then she unwound the cloth binding her hand. All she needed was a few drops. If she could just reopen the wound—

A hand reached from behind her, clamping her wrist in a firm grip. She whirled to face him.

"What do you think you're doing?" Her husband's eyes narrowed in suspicion.

"I—" The fury in his face closed off her throat. She'd defrauded him on their wedding night. How could she admit she was about to falsify evidence of purity lost?

His fingers tightened on her wrist till she dropped the blade.

"You're hurting me," she whimpered.

"That's the least of your worries considering the hurt you were about to do yourself." He released her and picked up the dagger. Then he shoved it into its sheath and tossed it back onto his pile of clothing. As Brenna watched, the fire ebbed from his eyes and he sank wearily down on the mattress, turning from her.

"I know you can't bear me, Brenna," he said softly. "But you don't need to do away with yourself to escape me. I'll not trouble you again."

Brenna's breath caught in her throat and she reached out, meaning to touch him on the shoulder, but drawing back instead.

Maybe 'tis better this way, she reasoned. If Jorand thought she didn't fancy him, perhaps she'd never have to tell him the real reason behind her refusal. She'd told the tale to no one but her father and it was like being eviscerated alive to speak the words even that once. She didn't think she could do it again.

"I thank ye," Brenna said, her voice small and quavering. She eased down to sit beside him, careful to avoid touching him.

His shoulders slumped and he leaned forward to rest his weight on his elbows, his hands on the back of his head. The urge to give in, to grant him the comfort of her body was strong, however painful it might be to her. Her heart ached for him and she suddenly knew this was the man she could have loved all her life, if only . . .

And she knew with equal certainty she couldn't let a lie hang between them.

"Ye are mistook on two counts," she said in a whisper. "I wasn't after doing away with meself. Only the Lord God Almighty can decide when 'tis time for me to leave this world. To take upon meself that which is His alone," she shuddered at the presumption, " 'twould have been a mortal sin. Did Father Michael not explain such things afore ye were christened?"

"Guess the priest missed some of the finer points of your faith," he said, still studying the stone pavings between his feet with complete absorption. "What else am I wrong about?"

" 'Tis not ye I cannot bear, Jorand," she said. " 'Tis meself."

His gaze slid sideways toward her, a puzzled frown knotting his brows. "I don't understand you, Brenna. But I want to."

Jorand flopped back on the bed, an arm draped over his eyes. "I thought and thought last night before I finally fell asleep. I had plenty of time to do it. That floor isn't as soft as it looks, you know."

Brenna felt a stab of guilt for making him bed down on cold stone.

He peered out from under his arm. "You wanted me last night, at least for a little while. I'm sure of it. What happened to change that?"

" 'Tis nothing ye did," she said. "Or didn't do."

"Then what, Brenna? I've watched you over the past weeks. You may be sharp-tongued, but I've yet to see you be cruel." He sat up and leaned toward her. "Do you love another? Is that what kept you from giving yourself to me?"

"No," she said, sighing. " 'Tis nothing to do with love. Only with lust."

"I told myself I'd never ask, but I've got to know. Who was he?"

"Like ye, he was a Northman," she said miserably. "I don't know his name and never want to. Ye misunderstood me before and I was content to let be, but I see I must tell ye all now." Her voice was broken by a sob and she covered her face with her hands and wept.

After a few moments she became aware he was stroking her hair, smoothing out the tangles and crooning something in Norse that sounded like the same thing she'd heard him mumbling to one of the horses when it shied.

"Tell me," he said simply.

" 'Twas me own fault," she said between sniffles. "Me stubborn prideful will at the root of it all. Ye see, Father Michael taught me to read and write and when I went to Clonmancnoise Abbey with me sister Sinead, I expected to spend me days happily in the vast library there."

Jorand's face screwed into a puzzled frown.

"But they wouldn't let me work in the scriptorium. Illuminating manuscripts wasn't a fit occupation for a woman. 'Twas just for the menfolk to do. The abbot judged me talents would be better used scrubbing the already clean pavings." Her chin quivered as she continued. "I disobeyed the abbot and crept out of the abbey after vespers. While walking the banks of the Shannon, I stumbled upon a Northman. I suppose I should be grateful there was but one of them at first."

She took a shuddering breath.

"I tried to scream, but nothing came out. I turned and ran, but he followed. Then on the path, I found me sister Sinead. She'd missed me and knew I'd hie meself to the river from time to time. We ran together, but he caught me. I tried to fight him, but he was too strong. I couldn't stop him." She covered her mouth with her hand, unable to go on. Wracking spasms shook her frame and she felt a warm arm slide around her. Suddenly her head was against his chest and he cradled her gently.

"Sinead leaped upon his back, fighting and biting like a she-wolf. That's when he let me go and turned on her. 'Run,' she said, and to me shame . . ." Brenna's face crumpled. "I did."

"I . . . I must have lost me wits, because there's parts I don't remember and parts I cannot forget, no matter how I try." She chewed her bottom lip, hearing again her sister's screams while she cowered in paralyzed terror in the nearby brush. "But by God's mercy, I must have fainted. When I finally came to meself, I found Sinead alone on the bank and a whole crew of *Ostmen* sailing away, just rounding the bend."

She'd never forget the livid red wool of the Northmen's sail. It matched the blood streaking her sister's thighs.

"The fault is not yours." Jorand's grip tightened around her.

"Is it not? If not for me, she'd be safe yet." Brenna trembled with guilt. "But for her courage, it would have been me. It should have been me."

There was worse yet to tell, but she couldn't bear it now. Even Da didn't know the rest.

"I can't undo your past, Brenna, any more than I can remember my own," he finally said. "So now what happens?"

"What do you mean?"

"It's plain you don't mean to be a wife to me." He made no move to release her, but he did loosen his grip. "I'll not bind you to me unwilling any more than I'd take you unwilling."

"Ye mean to turn me out?" It would shame her as badly as the truth for him to repudiate her after spending the night with her.

"No, I ... This changes everything. I don't know what you expect me to do." His eyes had taken on a faraway look.

He meant to sail away. "If we're not married," she whispered, "ye fear ye'll not be given leave to go."

He shrugged. "There is that."

"Me father can be a hard man when he believes he has cause to be," Brenna admitted.

Brian Ui Niall tried to be a genial man of peace, but he was also capable of demanding and getting the blood of a rival's firstborn. Brenna wondered sometimes at the tales of ferocity in battle she'd heard about her father. When Brian's slate-gray eyes blazed in anger, she realized the tales were undoubtedly true. Her father would see Jorand dead before he allowed Brenna to be shamed. She couldn't let that happen.

"I know your freedom is important to ye. I would not keep ye from it."

"What are you proposing?" He cocked a brow at her.

She ventured a hand on his arm. "No one but we knows what passes between us."

"Or doesn't pass between us," he said, his lip curling.

"Aye," she conceded. "But in the eyes of the world, we are husband and wife. Could we not continue as such? In the fullness of time, ye may have your freedom and I will bear your name. If ye can bear such a coward as meself."

"For at least a year and a day," he said, looking at the bandage on his hand.

"Aye," she said.

Outside the hut, Brenna heard hacking coughs and the slamming of the heavy keep door, the first stirrings of the wedding guests.

"They'll be here soon," she said.

"Who will?"

"Those who mean to make sure a true marriage has been made." Her eyes met his. "The linens are in disorder. If we act the part, they'll believe."

She'd told him her hardest truth. It was time for another.

"When ye caught me with your knife, I was after leaving a blood stain in the bedding." She looked away. "I was trying to cover me shame."

"The shame isn't yours, Brenna," he said, cupping her chin in his hand, forcing her to meet his gaze. "You didn't intend to deceive me. There's no reason for the rest of the world to know if you don't wish it." He spat the words out as though they pained him as they passed through his teeth. "Who else knows the truth of this?"

"Only me da."

"Good." He stood and unwound the cloth on his palm with purpose. When he flexed his hand, the gash broke open and beads of red welled up along the cut. He smeared the center of the bed with several drops of blood. "Will that do?"

Tears pressed against her eyes. She'd hurt him by her refusal to bed him, and yet he protected her. "Again, I thank ye. Ye have covered me shame. Honor is satisfied."

He looked at her blankly. "I'm glad something is."

CHAPTER SIXTEEN

"Brenna, me heart, a word in your ear."

"What is it, Da?" She balanced the full basket on her hip and waited for her father to join her on the path. When he came even with her, Brian Ui Niall swept up the weight of her load and balanced it on his own shoulder.

"Is it fresh bread I'm smelling?" The king sniffed appreciatively. "I'm thinking your Northman's big enough already. If ye keep feeding the man this well, daughter, there's no telling how tall he'll grow."

"I only hope I can get him to stop long enough to eat. Unless I take food to him, he'll work on that infernal boat without a scrap of supper and not even notice his belly's complaint." Brenna glanced sideways at her father. "Are ye after giving me advice on the care and feeding of husbands, then?"

"Not exactly, but now ye've brought the subject to the fore, I've wondered how married life is agreeing with ye."

"It'll do," she said with a shrug.

"It'll do? Ye sound less than pleased. Ah, Brenna, that's not what I'd hoped for ye." Brian's dark brows drew together over his fine straight nose and a murderous glint sparked in her father's eyes. "Has the man been mistreating ye?"

"No, Da."

"Good then. I'm glad I've not lost me touch when it comes to judging a man's character." The king filched a small barley bun from the basket and bit into the warm pastry, rolling his eyes in delight. "Still, I thought the Northman would be the right one for ye," he said between bites.

She arched a brow at him. "Don't be playing the doting father with me. This pairing was for your convenience. Ye needed me safely wed so ye could make Moira's match, and there's the end of it. None of the local lads were to me taste and ye know it." She wrestled the basket back from him. "Jorand was me only choice."

She glared at her father, further irritated when Brian's shoulders hunched in agreement. He didn't bother to object to the obvious, but the truth still stung.

"But, Brenna, did ye never think your Northman was also the fitting choice?"

"How do ye mean?"

The king sighed. "I know ye've been hurt, daughter. No maid should see what ye've seen. But I thought marrying the same kind of man as hurt your sister might help ye heal. Sinead would want ye to go about whole hearted again. Have ye not found solace in the Northman's bed, then?"

"I very much fear he'd say he's found none in

mine." Brenna pursed her lips together. If Da wanted to have it direct, then she'd give it to him.

Brian frowned and ran a hand across his mouth, tugging at his chin as if that would help him find the right words. "I know 'tis not the sort of thing a girl wishes to speak of with her father, but—"

"Mother's not about to speak of it with me, now is she?" Brenna interrupted him with a trace of annoyance and more than a little embarrassment. Still, when her father's shoulders sagged, she wished she hadn't spoken so quickly. Una had shown a brief flicker of interest in life when Jorand repaired her chair. Everyone hoped it would last. But the queen of Donegal retreated once again into her dark, solitary sadness where none could touch her. Brenna felt guilty for reminding her father how alone he was.

"No, daughter, your mother's not much help to ye, I'll grant it."

Brian reached for another barley bun and Brenna narrowly resisted the urge to slap his hand away. She'd baked them for her husband, after all.

"Your mother, God grant her peace, is no help even to herself. Which is why I feel bound to take it upon meself—"

"Da, I mean no disrespect to ye, but given the state of your own marriage, I don't think ye are the one to be giving advice to me."

"Ah, but 'twas not always thus with your mother and me. Loved each other fine, we did." Brian's voice trailed away as he seemed to follow the wisp of a nearly forgotten time. "I only wish the best for ye, me heart. And the way of a man with his wife is truly one of God's wonders in the world."

"The wonder 'tis so many women put up with it," Brenna said bluntly.

Brian raised a questioning brow at her. "I thought ye said he hadn't mistreated ye. If that man's given ye even a moment's pain—" The king grasped her shoulders, forcing her to face him. "Say the word, daughter, and I'll fetch me ballocks shears and see the blackguard unmanned before sunset."

Her father would do it without a qualm. Brenna felt the blood run from her head at the thought.

"No, Da," she struggled to keep her voice even. "He hasn't … I mean, I wouldn't let … There's no need for ye to take such a notion." Brenna heaved a sigh. "Ye may as well know our wedding night was a fraud. Jorand hasn't been near me because I won't allow it. I told him what happened at Clonmacnoise and he's stayed away from me ever since."

"But that was none of your doing. Don't tell me the man holds it against ye?"

"No, Da," she said, avoiding his direct gaze. "I'm holding it against him. And whatever else Jorand is capable of, he at least hasn't forced himself on me."

"Brenna! He shouldn't have to. The man is your lawful husband." Her father's tone was reproving. "Did ye not take the vows?"

"Aye, but—"

"No buts, daughter," Brian said. "Ye swore before God Almighty to give the man your body, and by all that's holy, ye must honor your oath."

Tears trembled on the edges of her eyelids, blurring her vision. She stumbled a bit and might have gone down, but her father caught her in time and held her in a tight embrace. The basket of food clattered to the ground, one of the buns falling out onto the long green grass.

"Oh, me heart," Brian crooned as he patted her head against his chest. "I can't tell ye how many times I've prayed to take this hurt from ye. But there's naught I can do. Ye must simply trust me in this, daughter. The little ye know of what passes between a man and a woman, 'tis not the whole of the matter, truly 'tis not."

Brenna's cheeks burned and she was grateful Brian crushed her against him so she couldn't see her father's face.

"If the Northman's willing to wait for ye, it gives me hope he's the one to see ye made whole." Brian pressed his lips to her forehead, then stooped to gather up the basket. He walked toward the sea once more, heedless of whether Brenna followed or not. "But ye must try, darlin'. Loving takes two."

Brenna shook her head sadly and trotted to catch up with the king. "I don't think I can, Da."

"There's not so much thinking as needs to be done about it, girl," Brian said. "Mayhap that's your problem. Stop thinking so much and just ... well ..." He cleared his throat uncomfortably. Then he squared his shoulders and nodded curtly. "Life is hard enough without love. If the man offers ye comfort and kindness, accept it, lass. Accept the love."

She ventured a weak smile as she pondered his words.

They strolled in silence to the head of the trail that led downward to the cove where Jorand was working.

"Right, then." Brian handed the basket back to her

and turned toward his keep. "Pass a good evening, daughter."

Brenna watched him go. Could her father be right? Her one view of experience with a man was as terrifying a thing as she ever wished to face. But would it be different with Jorand? He'd certainly made her feel different on their wedding night. Until she'd demanded he stop.

What if she'd been wrong?

She turned to look down at her husband in the cove below. He'd stripped off his tunic and was working only in his trews. Jorand's fair skin had burnished to a golden bronze from long hours in the sun, but Brenna knew that his thighs were still pale in comparison.

For just a moment, she remembered how he looked in the flickering light of the fire in their bridal bower—strong, potently male, with a hint of the same wild glint in his eyes Brenna had seen in her father's stallion when the mares were in season. She swallowed the rising lump in her throat.

A vise tightened on her chest. Jorand was exceedingly fine to look upon. She'd seen more than one of the neighboring women rake him with their gaze and find reason to linger.

Perhaps her father was right. Sinead wouldn't want her to go about cringing in fear all her life. Even though he was a Northman, Jorand wasn't the least like the man who'd raped her sister. Accept the love, Da had said.

If only she could screw up the courage to try.

Chapter Seventeen

Jorand bored another hole with the auger and slid the iron rivet home. He gauged the depth perfectly and the metal he'd worked the night before fit snugly into the opening. The iron and oak came together with the neatness of two things designed for each other.

Pity he couldn't have that kind of precision in his marriage . . .

He shook his head and shoved the unproductive thought aside. He needed to concentrate on his boat. The more he worked the wood, the more malleable it became in his skilled hands, and the small craft was taking shape beautifully.

As he labored, memories came to him in rushes, vivid flashes of sight and sound. They were jumbled up—brief glimpses of strange places, snippets of conversations, faces that seemed to melt into one another so he wasn't sure who or what he was seeing in his mind. Always the new memories were accompanied by a pounding in his temple that threatened to send him into dizzy oblivion.

It was exhausting to try to make sense of the disjointed images, but he slogged away at it even as his hands kept busy building the boat. He hoped remembering would help, but nothing in his past seemed likely to show him what to do about his present. He was totally lost.

He felt like a swimmer nearly spent, clawing his way toward the surface of the water, lungs bursting and mind tunneling for lack of air. If only he could break through, feel the cleansing breath of a clear memory, piece together a true sense of himself, maybe then he'd be able to make sense of the rest of his life.

"Brenna." He whispered her name like a prayer.

When the strange images in his brain proved to be too much, he filled his mind with her instead. Brenna, acid-tongued and saucy, working as hard as any man in the keep. Brenna, frail and vulnerable, singing sad Irish songs when she thought he didn't hear her. Brenna, round and soft, sighing in her sleep while he gritted his teeth on his pallet across the room.

He hadn't made any more advances toward her since their wedding night, though not for lack of wanting. He was beginning to crave her the way a starving man lusts after a crust of bread, but he pushed the urge down.

Her threat of a knife in his ribs wasn't what kept him away. It was the glint of terror reflected in her eyes, the way she drew away from him inside her clothes whenever their bodies chanced to brush against each other in the small confines of their hut. If he had to hurt her to have her, he was determined to wait.

The hunger grew in him like a suffocating vine.

Brenna was either going to be his salvation or the death of him. He wasn't sure which.

"That boat doesn't care if ye fall down from overwork, ye know."

He turned at the sound of her voice. "But you do?" He couldn't resist needling her.

"Sure and ye'll make yourself sick if ye don't stop for a bite now and again."

"I'm glad to know you care."

"Of course, I care." Brenna set down the basket she had balanced on her hip and rummaged through it. She drew out a small jug, pulled out the bung, and handed it to him. "If ye fall ill, who'd have to drop her work and tend to ye, I'd like to know? 'Twould be me, and then what would become of the rest of them?"

He downed a swig of ale and found it cool and soothing to his parched throat.

"I expect Moira could pick up where you left off giving orders," he said dryly and was rewarded by the dangerous glint in her eye.

"Aye, well . . . someone needs to see to things." The steam seemed to go out of her as she turned her attention to the boat. "How is this cursed contraption coming along? Will it be finished soon?"

So, she's anxious to be rid of me.

"I can try it now if you like."

A panic-stricken look crossed her face. " 'Tis not done yet, surely."

"No, I need to add a mast and finish the inside of the hull with some flooring to make her more comfortable, but I intend to see if she's seaworthy today."

"You're not leaving?" She caught his arm as he turned away, then dropped her hand when he looked back at her.

"Would it bother you if I did?"

She didn't meet his gaze. "Ye promised me da not to go without his leave."

"I'm a man of my word," he said testily. "I'll not go yet. No, princess, you're not that lucky. Today I only intend to try her in the lagoon to make sure the joints hold."

He put a shoulder to the stern and shoved the craft toward the smooth water of the sheltered cove. When the prow lifted in the light ripple of a wave, he turned back to face her.

"Can you swim, princess?"

She hesitated for an instant. "I expect I can make do."

"Come, if you like."

To his surprise, she walked toward him still carrying the dinner basket. When she reached the water's edge, he lifted her gently into the swaying craft. Her hem rode up for a moment and he caught a tantalizing glimpse of a slender ankle and calf.

"Better have a seat," he ordered before he gave the boat a final push and clambered over the side to join her. Jorand slid the twin oars into the ports and bent to his work, rowing against the slight swell of waves in the small cove. When they reach the center of the lagoon, he shipped the oars and tossed out the anchor stone.

"That should do it," he said, settling himself so he could see Brenna. Her face paled and she gripped the sides of the small craft so hard her knuckles were white.

"Now what?" she asked.

"We wait to see where she leaks."

"What do you mean 'where' she leaks?"

"I think I sealed all the joints," he pointed to the bits of tar and moss jammed between the strakes. "But I might have missed a spot or two. Anything made by human hands is prone to failure. So we have a trial run in a shallow spot to see if she'll hold."

Her eyes widened. "How shallow?"

He leaned over the side, looked down into the clear gray water, and counted the number of knots left on his anchor rope. "Not more than five spans." He spread his arms wide, then leaned back against the stern.

"But that's over your head."

"And yours, too, even if you stood on my shoulders," Jorand cocked his head at her. "What's the matter, princess? I thought you said you could swim."

"Well, are ye telling me I'll have to?"

"Not likely," he said. "Even if she leaked like a sieve, it takes a great deal of water to swamp a boat like this. We're close enough to shore that I could row back before she sank. Anyway, I'll warrant she'd stay afloat even half full."

"Let's not be trying to prove it, shall we?"

He peeked under the clean cloth covering her basket. "What have you brought me?"

"Just a bite of supper." She relaxed enough to let go of the sides of the craft as she pulled off the cloth and displayed her offering. "I'll not have anyone saying I neglect me husband's appetite."

"Not all of them anyway." He bit into one of the barley loaves and wished it had been his tongue instead.

"What do ye mean?" She narrowed her eyes at him.

He moved toward her in an easy half crouch so as not to make the boat sway more than necessary. "Just that a man has other needs besides a full belly."

She cast her gaze downward.

Why did he say that? It sounded demanding and pathetic, but when he looked at her he couldn't help himself. His gaze was drawn to the swell of her breasts pressing against the thin fabric of her linen tunic. He forced himself to look away. She couldn't bear his touch and he couldn't keep from wanting to touch her. What a fix he'd gotten himself into.

He had to change the subject, and quickly.

"*Ja,* a man needs to feel the wind on his face and a brisk sea breeze at his back from time to time."

"Then you'll be leaving soon?"

"I mean to." He offered her the jug of ale. When she declined, he tipped it back and let the warm bite of the golden liquid soothe his throat. "My boat isn't finished yet though."

"It wanted a mast, you said."

"*Ja,* and a sail to hang from it." A light breeze rippled over them. He adjusted the steering oar and the prow turned in the water. "If she had a sail, she'd be a fine boat. It needs to be of heavy wool, tightly woven. Can you make one for me?"

"I have a length of yellow wool on me loom now that might do," she offered. "How does it all work?"

"Come." He led her, walking carefully down the spine of the boat to the midpoint where he'd already built the housing for the mast's base. He explained in layman's terms how he'd harness the wind and bend it to his will.

"Ye've remembered all that?" she asked.

He nodded.

"And the skill it took to build this?"

"Some of it was hit or miss, but most of it came

right back to me. It was almost like my hands did the remembering."

To his surprise, she took one of his hands in hers and turned it palm up. He held his breath as she traced her fingertip over his callouses and along the new red scar knifing across his palm.

"Ye certainly are clever with your hands, Jorand," she finally said. Traces of a blush bloomed in her cheeks.

Was she thinking of how his hands had molded to her body? How he'd explored her like a newly discovered inlet? He felt himself rouse to her, wanting to take her right there in the swaying craft. But she dropped his hand and eased away.

A small swell sent the craft rocking and Brenna wobbled uncertainly. He caught her before she could topple over. By the gods, she felt good in his arms, soft and delicate, and the top of her head fit snugly under his chin. When she didn't jerk away, he pulled her closer, the need to hold her overriding his better judgment. He struggled to control his breathing, afraid even that small movement would spook her and she'd wrestle free.

"Me da says I'm not fulfilling me promise," she said, her voice small and hesitant.

"What promise?"

"To bed ye, as a proper wife should." She looked up to meet his gaze, her eyes darkening as the pupils dilated. The fear was still there, but he could see she fought to master it. "I took a vow before God and man and must needs honor it."

He felt his pulse quicken as his shaft hardened.

"I've no great need to wait for a bed, princess."

He tightened his grip, taking care not to crush her,

and reveled in her softness. For a blink, he thought he felt her stiffen but he shoved that possibility away. He buried his nose in her hair, inhaling her scent, sweet as rain-washed grass.

"Brenna," he murmured. "I've wanted you so."

His lips found her neck, her earlobe. He narrowly resisted the urge to bite down on the soft flesh.

He took her mouth and poured all his frustration and longing into the kiss. Her mouth softened under his, but there was no mistaking now. Her body was tense as a drawn bow.

Her arms were clamped to her sides, so he took one of her hands and brought it around him. Her icy fingers trembled on his ribs.

When he cupped her buttocks with his palms, her breath hissed in over her teeth. Her whole frame shuddered.

Jorand grabbed her by the shoulders and held her an arm's length away. Brenna's face was pallid as a corpse and a shudder rippled over her. He felt himself shrivel.

"By Loki's unwashed backside, woman!" He pushed her away. "What are you trying to do to me?"

"I thought ye wanted to—"

"What makes you think I want to lie with a shivering, whimpering—" Jorand bit back the harsh words threatening to explode out of him. He stomped away from her, heedless of the wild rolling of the craft under him, and plopped down next to the steering oar.

Brenna dropped to her knees and grasped the sides of the boat. A single tear was swiftly followed by a flood of others, but she covered her mouth to muffle her sobs.

"Stop crying," he ordered, dragging a hand through his hair in frustration. "Brenna, please."

"You're ... leaving." The words slipped out between gasps for breath. "I'm sorry. I'm so sorry. And now ye won't take me with ye."

His face scrunched into a confused frown. He'd never understand this woman. "You still want to come?"

"Aye," Brenna said, breathlessly. "Give me another chance. I can do it, I know I can. Use me body as ye wish. Only please take me when ye leave. I have to go to Clonmacnoise."

"Why?"

She swiped her eyes, but refused to meet his gaze. "Because I must."

"*Ja,* I'll take you with me." Jorand dragged a hand over his face. Why was he agreeing to more of this? He began to suspect Brenna was more a witch than a follower of the Christ, a dabbler in *seid* craft who'd learned to control those around her. She only need shed a few tears and he was willing to do anything to make her stop.

To his surprise, she lurched over to him in the swaying boat and covered his hand with kisses.

"I thank ye," she repeated. "I'll serve ye well, ye'll see."

"You don't have to do anything." He pulled his hand away. "I don't want you to do anything. We'll go on as before."

His chest constricted at the look of stark relief flooding her face.

"Thank ye, Jorand."

"You may not thank me once we get underway." His voice sounded more gruff than he intended, so he softened it as he went on. "As you can see, traveling in this boat means close quarters. You're going to have to get used to being near me."

He settled to lie down and lifted a hand to her. "Come, princess. I'll not harm you. If we're going to travel together you'll at least have to sleep near me for warmth and protection."

She took his hand and he steadied her until she settled herself beside him.

"Lay your head, girl," he said wearily.

Brenna slid closer and haltingly rested her head in the hollow of his shoulder. She still held herself stiff and brittle as a piece of weathered oak.

"Be easy," he said, patting her head as though she were a two-year-old. "Nothing will happen to you, I promise. I won't hurt you, Brenna."

"I'm sorry."

"Hush," he said, tired to his bones. "Just get used to being near me. I won't bite you." He grimaced, remembering his urge to nip her gently on the ear.

"Ye truly are good to me." She sighed.

Little by little, he felt the tension drain out of her limbs as she relaxed against him. Their breathing fell into rhythm.

"Am I not pleasing to you, then?" she asked.

He inhaled deeply, willing himself not to voice the frustration he felt. "Brenna, you're more than pleasing to me. I want you so badly, it's like a sickness. But it must go both ways, you see. If you don't want me, what pleasure can there be for me in that?"

"Other men—"

"When are you going to learn that I'm not other men?" He allowed himself to stroke her hair, tormenting himself with its softness. "I'll never take you unwilling, princess. In fact, I'll make you a promise. I won't take you till your wanting exceeds mine."

She expelled her pent-up breath in a satisfied sigh.

As soon as the hasty vow passed his lips, he realized his mistake. By that measure, he'd never bed her. She'd never get over the panic of her past long enough to enjoy dallying with him in her present. He had no reason to expect she would ever let him love her, but the way his heart still thudded against his ribs when he tugged her closer, he knew he still hoped.

"But you have to promise me something in return," he said.

"What?" she asked warily.

"You have to agree to spend time with me like this." He tipped her chin up so he could look into her eyes. "Close. Me touching you. You touching me. And starting tonight, we sleep in the same bed. Agreed?"

"And you won't . . ." Her eyes widened and she bit her lower lip.

"Not until you want me, too."

He brushed her forehead with his lips and she settled against him again. He ran his hand from her shoulder to the small of her back. He was painfully aware of the softness of her breasts pressed against his side. His body roused to her again, but he forced himself to lie still. It was agony, but he wouldn't chance frightening her again.

Perhaps when Brian Ui Niall had spared his life, he did him no favors after all.

CHAPTER EIGHTEEN

Brenna gulped a tepid sip from the waterskin, then swiped her mouth with the back of her hand. Her stomach cavorted wildly. Sweat gathered on her upper lip as she fought to quell the rising nausea.

"For the love of God, can we please put in to shore tonight?"

"*Ja*, princess, as you wish," Jorand said as he cast a squinted glance toward the westering sun. He reefed the coracle toward the opening of a small cove. "We've covered a goodly distance today."

Brenna nodded, nearly quaking with relief at the idea of solid ground under her feet. A swell rose beneath them and the boat surged forward, leaving her stomach behind. Brenna gave up and emptied her belly into the greenish waves.

"That'll make you feel better," Jorand said with unsympathetic cheerfulness as he handed her a small cloth. " 'Tis no shame, you know. Until you get your bearings, it's bound to happen. Another couple of days and you'll be fine. We'll make a sailor of you yet."

"If ye don't make a corpse of me first," Brenna muttered. She dipped the cloth over the side and dabbed the coolness over her face.

Remember why ye wanted to go, she commanded herself.

They'd left Donegal immediately after Moira's wedding feast. The boat had been finished two weeks earlier, but Brenna insisted on waiting till she saw her sister safely wed.

The night before the ceremony, Moira came to her with panic in her usually carefree face. "Mother tells me nothing. She expects me to go to the marriage bed ignorant as a nun, but ye must help me. Tell me how to please a man, Brenna."

Brenna was at a loss for an answer. "All men are different," she finally said. "Ask your groom. He'll have an inkling what he prefers, I'll not doubt."

It was a beautiful ceremony, a full mass with Father Michael in exceptional voice. The chiefs of the clan Ulaid came to witness the marriage and subsequent coronation of Moira as their future queen. They roared their approval when the circlet of bronze glinted amid her sister's fiery curls.

Her father asked Brenna if she regretted her simple handfast ceremony after Moira's grand rite. She had no complaints on that score. Brenna remembered the look on Jorand's face as he said his vows and contrasted it with Domhnall's son, Fearghus.

If she feared for Moira's happiness, she couldn't say it eased her mind.

Even when her sister was in the room, the heir of Ulaid had a disconcerting habit of eyeing the children who cavorted about the keep as though they'd left their shifts behind. He was clever enough not to let Brian Ui Niall catch him at it, but seemed to delight in Brenna's discomfort whenever she met his cold-eyed gaze.

Jorand disliked the man as well, though she was sure he didn't know exactly why. Brenna's marriage might not be a love match for the ages, but at least Jorand didn't have a roving eye. Against all her expectations, he treated Brenna with courtesy and respect.

Still, Moira was a bride. She was deliriously happy on her day, the queenly title that accompanied her match sending her into raptures. Brenna hoped it would be enough.

"Feeling better?" Jorand asked.

She nodded. Strangely enough, she did, and when the bottom of the boat scraped against the sand, she nearly did a jig.

When they sailed south from Donegal Bay, the coastline was rocky. Sheer cliffs made it impossible for them to beach the craft last night. Jorand had tossed out the anchor stone and they lay side by side in the curved hull of the boat. If Brenna hadn't been fighting a queasy stomach, she'd have enjoyed watching the stars winking on one by one, like candles being lit in a chapel vestry.

To her surprise, she was beginning to enjoy sleeping next to the big Northman. Of course, the sturdy bed at home was more pleasant than the swaying coracle, but she was comforted by Jorand's deep, even breathing and solid warmth. Once in his sleep, he reached for her and pulled her close. His breath caressed the back of her neck and she felt the steady thump of his heart against her spine. The contact was so basic and simple, just a small thing really, but it made her chest ache. She found herself wishing things were different between them.

Brenna climbed over the side of the boat, splashing up to her knees in the surf. Jorand was already out and shoving the prow as far up onto the beach as he could. Then he came around to the front and hauled the boat out of the water with a stout rope. Brenna shook out her tunic and found it stiff with crusty salt.

"That should hold it," he said, tying off the line on the smooth trunk of a red arbutus. "If you've found your land legs, we'll walk a bit." Jorand pointed into the distance. "There's a stream emptying into the cove and the water will be less brackish farther in."

When Brenna nodded, he shouldered a pack with their food and gear. They found a game trail wandering alongside the watercourse and followed it into the deep shade of an ancient forest.

The night would be chilly, but now the air was filled with a drowsy warmth and the rich, fecund smell of fertile earth. Brenna inhaled deeply, satisfied with solid ground underfoot and the familiar comfort of a glade.

The stream rioted beside them, sometimes leaping, sometimes widening to a sedate ripple, and once eddying into a deep pool as it rounded a bend. Brenna made note of the clear water. She'd be back later to wash the brine off her skin and hair. They continued to hike for another twist or two in the stream.

" 'Tis far enough, surely?"

Jorand bent to scoop up a handful of water and brought it to his lips. "*Ja*, it'll do."

Brenna gathered dry limbs for a fire while Jorand constructed a lean-to of deadfall and cedar boughs.

"Not exactly a palace," he admitted, surveying his handiwork with his fists on his hips. "But it should turn the rain. Someday, I'll build you a fine longhouse."

"Someday? Remember ye are bound to me for only a year and a day. If ye intend to build me a house, we'd best not tarry long in this Dublin ye seek."

His eyes darkened to deep indigo. "If you're in such a hurry, perhaps we shouldn't stop at that abbey you are so hot to visit."

"No, Jorand," she protested. "Ye must take me to Clonmacnoise. Ye promised."

"*Ja,* I did. I've never asked, but I'm thinking it's time you told me why." He knelt to strike flint to steel, pausing to blow on a spark in hopes it would ignite the small pile of tinder. "You hate sailing. You barely tolerate me. But nothing could stop you from coming. What's so important at Clonmacnoise?"

She pressed her lips together in a hard line. "At first I thought my life was there. I spent the better part of a year at the abbey, intending to work in the scriptorium. I had such hopes, but..." Brenna gulped. No. She couldn't tell him the truth. He might not help her if he knew. She needed a diversion. "I... I wanted to learn more of my craft. I did tell ye I can read?"

"You might have mentioned it."

"Aye, and write, too. Father Michael taught me."

He leaned over the glowing embers and blew softly on them, urging them to a lively blaze. "Show me."

She smoothed a patch of dirt with her foot and wrote in the soft turf with a twig.

"What's that say?" He left the fire long enough to study the marks in the dirt.

" 'Tis your name." She underlined the letters as she voiced them. "Jor-and."

"If you say so," was his noncommittal reply, but he narrowed his eyes as he studied the letters. Then he turned his attention back to the flames for a moment before he pinned her to the spot with a steady gaze. "You still haven't answered my question."

She looked away.

"I guess you'll tell me when you're ready," he said. "But that's part of being husband and wife, you know. We may not share much, but we can at least trust each other enough to bear each other's secrets."

"And what secrets have ye shared with me?"

"All I know," he said sadly.

Brenna felt guilt for reminding him of his memory loss.

"Forgive me." She laid a hand on his arm. "No more has returned to ye?"

"I don't know if it's a memory or not, but lately, I have been seeing a face in my dreams that seems familiar." Jorand stretched out his legs and leaned back against a fallen log.

"A woman?"

He chuckled. "No. It's a boy, a dark-haired boy. In my dreams, he's a few years older than me and it seems we're in trouble together most of the time."

Brenna let a relieved giggle slip out. She was comforted the face didn't belong to another woman. She'd been trying to guard her heart, to not let Jorand come to mean too much to her since she expected he'd leave her eventually, but her reaction proved her defenses against him were crumbling.

"Mayhap he's your brother."

"Maybe, but I don't think so. It seems like in the dreams, the dark-haired boy has a brother, a mean-spirited lad who bedevils the two of us most of the time." He launched into an account of his dreams with as much accuracy as he could muster.

Brenna added dried meat and root vegetables to a stew pot dangling over the flames while she listened. Given the depth of detail Jorand described, it seemed clear some memories must be bubbling to the surface. "And in your dreams, do ye not see your family, your parents?"

"No, but it's like . . . like the boy is all the family I've got." A deep cleft formed between his brows and he cocked his head as though listening to a voice Brenna couldn't hear. "I was fostered out to his family. Part of his family, but not really. *Ja,* that must have been it." Light shone in his eyes and a smile spread across his features. He cast its radiance on Brenna. "I remember. The boy's name was . . . Bjorn."

Suddenly, like water springing from a rock, Brenna could almost see a flood of memories burst in Jorand's mind and out of his mouth. He spoke quickly, eager to voice the thoughts as though he was afraid they'd retreat into darkness again. He told Brenna about his childhood in the *jarlhof* of Sogna under the care of Harald the Jarl, which she supposed was a level of nobility roughly equivalent to her father's kingship, about playing "Gnomes and Elves" with young Bjorn in the deep Norse forests, and climbing for gulls' eggs on the craggy side of the fjord.

When he reached the end of his litany, he subsided into silence.

"Is there more?"

"No." He put a hand to his temple and rubbed. "Nothing more. It seems I remember I was ten once, but that's it. Lot of good it does me."

"Of course it does," she said. "You remembered something, at least. Surely more will follow. You look tired. Why don't you rest here by the fire and watch the stewpot for me? I'll be right back."

She gathered a change of clothing and slipped back to the path by the stream, heading for the quiet little pool they'd passed by.

Her heart was banging in her chest. At first she could think of no reason why she felt so unsettled, but then she realized it was because Jorand's memory was returning. True, there was no woman yet in his past, but that didn't mean one wasn't there, waiting for him to find her in the closed-off part of his mind. And when he did . . .

Brenna flung down her *brat* from off her shoulders and stooped to lift her hem up over her head. It felt good to strip out of her briny-stiff clothing and stretch in the last rays of sunlight. She'd rinse them out and put on her spare tunic before going back to Jorand and the fire, but for now, the water called to her. She eased into it up to her hips.

Brenna scooped up handfuls of the clear liquid, splashing it on her face and shoulders. Rivulets of pleasure coursed down her arms, over breasts and belly. Weariness sloughed off with the salty grit and her skin tingled in the fresh water. She waded out farther and discovered the pool was even deeper than she thought. The bottom of the stream retreated under her and she slid beneath the surface.

Brenna clawed back up, sputtering and floundering. No matter what she'd told Jorand to coax him into bringing her with him, she really was not much of a swimmer. When her toes found the bottom again, she was able to relax and push her hair out of her eyes. Brenna looked up to see Jorand sitting beside her pile of discarded clothing.

"How long have ye been there?"

"Long enough."

He stood and yanked his tunic over his head.

"What in the name of all the holy angels do ye think ye are doing?

"You're not the only one who likes to be clean, princess." He pulled a face at her. "Besides, I always knew you'd lure me into the water one day."

That day long ago when she'd spied him at his bath flashed in her mind. She decided she really couldn't fault him for peeking at her. Besides, it wasn't as though he'd never seen her naked, and they were married, after all. Modesty was a shame between husband and wife.

Jorand tugged down his leggings and stepped out of them. Brenna found herself staring and turned around lest he catch her at it. From the top of his golden head to the strong muscles in his calves, the beautifully shaped feet, the man was disturbingly well made.

She heard him enter the water with a splash and then saw his sleek form glide past her under the surface. Broad shoulders tapering to his narrow waist and tight buttocks, powerful thighs—he was a delight to watch.

"Careful," she said as he surfaced. "'Tis deeper than it appears."

"Don't worry, princess, I'm a strong swimmer."

His gaze flickered over her shoulders and down to

her breasts bobbing on the surface. She waved her hands before her to stir up the water, sending a light mist his direction.

"Ye needn't stare so."

"*Ja,* I do need."

His smile made her heart skip like a spring lamb, but alongside the pleasure his admiration gave her, panic rose in equal measure. She swiped at the water and splashed him.

Jorand made a low growling sound and dove beneath the surface, heading straight for her.

She cried out as he came up under her and tossed her into the air. She sailed about the distance of two spans and landed bottom-first with a splash. When she sputtered to the surface, all she could hear was his laughter bounding off the trees and rocks around them.

"Why, ye *Finn-Gall* demon! I'll teach ye to mishandle a daughter of the house of Ui Niall." Brenna lunged at him and shoved his head below the surface. He came up shaking his mane and roaring with laughter.

Brenna giggled like a little girl and pushed him down again. This time he grabbed her legs and emerged with Brenna perched on his shoulders. She struggled for balance, grabbing at his slippery skin and settling for latching on to his ears.

"Ow!" Jorand howled. "Lots of women claim their husbands never listen to them. Better leave my ears attached or you'll have no room to complain."

Brenna released him and he ducked beneath the surface again, pushed off the bottom, and shot her up into the air. This time she landed in the deeper part of the pool, where she floundered and bobbed. She stiffened, feeling herself sink. In her panic, she sucked in a mouthful of water and disappeared beneath the surface like an anchor stone.

The dying sun flashed through the water in long shafts, illuminating the fine grains of silt floating before her eyes. She flailed her arms and legs, but made no progress toward the sun and the world of light and air. Her chest ached, but she fought against the urge to inhale.

Then suddenly a hand gripped her and yanked her upward. She broke the surface and blessed air rushed back into her lungs. Jorand's arm was around her, pulling her with sure strokes back to the shallows. She coughed out the liquid and dragged more air in over her teeth. It never tasted so sweet.

As soon as Jorand could plant his feet, he stopped and held her close. With a shock, Brenna realized he was trembling more than she.

"I'm sorry, princess." She felt the warmth of his breath in her ear. "I thought you told me you were a swimmer."

"I can usually keep meself afloat, but ye … ye make me weak," she admitted.

"Forgive me. I played too rough." He put a hand to her head, stroking her gently.

He was playing anything but rough now, Brenna thought. Pressed against his chest, buoyed by the light current, she'd never felt such safety, such peace. When she looked up at him, his features were marred with concern.

"I'm fine," she said. "No harm done."

One corner of his mouth turned up. "No harm," he repeated. "You scared me to death. But if it gets you into my arms naked, it was worth it."

Brenna blinked. She *was* in his arms naked. They floated together, skin on skin, her taut nipples grazing his chest, his erection hard against her flat belly, and—miracle of miracles—she wasn't afraid.

She turned her face up to him, inviting him. He answered her summons by covering her mouth with his.

When he released her, she smiled up at him with promise.

"Aye, 'tis worth it."

CHAPTER NINETEEN

The cool of the brook, the heat of his mouth, the way his hands slid over her skin, Brenna was drowning in a steady stream of new sensations. Together she and Jorand rolled beneath the rippling water, locked in a kiss so sweet, she'd rather have died than break it off. Like a pair of otters, they twisted together in love-play.

Jorand regained his feet and pulled her back to the surface with him.

"Are you sure?" he asked intently. "I don't think I can bear it if ... I don't want to hurt you, but I'm not sure I'll be able to stop again if this goes much further."

Ye swore before God Almighty to give the man your body, and by all that's holy, ye must honor your oath.

Her father's admonition rang in her head. Somehow the prospect of joining with this man, this husband of hers, seemed less daunting than before. Especially since Jorand's kiss roused such fire in her. She'd feared passion before, maybe even more than her dread of pain, afraid of dancing too close to the flames. Now, looking into the cool, blue depths of Jorand's eyes, she knew he'd keep her safe, no matter what kind of madness he led her into.

"I don't want ye to stop," she said. "Not ever."

With a groan, he clasped her to him again and kissed her, this time with all the urgency of a starving man at a banquet.

"I don't know what ye want of me." Brenna gasped, both for lack of air and for the tingling feel of his mouth on hers. "What must I do?"

"Trust me, princess. Just trust me." He cupped her bottom, tugging her closer. Brenna felt his chest swell in a ragged breath as he struggled to control himself. Like one of her father's huge workhorses in harness, Jorand was the image of bridled strength.

"Be easy now," he whispered into her ear, his breath sending tendrils of pleasure down her neck, "and let the water bear you up."

He lifted her gently, hooking an arm under each knee. Under his direction, she circled his waist with her legs, then released her hold on his shoulders, letting him guide her. Lying back in the water, her hair floated around her, gently swaying in the current, tickling her bare skin.

She puzzled over what might come next. Since she'd given him her word not to stop, Jorand seemed intent on taking his time.

"What a wonder you are, Brenna," he said, his voice husky with desire. "I never know what to expect from you."

"Are ye not pleased with me, then?" She squeezed her legs tighter around him, reveling in the way his eyes widened. So, she could feed the fire in him, too.

The knowledge gave her a little thrill of power. "Would ye rather I finish me bath and go tend the supper?"

"Let it burn," he said hoarsely as his gaze devoured her. He slid his hands over her hips, up past her waist, to trail lazy circles around her breasts. "You're so fair, princess."

She forced herself not to try to cover her nakedness and hide from his admiring eyes. His earnest expression made her feel his words were true. She *was* fair. If the hunger in his face was any measure, she was beautiful and she felt it.

Brenna closed her eyes and let her arms float away above her head, secure in knowing he held her safely.

His fingers sent swirls of pleasure over her as he explored her body, tracing the curve of her belly and skimming along the underside of each breast. Her nipples hardened, aching for his touch as his hand danced past them.

"You're soft as silk, you know," Jorand said.

"What's silk?" Brenna caught her lower lip with her teeth, fighting against the urge to bring her own hands to her throbbing bosom. Anything to still the bewildering need.

"Silk is a fabric so fine, it feels like water on your skin." He lifted his hand and let droplets patter down onto her belly, then returned to graze her breasts with his fingertips.

"Then by those lights, we're neither of us naked, we're wrapped in this silk ye speak of." She squirmed, trying to position her nipples into the path of his hands.

"What do you want, Brenna?" His voice sounded far away, muffled by the stream she floated in.

"Everything." She released a shuddering sigh when he finally captured a breast and massaged its swollen tip. Her eyes flew open and she searched his face, satisfied with the acceptance and encouragement she saw in his heavy-lidded eyes.

He was leading her into a strange new country and she followed willingly, surrendering to his hands, his voice, the growing maelstrom of delight sweeping her up. There was no pain. No fear. Only him.

"Oh!" She moaned when his thumbs found the soft crevice on the inside of her thighs. Her mind spiraled, as though she were floating away from her body. She needed to focus on something or she'd burst right out of her skin. "Tell me more of this thing called silk."

One corner of his mouth turned up in a knowing grin. "They say it's spun by magic in far away Cathay, the weaving done in greatest secrecy."

Given the wild surges of bliss his hands sent through her, she wouldn't have doubted him if he claimed to have produced the wonderment of silk out of pure air. "Where did ye see this miraculous cloth?"

A shadow passed over his features and Brenna wished she hadn't asked. Obviously, a partial memory had broken through, but not enough for him to answer her question.

"Don't know, and right now I don't much care." He teased the curling hairs between her legs. "But I know I've run a bolt of silk through my fingers and it doesn't begin to match you for softness."

What is he doing to me with those fine clever hands of his?

It was the last coherent thought Brenna mustered

as Jorand claimed her secret place, gently exploring and stroking. A surge of warmth flooded her belly, a deep rhythmic throb begging for … what? She had no answer for this need building inside her. She could only trust him to lead her aright and if she but yielded to his touch, all would be well. But oh! How her insides twisted into knots. She was wound tighter than a spool of new yarn.

Brenna arched her back, thrusting her hips up to him, heedless of the way it forced her head beneath the surface of the water.

"Ho, now, none of that," he said, pulling her upright.

"Ye're not stopping, are ye?" She bit back the groan of frustration threatening to erupt.

"No fear of that," he promised. "We just need a change of scenery."

He gathered her up as if she weighed less than an armful of posies and climbed out of the stream.

"What of our clothes?" Brenna asked as he swept her past the discarded piles.

"Don't worry." He gave her a squeeze. "They'll be there when we have need of them again."

As he carried her through the deep woods, she rested her head against his chest, listening to the banging of his heart. She smiled, realizing her own was doing a considerable jig as well. The heat of the day had dissipated and the evening air was cool on her wet skin. But the fresh green breeze did nothing to quench the fire rampaging through her loins.

Jorand laid her down beneath the lean-to he'd fashioned, settling her on his capacious cloak that covered a nest of pine boughs. She sank into the fragrant bower, letting her gaze rove over the body of her husband.

Husband. Bathed in Jorand's tender caring, she was pleased to be his if only it meant he'd keep touching her with those twice-blessed hands of his.

But he didn't move to stroke her again.

Instead, he stood over her, potent and ready, his gaze traveling the length of her body, starting with her curled toes and finally settling on Brenna's eyes. The steady drumbeat in her belly started afresh.

"Come to me, husband." Brenna stretched her arms toward him. "Love me."

He covered her body with his. Brenna welcomed the weight of him, thrusting her hips up to meet his, glorying in his hardness against her softness.

"Brenna." He breathed the name into her neck, then began trailing feather-soft kisses from her earlobe to the hollow at the base of her throat.

All the tender, sensitive places his hands had invaded, his mouth now conquered. He covered her breasts with kisses and when he finally took an aching nipple between his lips, she cried out for the joy of it. A jolt of desire shook her as she felt the inner connectedness of her breasts and her throbbing womb. With each suckle, the tremor of a contraction deep inside flooded her with need.

Jorand trailed his mouth down her ribs, stopping to tease her navel with his tongue. Brenna felt she'd crumble to bits in anticipation, but in anticipation of what she had no idea.

"What in the name of all the holy angels are ye doing to me?" she gasped.

"Loving you, princess. Just loving you."

Then he gently parted the delicate folds between her legs and claimed her with his mouth.

"Mercy," she breathed.

"I have none," he answered and returned to sweetly savaging her.

All semblance of control fled and Brenna quivered with wanting. She felt as if she were being pulled into a long, dark tunnel. She heard someone moan and realized without shame that it was her. Brenna knew she was naked before him, but Jorand was stripping her soul bare as well.

And she didn't care a whit.

Part of her training with Father Michael included learning to create the decorative patterns that curved and swirled in never ending convolutions. Now, her insides were more twisted upon themselves than the most intricate interlace she'd ever designed on vellum. Tighter and tighter, the knot curled in on itself, stretching Brenna thinner than the finest parchment. She drew a ragged breath. Downward she spiraled in an agony of need.

Then, suddenly, the knot shattered in a blinding wave of pleasure, followed hard on by another rolling spasm of bliss. Her body bucked with the force of her release as the contractions continued to suffuse her with delight. As dark as the tunnel had seemed when she was traveling along that bewildering corridor, she was now bathed in warmth and light, hearing nothing but the siren song of joy.

When she finally returned to a sense of herself, she was aware that Jorand had snugged in close beside her, his hand splayed possessively over her heart.

"Is all well with you, princess?"

She rolled her eyes at him and sighed. "Aye, entirely and completely well, as if ye didn't know it." She traced a finger over his cheek and jaw, amazed at what he had done with just his two clever hands and blessed sweet mouth. "I thought for a moment the angels had come to carry me to heaven. I had no idea a *Finn-Gall* demon such as yourself could do it as well."

His smile glinted at her in the failing light. Brenna turned her head to kiss him and found to her surprise that her newly spent body quickened to him again. But this time she welcomed the pleasant ache, knowing it was but the harbinger of future delight. She was aware of the length of his erection pressed against her thigh, sliding over her skin in a slow knock that would not be denied.

"I promised to wait till your wanting exceeded my own," Jorand said, his voice ragged with need. "Are we there yet?"

"Oh!" She ran a teasing hand over his chest, giving some of the hairs around one nipple a light tug. " 'Twould seem we're not quite done, are we?"

"Not if there's a god in that Christian heaven of yours, we're not."

He covered her mouth with his, taking her lips with a feverish urgency she answered with passion of her own. As the kiss deepened, she slid a hand down and brushed the side of his stiff phallus.

"What are you doing?" He grabbed her hand.

"Only what ye did to me," she said with feigned innocence. "I'm a gifted student, Jorand. I learn very quickly. Did I never tell ye that?"

When she stroked him again, his eyes rolled back in their sockets. "You're gifted all right."

"Then let me pleasure ye." He allowed her to push him onto his back and then folded his hands under his head with the air of a man about to undergo torture. She touched his shaft again, enjoying the smoothness of his taut skin and the way the big thing raised itself, seemingly of its own accord, to meet her hand. Brenna had the feeling she was making friends with an unknown beast, one she wasn't entirely sure was safe.

He is monstrous big.

How in the world was she to take him in? She chewed her bottom lip. After all the pleasure he'd shown her, would it still end in the pain she dreaded?

"Stop, Brenna."

"Have I hurt ye?" She jerked her hand away.

"No, I can't take any more, and I don't want it to be this way."

"Then how is it to be? What would ye have me do?"

"I've given that some thought." He lifted her and set her astraddle his hips. "Don't do anything that hurts you. But do something soon," he said through a clenched jaw. "Please."

Brenna looked down at him, wondering at his willingness to let her take the lead. She had no clue where to start. So she leaned forward to kiss him, finding honey under his tongue. His hands massaged her breasts again and warmth spread down to her womb. She gasped as she felt the tip of him enter her.

Their eyes met.

"Trust me, Brenna," he said. "I'm trusting you."

She nodded wordlessly and sat back, letting more of him in. He filled her snugly and she expanded to hold him. But his forward progress was stopped by her thin barrier. Brenna knew there was much more of him to come. She pulled forward and he slid out.

They groaned together, each despairing of the lost connection.

Brenna suddenly realized why she ached. She longed for him to fill her, whether it hurt or not. Using her hand, she guided him in again.

"It doesn't hurt," she said with wonder. "Saints above, it doesn't hurt."

She threw her head back and impaled herself on his full length. A cry escaped her lips.

"Brenna?" He reached for her.

When she looked down, a single tear slid down her cheek. "I only hurt for a moment. Now 'tis wonderful. You're wonderful."

She leaned down to kiss him again and they began the ancient dance, old as Eden itself, starting slowly and building to a new fevered pitch.

His breath came in ragged gasps as he strained under her, meeting her with strong thrusts. He gripped her hips as he suddenly held her still. Deep inside her, his seed erupted in satisfying jolts and, as if in answer, her secret place contracted around him in welcoming joy.

She sank down to rest her head on his chest, comforted when the wild thumping of his heart returned to a steady rhythm.

"Will that do, then?" she asked.

"*Ja*, princess, that'll do," Jorand said, running a hand over her damp hair. "But only if we do it often."

Chapter Twenty

"The rabbit is nearly done," Brenna announced as she turned the roasting carcass on an improvised spit.

"Good." Jorand came up behind her, pushed her hair aside, and planted a kiss on the nape of her neck. His lips sent little shivers of delight down her spine. Brenna wondered if he tasted the saltiness of the light sheen of perspiration on her skin from the exertion of their most recent tussle.

"You've worn me out again, woman. I can see that as your husband I'll need to keep up my strength."

Brenna smiled. She'd always been a quick student, but who'd have guessed she'd be such a willing pupil of the carnal arts. In the last few weeks of their travels, he'd taught her all he knew of the game of love. Once she understood the basics, she dreamed up some exquisite variations for their lovemaking. Brenna surprised herself by being more than willing to add her own creations to her husband's repertoire of pleasures. Where she had once been fearful, she was now bold. Once terrified of being taken, she now gave—and took—willingly.

They sailed on each day, carefully avoiding inhabited coves. Brenna feared it would be difficult to explain that the Northman she traveled with was her husband before some Irishman tried to put an arrow into him. The little boat Brian Ui Niall had christened the *Una* proved sturdy and seaworthy, rounding the rocky points of Erin and finally slipping into the wide estuary that narrowed into the river Shannon.

Before they left Donegal, Brian Ui Niall had lent Brenna the only map of the island he possessed and she copied it faithfully. So far, the landmarks proved accurate. Brenna wasn't sure, but judging from the symbols on the leather chart, she thought Clonmacnoise was nearby.

"Don't you think it's time you told me?" Jorand tore a piece of stale flat bread in half and handed her a portion.

"Told ye what?"

"What's so important at Clonmacnoise?" He took a bite of the bread, chewing it without much enthusiasm. The map of Erin was spread out before him and he traced a finger around the outline of the landmass. "If we'd kept going round the island, by my reckoning we'd have been in Dublin by now."

"Ye promised me we'd divert to the abbey."

"It's not that I mind the diversion." He slid a hand up her arm and back down to link fingers with her. "In fact, I've greatly enjoyed the diversion, but," his face grew serious, "I think the time for secrets between us has passed, don't you? What compels you to Clonmacnoise?"

Brenna sighed and slipped her hand away from

his. This was one secret she'd carefully guarded because it could end all others they might someday share. But Jorand was right. He was her husband. He, of all people, should know the whole truth.

"I've told ye what happened to me sister at the abbey."

He nodded soberly.

"I haven't told ye what happened after. Not even Da knows of it."

His eyes blazed on her behalf. "Did the Christians there blame you?"

She had no doubt that if she asked him, he'd personally sack the abbey in retribution for her.

"Aye, they did, and rightly too. If not for me, Sinead would have stayed safe behind the abbey walls. But that's not the worst of it. The blackguard left me sister with child."

Jorand remained silent, his face unreadable. What if her shameful revelation turned him from her? She swallowed hard and decided to keep going. If she was going to be damned, better to be damned for the truth.

"When I first realized Sinead was bearing, I tried to convince her to rid herself of it." She cast her gaze into her lap and folded her hands together to keep them from shaking. It still hurt her heart to remember urging Sinead to make that solitary trip through the glen.

"There's an old wise woman who lives not far from the abbey," Brenna explained. "She makes potions and such. Much as we hated the bairn's sire and the manner of its getting, I thought Sinead would be tempted."

"But she wasn't?"

"No, she wasn't. Sinead saw the coming child as a gift, a way for God to bring some good from all that was vile and ugly." Brenna hung her head. "Me sister was made of much finer stuff than I."

Sinead had given birth in the abbey, she told him, attended by women for whom men were a mystery and childbirth an unthinkable event. The nuns were kind and full of pious advice, but uniformly unhelpful.

After Sinead languished in childbed for the better part of two days, the abbot relented and called in a midwife, the very wise woman Brenna had counseled Sinead to see about doing away with the child. The crone reputedly knew as much about bringing a bairn into the world as sending one off to the next, and her sister delivered a healthy babe. One that was whisked away from her before she'd even held it once.

Brenna stared at the fire without really seeing it, the remembered scent of the blood and birthwater fresh in her nostrils. "She was pale as dawn, Sinead was." A shudder wracked her frame. "She told me to see to the bairn and then between one breath and the next, she was gone."

"And your father doesn't know your sister is dead?"

"Once a novice takes the veil, she's dead to her earthly family. Da thinks Sinead is a true Bride of Christ, safely beyond the shame of the Northman's rape. I couldn't bring meself to tell him different." Brenna thought she'd cried every tear she had for her sister, but a new spring of guilt welled up. Jorand reached for her, but she straight-armed him. She didn't deserve the comfort he might offer.

"The abbot tried to bring the babe to me, but I refused. The little demon killed me sister, I said, and I'd have nothing to do with it." She hid her face with her palms. "I was mad with grief and, God help me, if they'd forced it on me, I might have done murder. So they took it away."

Jorand moved closer to her, near enough for her to feel his heat, but not close enough to touch her.

"At first, I was glad not to have seen it, glad not to have the babe there a constant reminder of the calamity me sin had wrought," she said, wrapping her arms around her middle. "Then, it started to fret me that I didn't even know if the bairn was a boy or a girl. The abbot would tell me not a word."

Silence stretched between them. Why didn't he say something, anything to let her know what he was thinking? She was afraid of what she might see in his face, so she kept her eyes downcast.

"I never knew what became of the babe. I've always assumed the abbot fostered it out somewhere. He kept saying 'twould be best if I knew nothing and put the whole sorry mess out of me mind."

Brenna passed a hand over her eyes, seeing for a moment the tiny wailing bundle the midwife swept away from her sister's bedside. A stone settled into her chest. Why had she not honored her sister's request and asked for the child right then?

"But I found I couldn't bear not knowing," she said, picking at a loose thread in her woolen *brat*. Anything to keep her from looking up and seeing disapproval in Jorand's face. "Sinead laid the bairn's care on me and I failed her. Again. Then when I began to bedevil the Holy Father about it day and night, he sent me home. Said I'd never make a nun if I couldn't obey his orders any better than that."

All Brenna heard was the steady clatter of the river as it rustled past them.

"Will ye not say something?" she finally asked.

Jorand touched her then, resting his hand lightly on her knee. She looked up at him.

"I have to agree with your abbot," he said wryly, one corner of his mouth lifted in a grimace. "You'd never make a nun."

The crinkling lines around his eyes told her he didn't despise her, even though she despised herself. Now, would he understand the rest?

"So ye see, then, why I have to go back."

"Of course," Jorand said. "You want to see about the child, make sure it's well. That makes perfect sense."

"No, 'tis not all. I mean to take the bairn away with me when we leave."

"Brenna—"

"No, me mind's made up." She tucked her knees under her chin and clasped her arms around her legs, rocking slightly. "I've been vexed for months, nearly a year now, fretting about this child. God forgive me, I tried to convince Sinead to end its life, as if that would take away me sin. And I was relieved at first not to have the bairn, still hating the man who gave it to me sister." She heaved a sigh. "But then the dreams started coming."

"Dreams?"

"Aye, in the night, the child appears out of nowhere. Always 'tis in some kind of danger and I have to save it." Brenna gnawed her bottom lip. "And in me dreams I usually can't. 'Tis a sign, I believe. The babe must be in peril and I must needs see to it."

"You can't set much store in dreams," he said, reaching to take the rabbit from the spit and slice off a chunk of meat for each of them. "Dreams are nothing but fancies."

"Nothing till they make a body see things clear. This child may have had an ill begetting, but it doesn't change the fact that 'tis me sister's child. Sinead's own flesh. Me own kin." She waved away his offer of food. "How can I not know how it fares?"

The life of a child, even one coddled and cared for, was a dicey thing. Between famine and plague, accidents and interclan warfare, children were the most vulnerable of beings. To raise a bairn to adulthood was an accomplishment even if the youngster was well-cosseted. For a fosterling, a child tossed aside, Brenna knew the odds of survival were even slimmer.

" 'Tis the burden Sinead laid upon me. Perhaps 'tis me penance for the sin of rebellion, but I must care for this child." She swiped her nose on her sleeve. "Perhaps ye can't see the reason of it, but I'll not rest till I can take the bairn back to me father's keep and show him his true heritage."

Brenna's lips quivered. Her marriage was still so tenuous. True, they had found delight in each other, but she realized she had no right to ask Jorand to take on another man's child. Even if it meant he cast her aside after their handfast time was spent, she intended to keep the child.

"I will raise this babe," she said with force, as if she were trying to convince herself as well as him. "And I will love it."

"Have you thought about what this means?"

"Whether ye agree to it or not, makes no difference." Her voice faltered, but her will was determined. "The child has a prior claim on me. I must see to it."

"That's not what I meant. I was thinking about the child's foster parents. Mayhap they care for the child. What if the babe is happy and safe where it is? Or . . ."

"Or what?"

"What if the child is dead? Would you really want to know?" he asked quietly. "Would it not be better for you to be able to think of it alive?"

"Why would ye say such a thing?"

"The way things are now, you can imagine the child however you like. Boy or girl, whatever you please. Strong, healthy, afraid of nothing." Jorand's faraway look told Brenna he might be imagining a child of his own. "You've been given a gift, princess. In your mind and heart, you can hold a perfect child for your sister."

"But what I imagine may not be true."

"Does it matter? When I first came to you, not being able to remember worried me day and night. Now, I've decided if my memory never comes back, perhaps it is for the best."

She stared at him incredulously.

"What if there are things in my past I don't want to know?" His brows nearly met over his straight nose. "What if I were a different sort of man altogether before I washed up on your beach?"

Brenna laid a hand on his arm. "We are what we are. I think ye have always been the same, Jorand. Ye are a fine, fine man. And I'll have words with any who says different. If ye have things in your past ye'd be less than proud of, it only means ye are a true son of Adam, neither more nor less."

He cast a lopsided smile at her, beaming under her backhanded praise. "If you want this child, I'll see that you have it, even if I have to snatch it for you from its crib."

"That's exactly what Mother used to tell us girls the Northmen would do to us if we misbehaved." She suppressed a giggle. "Who'd have thought I'd have need of *Finn-Gall* cradle robber meself?" Then she sobered. "But I'm hoping it won't come to that. I've brought the silver that was me dowry and stand prepared to compensate whoever is fostering the babe. The real trick will be making Father Ambrose tell us where to find the child."

"I think you can safely leave that to me," he said, the set of his jaw leaving no doubt he'd enjoy forcing the information from the abbot. He caught up her hand and dropped a kiss into her palm. "Haven't you learned you can trust me yet, Brenna?"

She felt herself falling headlong into the blue depths of his eyes. Aye, here was an ocean she could launch herself upon and fear no hurt. Brenna pressed a palm to each of his cheeks and poured herself into a kiss.

The rabbit was cold and greasy by the time they got around to eating it.

Brenna wasn't sure what actually woke her. One moment, she was curled up beside her husband and the next she was lying, body tense, ears pricked, straining to catch the sound again.

The moon had risen, cold and full, every blade of grass doubled by its own sharp shadow. Their fire had sunk to dully glowing embers. She raised her head to listen. There, she heard it again.

It was a voice, low and full of guttural grunts and sibilance. She couldn't make out the words. The sound faded in and out as if it were sometimes amplified by water, sometimes buffered by the thick woods.

She eased herself away from Jorand without waking him and glided in silence to the river's edge. The voices were louder now and she realized why she couldn't understand the words. The men were speaking a foreign tongue.

Norse.

A rough laugh broke the quiet of the night, unnaturally loud on the water. It wasn't a pleasant sound. It was the sound of one who rejoices in another's suffering.

Brenna's soul froze within her. She knew that laugh.

A longship drifted into view around a bend in the river and standing in the prow, behind the serpent head, was the man whose face had haunted her nightmares. The silvery light made it impossible for her to see the dull russet of his hair and beard, but his coarse features and unmistakable laugh were burned on her mind. She'd watched him violate her sister not just once, but over and over again in a thousand evil dreams. She'd know him anywhere.

Suddenly Brenna felt the weight of a hand on her shoulder. She sucked breath in over her teeth, ready to scream, when another palm clamped over her mouth.

"Be easy, girl," Jorand whispered in her ear. "Keep still."

Brenna watched, motionless, as the raiding party glided by them, too caught up in their own conversations to notice the glint of two pairs of eyes tracking their movements from shore. The Northmen started a grunting chant and she recognized with a start it was the same song Jorand had sung in snatches when he first came to her.

As the dragonship disappeared around a turn in the waterway, the aftershakes of terror hit her. Jorand folded her into his arms to still her shuddering.

"Hush now." He murmured endearments into her hair, trying to soothe her. "They're gone."

"I know, but—"

"I won't let any hurt come to you, Brenna."

She stopped shivering and clasped him tightly. Finally, she felt him pull away.

"Wait here," Jorand said. "I'll be back.

"Where are ye going?"

"After them." He turned and headed toward the hidden coracle. "Those men are familiar to me. I mean to get some answers. I'm not sure how, but I know their leader."

"So do I."

He stopped and spun on his heel then. Slowly, she saw understanding dawn on his face.

"He's the one." She wrapped her arms around herself and rocked in hopeless misery. She felt her muscles constrict as she struggled to maintain control.

Brenna saw a cold shadow pass over Jorand's features as his mouth settled into a grim line.

"I will kill him for you," Jorand promised with cold fury. He turned and continued toward their small boat. He had hidden the craft beneath brush and broken boughs in case they encountered unwanted traffic. Now he tossed the concealment aside and untied the prow from the gnarled oak.

"No, don't go." Brenna threw her arms around his waist and buried her face in the middle of his back. "There are too many of them."

"Woman, let me be," he growled, twisting out of her grasp. Then he softened his tone. "Wait here. I'll try to be back before dawn."

He put a shoulder to the coracle and began shoving it back into the river Shannon.

Panic cast its tentacles over Brenna. She'd thought never to be free from the terror and guilt of her sister's violation, but her wounded soul was beginning to heal. Already, Jorand's tenderness wiped away all but the deepest scars on her heart. But if he got himself killed, she knew she'd never recover. She had to stop him.

One of the bits of brush Jorand had used to hide the ship was a stout limb as big around as her arm. She picked it up and, in a flash of inspiration, realized it would make an admirable club.

She took aim at his head and swung with all her might. The branch connected with his temple with a sickening thud.

He never saw the blow coming.

"I'll not lose ye to the likes of them," Brenna said as her husband collapsed in an unconscious heap.

Chapter Twenty-one

Light mist dripped from the edges of the lean-to. Brenna dipped a cloth into the leather bucket and held it to the egg-sized knot swelling Jorand's brow. His eyes were still half-closed. He hadn't stirred beyond a groan or two when she dragged his body up from the riverbank toward their little camp.

Halfway back to the smoldering fire, she'd remembered the boat. She left him splayed on the long grass while she splashed into the Shannon after the coracle. She managed to snag the tow rope before the small craft drifted out of her reach. Now it was bobbing in the river at the end of its tether, but at least it was securely lashed to the oak again.

When she got him settled back at their camp, Jorand's hands were cold and his lips an unhealthy shade of blue. In an effort to warm him, Brenna rebuilt their fire. She watched the steady rise and fall of his chest as the night wore on, trying to tell herself that was a good sign.

A lark trilled in a nearby tree and was promptly

joined by his neighbors in a chorus of rejoicing over surviving the terrors of another night. Overhead, Brenna saw streaks of pearly gray slashing the darkness. Dawn was fast approaching.

Maybe daylight would open Jorand's eyes. She hoped so. How could he have thought of leaving her in the wilds to chase down that pack of rabid dogs?

"Men," she muttered under her breath.

Why did he have to race off to avenge Sinead now when the deed couldn't be undone? What good would it do? His getting killed wouldn't bring back her sister, wouldn't erase her guilt. She tried to feel upset with him, but couldn't.

Instead, she flagellated herself. How could she have struck him in the exact spot of his previous hurt? Perhaps she'd done him a serious injury. What if he lost his memory again? What if he forgot her? In her panic, she hadn't taken the time to consider the consequences.

Her gut twisted in knots as she fingered the tender bruise. His skin was still cool under her touch.

"O God, I didn't mean to hit him that hard," she prayed. "Lord of Heaven, be merciful and forgive me."

"Maybe you should be more concerned about me forgiving you." One blue eye squinted up at her. Jorand struggled to sit up, then groaned and fell back on their bedding. His hand flew to his temple.

Brenna released the breath she hadn't realized she was holding.

"Ah! Ye're alive and in your right mind! God be praised." She leaned down and peppered his face with kisses. " 'Tis sorry I am, but ye see that I had to do it."

"Why?" He pushed her away and dragged in a deep breath.

"Why indeed." She sat back on her heels, hands fisted at her waist. "For one thing, there were too many of them and only one of ye, in case ye hadn't noticed."

"You think me so powerless?"

"I think ye dim-witted to barge into danger against such odds and to no purpose."

"No purpose, she says," Jorand grumbled. "Don't you want to see him dead?"

"Aye, of course I do." She softened her tone and leaned down to caress his stiff jawline. "I've wished the man dead every day since I first clapped eyes on him, but I had rather see ye living."

"I told you I'd be back," he said, refusing to be mollified. "My word is my oath. I'm not in the habit of making promises I don't intend to deliver."

"And I'm not in the habit of standing by, wringing me hands, while someone I care for heads for disaster."

He glared up at her. "Interfere again and the disaster will be my hand on your backside."

She flinched, but anger flared to life in her. She was prepared to argue more when she noticed how pale he was. She really had struck him a blow.

"'Tis sorry I am. Ye know I trust your word." Brenna read frustration in his clenched jaw.

"I recognized them, Brenna. Somehow, those men are a part of my past and I needed to know how. Can you not understand that the key to my memory might be with those men?"

"Did ye not tell me just last night if ye never remembered 'twould be no bad thing?"

"Don't twist my words. I only meant—" Jorand tried again to sit up. This time he had to grab his head with both hands. "Thor's hammer, woman. What have you done to me?"

The pain was more intense than anything he'd ever endured. White-hot waves rolled over him accompanied by a pounding drumbeat matching his heart stroke for stroke. The agony blinded him for a moment. Then colors poured back into his brain, swirling in a maelstrom of bloodred against the backs of his eyes. Voices assaulted him from all sides, muffled at first and then distinct and crisp, but so numerous, he couldn't make out what any of them were saying.

A flood of smells engulfed him, warm bread and exotic spices mixed with steaming piles of dung. One after another and jumbled together, the scents swarmed over him, both pleasing and repulsive, all equally unreal.

Every nerve in his body screamed in unison and he rolled into a tight ball, still clutching his head.

Then just as suddenly, everything came clear again and he was aware of the sweet grass under him. He felt Brenna's arms around him, rocking him gently. She whispered a furious repetitive prayer.

"Brenna." His voice was hoarse and raw. Jorand realized he must have cried out in the throes of the fit.

"Aye, I'm here, husband," she answered. "Rest ye now. All will be well. Ye'll see. All will be well."

He let her continue to rock him, but he knew the truth. All would not be well.

He remembered. He remembered everything.

Chapter Twenty-two

Brenna stood in the stern of the boat, gazing intently down the wide ribbon of water.

"According to the map, we should be there. Does anything look familiar to you yet?" Jorand bent forward and gave the oars another long-armed pull. They were traveling against the current and the wind that favored them up to this point had all but died.

"Nothing," Brenna admitted. "I don't recognize a thing." She plopped back down on her seat and adjusted the steering oar to keep them as close to the center of the river as possible. She'd left Clonmacnoise less than a year ago, but she'd tried to force the ugliness that had occurred there from her mind. She found it difficult to call the place back now. "Maybe that hillock yonder, but I cannot be sure. Ye must understand, we were not encouraged to go a-wandering beyond the walls of the abbey. 'Tis me sorrow that I did."

"Why did you ever leave your father's keep, Brenna?"

"Many reasons," she said. "For one, I didn't want to be forced into a marriage."

"Sorry about that," he said, pulling a face at her.

She swatted at him playfully. "Ye know ye're not in the least."

Jorand's lovemaking had a furious, urgent quality since she'd kept him from chasing those raiders by striking him down. He showed no ill effects from the blow, save for that initial massive headache. His interest in joining his powerful body with hers wasn't abated one whit. He seemed more taken with her than ever, and yet he'd not spoken any words of love to her. Not once. It might have troubled her more, except for the tender expression on his face when she caught him looking at her.

"And I'm not sorry, either. Ye have the makings of a fine husband, Jorand," she said impishly. "Once ye're properly trained, of course."

"Hmph!" He threw himself into rowing with renewed vigor.

"The threat of an arranged marriage wasn't the only thing that drove me from Donegal," Brenna continued. "The main reason I went to Clonmacnoise was for the library."

Her voice caught as she remembered the shelves of precious volumes lining the walls. "Ever so many books and parchments. 'Twould take a lifetime to read them all and I fully intended to do it." She sighed. " 'Tis a grand place. I've never asked ye before. Can ye read?"

"A little," he said. "I know some of the runes. There's a trick to them, you see. Sometimes, they stand for a sound and sometimes for a whole word or idea. A person has to study hard to decipher a rune stone."

"That does sound needlessly complicated." Brenna watched in fascination as the muscles across his strong shoulders bunched and flattened under his smooth skin. He'd tied his hair back with a leather thong and her gaze was drawn to the spot behind his ear she loved to kiss. His hairline glistened with perspiration. Brenna ran her tongue over her lips, almost tasting the saltiness of his skin.

"I could teach ye to read," she offered, trying to ignore the way her lips tingled with the urge to kiss his neck. If they stopped to dally every time she yearned for him, they'd never reach the abbey. "Ye have taught me a great many things in a short time. Turn and turn about, I say. Mayhap I'll return the favor."

"And very pleasant lessons those have been," he said, his voice a low rumbling purr.

She felt her body clench and forced herself to look away. Marriage was turning her into a terrible wanton, she decided with a secret smile. Father Michael had always preached subjugation of all appetites of the flesh, but her craving for this Northman didn't lend itself to modest consumption.

Oh, devil take what Father Michael says! She leaned down to plant a kiss on that tender spot and stayed to nip playfully at his earlobe.

The oars were left trailing in the river Shannon, as Jorand let them fall slack in the oar ports. He turned and gathered her onto his lap, returning her kisses with fiery ones of his own.

When he finally released her mouth, he sat still, searching her face for a moment. She was unable to decipher the meaning of his intense look. It was as if he were trying to burn her image into his memory. Surely he'd have no trouble remembering her now, she reasoned. A lazy smile creased his face and she dismissed the niggling twinge of worry.

"Not that I'm complaining, but what brought this on?" His hands roved over her, sending flutters of longing dancing along the surface of her skin.

"Are ye displeased?"

"Of course not," he said before nuzzling her ear. "I only want to know what I did so I can be sure to do it again."

"'Tis just ye. The look of ye, the smell, the feel, even the growling sound of your voice." Brenna sighed and snuggled into his chest. "Whenever I'm near ye, I'm like a child with a sweet tooth and ye are a tray of honeyed fruit."

He kissed her again, long and deep.

"Do ye have any idea how fine ye are?" She trailed her fingertips along his jaw down to his collarbone. "I'm the most blessed woman in the world to be having ye for a husband."

"Brenna—"

"Not another word till I finish, or I may not be able to." She drew in a ragged breath. "After what happened at Clonmacnoise, I never hoped to feel this way for any man. I'd go anywhere with ye. I don't even mind ye are dragging me to that den of Northmen called Dublin—"

He clamped a hand over her mouth to stop her in mid-thought. "Let's not go."

"What?"

"I don't need to go to Dublin. We'll see about the child at the abbey, and once we have him, we'll sail north, back to Donegal."

"But ye were so set on going to see if ye've kin there."

The odd expression passed over his face again so quickly Brenna thought she might have imagined it.

"I've changed my mind," he said with a smile that seemed forced.

"So be it," she said, hardly daring to believe her good fortune. She'd embraced traveling to Dublin with the same enthusiasm the early Christian martyrs must have felt about their visit to the Roman lions. "I'll be more than pleased to be heading home. But ye haven't let me finish what I needed to tell ye. 'Tis how I care for ye. Do ye not know that I . . ." She drew a deep breath.

Smoke.

The acrid odor invaded her nostrils and sent a tingling premonition down her spine. It was far too strong to be a crofter's cooking fire. "Do ye smell that?"

She slid off his lap and looked upriver, hand raised to shield her eyes. The glare of late afternoon sun turned the river to molten gold. A tall gray plume rose in the distance, beyond the next bend in the waterway.

"Whatever's ablaze, it's big," Jorand said solemnly as he returned to the oars.

Brenna's heart hammered a warning. A large flat granite boulder next to a trio of shuddering aspens caught her eye as they glided by. A stab of recognition coursed through her.

" 'Tis the abbey," Brenna said flatly. "Someone has sacked Clonmacnoise."

They broke free of the trees and in the barren land of Offaly, the cloister came into view on the bank of the wide river. Light ash fell in the air around them. The gray stone walls seemed intact, but the heavy oak portal had been smashed to kindling, its remains swinging drunkenly on one iron hinge. Clonmacnoise was a double monastery, home to a community of monks and nuns who lived in separate enclaves but worked and worshipped in the same place. Inside the walls the compound was dotted with little beehive-shaped cells, the homely houses of the monks who tended the grounds. Most of them were made of stone, but the ones that were wattle-and-daub sent spires of smoke flying.

The fine chapel's thatch roof was gone, leaving only a blackened skeleton of charred beams. Of the little church built by St. Ciaran himself, there was no trace. The stone tower that overshadowed Clonmacnoise belched out dark fumes. Brenna heard the crackle and hiss of flames before she saw them dancing at the far end of the compound.

"The library," she whispered, not daring to trust her voice further. It would burn for days. The exquisite volume of Saint Augustine's *Confessions* bound in Spanish leather, the ancient Greek Septuagint, the fabulous jewel-encrusted Skellig Michael codex, all the treasures of art, wisdom, and devotion hidden between the bindings in the library of Clonmacnoise Abbey were reduced to smoldering ash. The loss was unimaginable. She swayed a little and was grateful when Jorand caught her in his arms.

Suddenly a new scent reached them, a sweetish smell that reminded Brenna of roasting meat.

Burning flesh.

She clamped a hand over her mouth, fearful she'd be sick. The faces of the kindly nuns, old Murtaugh the sexton, and even imperious Father Ambrose reeled before her eyes. They were all totally without harm and obviously without any defense as well.

"Sweet Jesus," she breathed. "Who could do such a thing?"

"We both know the answer," Jorand said, his mouth tight. "Northmen."

"Aye, the raiding party," she nodded. "But that was days ago. Surely something could be saved. The nuns and monks wouldn't let the fires burn unabated unless . . ."

"Unless they're all dead," he finished for her. Firm hands on her shoulders, he turned her from the bleak vision. "There's nothing for you here. Let's go home, Brenna."

"No, someone may yet be alive and need our help."

Jorand manned the sculls while Brenna leaned against the steering oar to bring the prow to the beachhead.

Someone must have been spared. Otherwise, she'd never know what had become of her sister's bairn. That little ghost would dog her dreams for the rest of her life.

Please, God, let there be someone.

CHAPTER TWENTY-THREE

Only the library was still ablaze, but smoke curled from the remains of a dozen buildings. Save for the pop and sizzle of flames devouring the literary wealth of the abbey, there was no other sound as Brenna and Jorand trudged through the abbey's broken arch. Even the birds seemed to have forgotten how to sing.

"Here," Jorand said as he draped a wet cloth over her nose and mouth and tied it behind her head. "This will help."

It did seem to block out smells and most of the smoke, but Brenna's eyes still stung.

The wooden structure that was home to the nuns and novices, the veritable rabbit warren of cells in which her sister had given birth, was a mass of charred rubble. On the far side of the tower, a smoldering pile caught her eye. When she recognized a set of blackened stubs as the remains of a human rib cage, she darted her gaze away, hand to her heart.

A scream clawed at the back of her throat, but she

choked it down. She had to maintain an illusion of calm. If she collapsed in a keening heap, Jorand would certainly carry her back to the vessel and she'd never know the fate of Sinead's child. Surely the babe had been fostered out, not hidden away in some secluded cell on the abbey grounds. Surely they wouldn't have been able to keep it from her if the child had been secreted there. Brenna prayed it was so.

Her ears pricked to a sound. It was faint, but regular, a rasping singsong.

"Do ye hear that?" she asked.

"It's coming from over there." Jorand pointed toward the graveyard, a small piece of consecrated ground dotted with standing stones.

Brenna lifted her skirt and broke into a trot. The sound was clearer now. Definitely a human voice, but one so marred with grief and smoke, she couldn't tell whether it was male or female. A broken string of words floated to her ears.

"O God of all spirits and all flesh," the voice droned, "... trampled down death and ... the devil, and given life to Thy world ..."

Brenna recognized part of the Matins for Those Who Have Fallen Asleep, an office for the dead. But matins were for the morning. The sun was sinking in the western sky. If worship was called for, vespers would be more appropriate to the approaching twilight.

"Lord, give rest to the souls of Thy servants," the voice croaked in a sad parody of chanting. "... in a place of light, in a place of verdure... whence all sickness, sorrow and sighing have fled awa—" The worshipper broke into ragged sobs. *"Mea culpa, mea culpa, mea maxima culpa."*

Brenna rounded the tallest of the standing Celtic

crosses and found the abbot, Father Ambrose, sprawled in a miserable lump, eyes covered by soot-begrimed hands. She knelt beside him.

"Father," she said softly.

He peered at her from between grubby fingers, nails all broken and torn. The abbot struggled to sit up, a questioning look of both recognition and disbelief on his pudgy, sallow features. When Jorand came into view, the priest cowered back, shielding his head with his hands.

"Deliver us, O Lord, from the terror of the Northmen. *In nomine Patri, et Fili, et Spiritu Sancto,"* he chanted with vehemence.

"Don't fret yourself, Father," Brenna said quickly. "This is Jorand. Ye've naught to fear from him."

"No more *Finn-Gall* demons, for Christ's pity," Ambrose nearly shrieked, crossing himself repeatedly.

Jorand let his arms dangle unthreateningly at his sides in an effort to look less imposing, Brenna supposed. She decided he was less than successful. With his height, coloring and strong Norse features, there was no disguising what he was. Even in a passive state, her husband had the look of a formidable warrior. She sent him an invisible plea for some privacy and he blessedly took the hint.

"I'll be nearby if you need me," he promised, and strode away, stopping within earshot, Brenna noticed.

"Father," she said, taking one of the abbot's shaking hands in hers. His eyes rolled wildly and there was no glint of recognition in them now. She was sure it was because she'd been in the company of a Northman. " 'Tis only me. Brenna of Donegal. Do ye mind me now?"

A faint light came into his rheumy eyes. "Oh, child, ye have chosen an ill day to return to the House of God."

"Tell me what happened."

"They fell upon us just after nones two days ago."

"Northmen?"

"Aye, the thieving hell-spawn," he said with force, clearly feeling braver now that her Northman was out of sight. "Of course, we barred the gate at once but they battered it down. We had no way to fight them. We are a peaceful community of scholars and saints." He sniffled into his dirty sleeve. "What did we do to deserve this?"

The same question had niggled at her for months following her sister's rape. Jorand's comforting words came back to her.

"'Tis not a question of deserving. Only bad luck placed ye in the path of evil," she said. "There will always be those who are determined to harm others."

"But how could God have allowed this to happen?" he bleated.

Brenna was amazed she should be giving lessons in faith to one who had been her spiritual guide. "The Almighty gifted us with the right to choose. Just because some choose evil in the world, it doesn't make God any less good." She stroked the back of his hand in an effort to soothe him. "That's what ye always tried to teach me."

"Did I?" His gaze darted about in a confused manner. "I think 'tis a long time since I taught ye anything. Why have ye come back? Has God given ye a true vocation at last?"

"No, Father. I'm a married lady now."

"Ah, well, that's grand then, isn't it?" His eyes fastened on hers with a more lucid gaze. "So God has been pleased to work everything for your good. Who is the blessed fellow He chose for your husband?"

"Ye just met him," she said. "Jorand the Northman. He's helped me see that not all Northmen are evil, any more than all Irishmen are saints." Her gaze swept over the desecrated abbey. "Though ye certainly encountered some wicked *Ostmen* here. Was anyone else saved alive?"

His round face sagged. "Only Murtaugh."

Brenna sank down beside him and wept for the loss of the nuns and monks who had been her friends.

"I suppose ye wonder how I was spared. 'Twas not for mercy's sake, I assure ye." He hid his eyes again as fresh spasms of grief washed over him. "They made me watch."

Brenna bit her bottom lip and patted his forearm in comfort. She'd never have dared be so informal with the abbot when she was a novice here, but suffering was a great leveler. It erased all difference in rank between them. They were just two victims of Norse terror, but the tables had turned. Now it was Brenna's turn to console and help him heal if she could.

The abbot dropped his hands and stared into the endless sky. "The ones they didn't kill in the first rush of the raid, they slaughtered later for sport. Mother Superior, they stripped and paraded around the chapel. Then they disemboweled her." His voice was flat, as though if he thought about the words and their terrible meaning, he'd be unable to go on speaking. "The novices … ye of all people should know what happened to them."

Brenna nodded grimly.

"I thought the heathen might carry them off as

slaves. 'Tis often the case," he said. "But after they'd been defiled, the Norse devils cut their throats. Just like spring lambs in an abattoir."

"What of the monks?" she asked.

"They were hanged alive from the top of the tower and then set ablaze." Father Ambrose clamped his hands over his ears, to keep out the remembered screams, no doubt. He shook his head slowly. " 'Twas my fault, all my fault."

The abbot slumped down on the grass and passed into delirium, babbling incoherently and beating his chest.

Brenna stood and motioned for Jorand to come. When the big Northman came into view, Father Ambrose gasped twice and lapsed into unconsciousness.

"We can't leave him here," Brenna said. "Can ye carry him?"

"Ja." He bent and slung the inert body over his shoulder as dispassionately as if the abbot were a sack of millet. "Where do you want him?"

"The sexton's cottage," Brenna strode away, leading Jorand back through the compound and out the battered gate. "Father Ambrose is in no shape for questions. Maybe Murtaugh will have the answers I seek."

Murtaugh lived alone in a tiny house snugged up against the abbey's stone walls. It was Brenna's firm belief that the wiry old man had cared for the grounds and the garden of Clonmacnoise since the Flood. If Murtaugh had a second name, no one had ever heard it. He was not a member of the religious order and was known to pepper his speech with outrageous blasphemies, but abbots came and went at Clonmacnoise while Murtaugh stayed on. He was as much a fixture in the abbey as the relics in the now desecrated library.

Behind the compound, Brenna saw the stone walls of his cottage still standing. Even the thatched roof remained intact. Murtaugh was seated on a stump near the open doorway calmly stirring a pot suspended over a small cooking fire.

Since they were upwind from the smoke, Brenna pulled the damp kerchief from her face so the old man might recognize her. A bobbing nod and loud *harrumph* told her he did.

"Is Himself dead?" Murtaugh asked loudly.

"No, only fainted," Brenna answered in an equally loud tone. The sexton often pretended to be deaf as a rock, though Brenna knew better. "Can we lay him inside?"

"Suit yerself," he said with a shrug and returned to his work.

Brenna led Jorand into the interior of the cottage. She had come here often to sip tea with the ancient gardener and glean what she could of plant lore from him. He did not part with his knowledge willingly. She had to bully and cajole him into sharing his wisdom with her on more than one occasion.

The cottage was still bursting with seedlings and oddments, the walls lined with shelves to hold all the old man's vining projects. But the packed earthen floor was swept clean of debris. There was a simple table with two stools, a chest for storage, and a fresh pallet in one corner. Jorand deposited the abbot there and followed Brenna back out. They rejoined Murtaugh by his fire.

"Always told Himself ye'd be back one day," Murtaugh said as he squinted up at Brenna. Then his still sharp eyes took Jorand's measure. "But God's feet, I never thought to see ye with a twice-cursed *Ostman* in tow."

"This is Jorand. He's me husband if ye don't mind, so ye'll kindly be keeping a civil tongue in that old head of yours," she scolded.

"Husband, is it? There be a strange tale worth the telling or I'm mistook." He ladled out a portion of stew and handed it to her in a wooden bowl. "Hungry?"

"Aye," she admitted, accepting the rich-smelling offering with gratitude.

"I supposed your Northman is, too," he said grudgingly and scooped out a bowlful for Jorand as well, jerking his hand back when the younger man took the food from him. Murtaugh leaned toward Brenna and asked in what passed for a whisper, "Is he safe?"

She stifled a laugh, then remembered the hair-raising tale Moira told of Jorand's *berserkr* fury against the men who had attacked her and the look of cold mayhem in his startling blue eyes when he started after the raiders.

"No, he isn't in the least safe," Brenna admitted. "But he can be trusted."

"He also doesn't appreciate being talked about as though he isn't here," Jorand said.

"Speaks the fair tongue, eh?" Murtaugh slurped at his bowl, dropping all pretense of deafness. "Can't be all bad, then."

That seemed to satisfy the sexton for the moment, and he turned his full attention to the stew. When they were finished eating, Brenna decided it was time for her questions. But something the abbot had said demanded explanation first.

"When we first happened upon Father Ambrose, he was saying *'mea culpa'*. Why does he seem to think all this is his fault?"

"Och, that's bad, it is." Murtaugh scratched absently at his balding pate. "I wasn't here, ye ken, being upriver seeing to the butchering of a couple of beeves for the abbey's winter table, but I got the tale straight from Himself."

Brenna gathered their bowls together to wash later in the Shannon and leaned in expectantly to hear the story.

"Ye see, the Northmen made to parley at first, the gate being barred and all," Murtaugh explained using his gnarled hands to gesture his meaning. "They demanded a certain weight of silver to let the abbey be."

Brenna looked askance at Jorand.

He shrugged. "It's not unusual. Most towns are willing to pay to avoid a raid. Coming to an agreement saves time," he paused "and lives. Did the abbot have the *wergild?"*

"I don't know about that foreign stuff, but Himself had the coin and no mistake. God's no pauper ye know," Murtaugh said. "But it didn't seem right to part with the Lord's bounty just on the say-so of a bunch of heathens."

Jorand made a snorting noise and the old man eyed him suspiciously. Brenna suspected it bothered her husband to be considered no better than the raiders.

"My Lord Abbot wouldn't part with so much as a mite, much good it did him. The Northmen got it all just the same. And, as ye can see, they put the rest to the torch."

After the lives of the people at Clonmacnoise, the

irreplaceable wealth of the library meant far more to Brenna than any amount of precious metal. "So nothing was saved then? None of the books?"

"What would a Northman do with a book? Them being all ignorant savages."

Brenna knew for a fact that Murtaugh was totally illiterate himself, but the old man did hold a reverence for the written word. He'd spent hours watching Brenna illuminate the pages she pilfered from the scriptorium. Since she was forbidden to work with the male scribes openly, the sexton had let her steal away to his cottage to practice her art.

"The *Ostman* devils destroyed it all," Murtaugh said.

"Not all." Brenna heard Father Ambrose' voice, faint and disheartened.

She turned to see the abbot wobbling in the doorway, a hand to his head. He must truly be losing his wits if he didn't think the destruction of Clonmacnoise complete.

"They didn't destroy everything," Father Ambrose said with surety. "The Northmen took the Skellig Michael Codex. I saw the leader carry it off."

"What's that?" Jorand asked.

"The Codex is a fabulous treasure," Brenna said, a tiny thrill running through her just thinking about the bejeweled volume. "It's a set of the Gospels and so much more. The art folios alone are worth more than . . ." she searched her mind for a staggering sum, "than all the rest of Clonmacnoise put together. The illumination is unparalleled."

"Then it's worth quite a bit?"

"Aye, ye could say that," Brenna said. "All the gold and jewels in Tara would seem beggarly by comparison. 'Tis too fine a thing even for a king to own. 'Tis truly a book that can belong only to God."

"And now it has fallen into the hands of the heathen." The abbot trudged over to join their circle, careful to position himself between Murtaugh and Brenna, as far from Jorand as possible. "But now, child, what brings ye back to us from Donegal?"

"Surely, ye must know, Father. 'Tis the babe birthed here. Me own sister's babe." Brenna folded her hands in her lap to keep them from quivering. "I've tried to put it out of me head, but I can't put it from me heart. I need to know once and for all. How fares the bairn?"

Murtaugh shot the abbot a glance that clearly said, "I told ye as much," but kept his lips in a straight hard line.

The abbot seemed to consider her request, then slowly shook his head. "No, 'tis best to let matters lie as they are. Ye must trust me for this."

Jorand felt the pain that flashed across Brenna's face, sharp as a knife to his ribs. The pudgy churchman may have been head of this smoldering abbey, but the abbot had no power over Brenna now. Not if he had anything to say about it.

He rose to his feet and, fists clenched, leveled Father Ambrose with a dead stare. "You will tell her what she wants to know and quickly, or no god will deliver you from the fury of this Northman."

To his surprise, Brenna leaped between them and planted her splayed fingers on his chest.

"No, not like this," she pleaded. "He's been through too much already."

"I haven't even started yet."

"No, no violence," she said with adamancy. "There has to be another way."

Jorand glared at the abbot. "An exchange then," he offered with grudging reluctance. "If I tell you the name of the man who holds the Codex, you must tell Brenna where to find the child."

Emboldened by Brenna's unexpected protection, the abbot dusted off his cassock and met Jorand's gaze. "And what good does a mere name do us here in the House of God? Think ye we shall pray for the blackguard after this desecration?"

"Is there nothing we can do to persuade you, Father?" Brenna asked.

"I can think of several things." Jorand bared his teeth in an expression he was sure the churchman couldn't mistake for a smile.

Brenna frowned and put a restraining hand on his forearm. "Please, Father. We've come so far and not knowing vexes me beyond bearing. I can't return to Donegal without finding out what became of Sinead's bairn."

"I sympathize, my child, but ye wanted nothing to do with the babe when it was born," the abbot said, placing a speculative finger to his lips. "Now if ye were to find and return the Codex intact, that might be an act of contrition worthy of reward. But alas! The Codex has passed from the hands of civilized men. How do you hope to retrieve it?"

"She can't," Jorand said. "But I can." He'd hoped to avoid this, to let his past sink back into forgetfulness, but if there was a God, as Brenna insisted, He seemed unwilling to let Jorand get away with it.

"How can ye do that?" Father Ambrose asked.

"Because I know the man who took it. His name is Kolgrim," Jorand said.

"Ye remembered." Brenna gaped at him.

"Ja, I remembered his name," Jorand said, hoping that much would satisfy her for now. He couldn't bear to tell her more.

Murtaugh glared at him, probably suspecting he was somehow involved with the sacking of Clonmacnoise, but the abbot was quick to jump at the chance to have his treasure restored.

"Ye may indeed know the villain, of that I've no doubt," Father Ambrose said. "But the world is wide. How will ye find him?"

Jorand felt an invisible noose tighten around his neck. "I know his homeport. I know where he'll be."

"Then by all means, go. God's blessing on ye and the worthy task ye have set for yourself." The abbot seemed to forget Jorand's unfortunate heritage for a moment and sketched a benediction with his right hand.

"Keep your blessings to yourself. All I want is your word," Jorand demanded. "The truth about the child's whereabouts for the book. Agreed?"

Father Ambrose hesitated for only a moment, then nodded solemnly. "I'll tell Brenna about the child."

Jorand wheeled around and stomped away, furious to be forced to this untenable position, but unable to run from it. He heard Brenna's light footfalls pattering behind him.

"Where are we going?" she asked when she caught up with him.

"*We* are going nowhere," he said without much hope. "You're staying here and I'm bound to retrieve that damned book."

"No, please, ye can't leave me," Brenna said, clinging to his arm. "Will ye be in harm's way?"

"Probably."

She had no idea how much.

"This concerns me, too. Ye're only doing this so I can find Sinead's child. If ye are going into danger because of me ... I'm your wife, Jorand. I must needs be at your side."

He stopped. He knew he should just keep going, but he couldn't bear to tear his arm away from her. Then he made the mistake of looking at her. Her hair was flying out in all directions, her face grimy from the smoke, but her soul shone shining clear and pure from her silver-gray eyes. She didn't have a clue what she was asking.

"Brenna," he said, cupping her cheek in his palm. "If you come with me, it'll be hard."

"When has it been easy for the likes of us?" She smiled at him, the little crooked smile that made his insides melt. So trusting. When she looked at him like that he wanted to slay dragons for her.

How would she feel when she discovered *he* was the dragon?

"Please," she said, worrying her lower lip with her little white teeth. "I cannot bear to see ye go alone."

Utterly conquered, he folded her into his arms and hugged her fiercely. "And I can't bear to leave you."

He kissed her hard, wanting to fall into the oblivion he found in her loving. But she was not so easily distracted and pulled back from him, fixing him with a determined gaze.

"So where are we bound?" she asked.

To Hell, most like, he wanted to answer. Instead he just said, "Dublin."

Chapter Twenty-four

The trip back down the Shannon and out to sea passed by in a blur for Jorand. If only he'd told her immediately, right when his memory came back, perhaps then she'd have understood.

Coward!

He cursed himself regularly. Each day, he told himself now was the time. Brenna needed to know the whole truth. But then she'd say something about her hopes and plans that made it impossible for him to speak.

He concentrated on navigation, on trimming the sail more often than it needed, anything to keep his mind off what waited for them in the Norse enclave on the banks of the river Liffey. And each night, as Brenna curled against him, he found himself unable to keep from reaching for her.

He made love to her with as much tenderness as he could, all the while feeling so desperate it was all he could do not to take her like a rutting beast. To claim her as his own, finally and forever.

Then morning would dawn and they'd be one day nearer to Dublin. One day nearer to the truth.

"Look ye, yonder there," Brenna said from the prow. "Smoke. Could your Dublin be burning?"

"No," he said morosely. "That's just cooking fires."

"But, are there so many?"

He grimaced. "I'd forgotten. You've never been to a town before. There are many people in Dublin. Probably more than five hundred souls."

He glanced down into the dark brown river, thick with sediment from its peat bed, and would have known the settlement was near even without the fires. This silt-laden river was as familiar to him as the curve of Brenna's waist, but without any of the sweetness. He dropped the woolen sail and stepped nimbly to the steering oar, turning the prow toward the grassy bank.

"We'll camp here tonight," he announced.

"But we're so close, and there's yet some daylight to travel by. The sooner we get to Dublin, the sooner we learn if the man we seek is there. Then we'll take the Skellig-Michael Codex back from him and be done with the cursed place."

"As easy as that, you think?"

She sighed. "Probably not."

"Certainly not," he assured her. "Something you need to understand about Northmen is that we don't believe in turning the other cheek. What a man has, he must hold. The monks at Clonmacnoise didn't fight to keep the book. Kolgrim believes the Codex is his by right. Even if he's in Dublin, he'll not part with it willingly."

"I know. I just keep hoping that somehow, something will turn out easy for us."

A small pang streaked through his chest at the way her shoulders sagged. He felt her weariness as if it were a stone around his own neck.

"Besides, I was looking forward to a hot bath and more of a roof over me head than a fir bough." Brenna shot one more wistful glance upstream. "We've come so far and 'tis only a little way farther."

That was precisely what he was afraid of.

"Brenna," he said, his tone commanding enough that she jerked her gaze toward him sharply. "We need to camp here tonight. I'll explain it all to you, but for now and for the next few days, I'm asking you to trust me."

"I think I know what ye're trying to say. 'Tis going to be difficult for me, being in Dublin amongst ... your people."

"I just want to be sure you understand a few things." The hull of his boat grated against the river bottom when the prow nosed its way up the bank. "First, very few of my countrymen speak your tongue. Our customs are different. You may find them a bit rough, but don't be afraid. You're my wife. I'll take care of you."

"Ye make it sound as if we're entering a bear cave."

"In some ways, we are." He stepped over the side of the boat and splashed to shore, tugging on the end of the coracle's tether. "This particular bear's name is Thorkill. Five years ago he led a force of sixty long-ships up the Liffey. He's the founder of Dublin, a strong leader, and not one to delay either judgment or punishment."

He tied off the boat and went back to lift Brenna out and carry her to shore. No need for both of them to have wet feet. She was as light as a child in his arms, but as his hand brushed the soft underside of one of her breasts, he knew she was all woman.

"But how do you know so much about this Thorkill?" A sudden light dawned in her eyes. "Oh! Ye remembered."

"I did."

She hugged his neck hard before he set her lightly down. "Has it all come back to ye then?"

"*Ja,* I think so." His gut twisted in knots.

"But that's wonderful. Ye must tell me everything," she said as she began to cut slices of peat for their small fire. "Why is it ye are looking so glum?"

He sank down on a gray-speckled rock and avoided meeting her gaze, studying instead his own long-fingered hands. "Because it's not all good."

"And how does that make ye different from anyone else?" Brenna ruffled his hair with one hand, then stooped to brush her lips across his forehead. Her small palm cupped his chin, and he looked up at her. He saw at once the strain behind her smile and realized that despite her forced cheer, she was afraid. "Start at the beginning and when it gets difficult, perhaps the stew will be fit to eat by then and ye can take a rest."

The beginning. That was at least safe.

"I was born in Sognefjord," he said. He told her the hazy memory of his parents' death at sea when he was barely old enough to heft a water bucket. Jorand's older brother Eirick took him in for a season, but Eirick's wife didn't like the thought of a rival heir to the family holding of tillable acreage so close at hand. So Jorand was fostered out to the *jarl,* the acknowledged leader of the fjord.

"Harald and his lady were good to me," he said.

"Seems Orn, my father, had saved Harald's life in battle, so I was treated like family, more or less."

In fact, Jorand had thrived under the slightly negligent care of the *jarl*, growing up wild as a wolf cub in the great longhouse. Gunnar, eldest son of Harald and heir to all of Sogna, couldn't be bothered with a twig of a fosterling except to play sly, cruel tricks on Jorand as often as he could. Bjorn, the *jarl*'s younger son, was only a few years Jorand's senior, but he stood solidly with the bewildered child and protected him as much as he was able. Bjorn immediately became the principal god in young Jorand's private pantheon.

"Bjorn was brother to me in ways my own kin never were," Jorand said. "When we came of age to go to sea, he became my captain. Bjorn was a natural leader. I'd have followed him to Hel with a light heart."

"Then ye have gone viking, haven't ye?"

"Ja," he said, fixing his mouth in a hard line. "I have been on raids of neighboring fjords. Usually in retaliation for an encroachment on their part, but sometimes not."

She waited, a question in her eyes as she added a bit of wild celery and onion to the cooking pot hanging over the smoky fire. His stomach growled at the aroma, even as his nerves balled his innards in knots.

"Then ye ... ye have done as was done to me sister," she choked the words out.

"No, never that," he protested. "I never forced a woman, or killed one either. Though I have killed my share of men on raids. The northlands are beautiful but unforgiving. The growing season is short and farmable land scarce. Second sons have no other choice but to sell their blades and pledge to one *jarl* or another. By going viking, we earn our place with the wealth we can hold and bring back to the fjord."

She sighed. "When ye put that face on it, I suppose 'tis not unlike the cattle rustling me da and the Connacht regularly practice on each other's borders. Still, Father Michael would likely name it a sin."

"Most likely," he agreed. Funny how he'd never thought of viking as wrong. It was just the way of his world. People needed to eat and the fjord could only provide so much. If he brought back a hoard of silver or a bony kine or a sow heavy with a litter of piglets, he was a hero. He helped his settlement survive the harsh northern winter. That was as right as it got.

"But my life wasn't all raiding." He went on to tell her of walrus hunts in the frostlands and learning the shipwright's trade. Her gray eyes sparkled when he told her of his wild trip down the rivers of the continent to the Black Sea and the fabulous city of Miklagard straddling the narrow opening to Middle Earth's great inland sea.

"Miklagard? Oh, ye mean Byzantium surely," she said with a rush of understanding. "I've read tales of that great city, but never believed the half of it. Oh, to see it, truly. What a wonderment."

The wonder of it was that they ever escaped with their skins intact, but Jorand wouldn't burst her illusions.

"So how, after traveling the wide, wide world, did ye ever end up on the beach of Donegal Bay?"

Now they were on boggier footing and Jorand felt the grasping undertow sucking him down. He was about to be lost and he knew it.

"Is the stew done yet?" He sniffed at it.

"Aye," she said, ladling up a bowlful and handing it to him. "And ye can have it, but only if ye can eat and talk at the self-same time."

His appetite fled, but he forced himself to swallow a mouthful and make appreciative noises.

"When Bjorn was settled in Sognefjord, I realized I didn't want to stay put. After all my travels, it didn't seem like home anymore. And the more I thought about it, the more I realized that the *jarlhof* in Sogna wasn't my home. Would never truly be my home. Even the family who raised me wasn't really my family. So I left my friend with his new wife and went in search of a place of my own."

Brenna rested a hand on his knee. "And have ye found it, then?"

He put down the wooden bowl and cupped her face with both hands. "I never knew what home was till I met you, Brenna. But I think something inside me knew the first time you called me Keefe Murphy that you'd help me find myself and my place in the world. You are my snug harbor." He kissed her deeply. "And I hope never to go viking again."

"Never tell a woman that, man," a voice said from the darkness. "At least not until you're so old your pecker's ready to fall off."

Jorand leaped to his feet, knife to hand. He shoved Brenna behind him and crouched to meet the newcomer who'd crept up on them.

Idiot!

This close to Dublin, he should have expected an outlying patrol. Why had he not been on guard?

There were four of them, all fully his match for weight and height, and bristling with weaponry. When they stepped into the circle of light, Jorand realized with a start that he knew the leader.

The big man wielded a hobnailed club, brandishing it over his head. He made a sound, a cross between a growl and an evil-sounding chuckle, then stopped and blinked twice. Suddenly, he let the club drop.

"Loki strike me blind!" he swore. "Jorand. We thought you dead."

"Not yet," Jorand said grimly.

The leader strode forward, baring his teeth in a wolfish grin and clasped forearms with Jorand.

"Welcome home," the man said, then turned his attention to Brenna. Even in the flickering firelight, Jorand saw she'd gone white as a fish belly. "Who've you brought with you?"

"This is my wife, Brenna," Jorand said evenly. "Brenna, this is Thorkill. My father-in-law."

Chapter Twenty-five

Brenna released the breath she'd been holding since the four Northmen invaded their camp. She shook her head, certain lack of air had led her to imagine things. The sweet green night stole into her lungs.

"What?" Her tongue felt thick as a sausage in her mouth. "What did ye say?"

"Thorkill is my father-in-law," Jorand repeated evenly. "His daughter Solveig is my wife."

The words pierced her ears and swirled around her brain, nonsense sounds to which she was unable to attach any meaning. Then the truth jolted through her and, swift as an arrow, impaled her heart.

Thorkill appraised her frankly, his gaze raking her form, as if she were no more than a new brood mare Jorand had added to his herd. Then the older man's ice blue eyes took on a lascivious gleam. It was a look she'd seen on a Northman's face before. Her gut churned, but she didn't feel fear.

She didn't feel anything.

She remembered the day old Seamus had his leg

severed in a battle with the Connacht. Armed with a rare Spanish sword, his opponent had sliced off the limb cleanly in a blinding moment. Men who'd seen it happen said Seamus himself didn't realize the leg was gone till he lost his balance and fell.

Her father and his men had rushed Seamus back to the keep, a strap of leather cinched tight to the bleeding stump. The shock of the injury numbed Seamus so he didn't feel a thing until the spurting wound was cauterized. Then he'd howled like a demon, shrieking and raving.

Now her heart was numb, just like Seamus's leg. At any moment, the burning would come. She forced herself to inhale again, and along with the cool, moist air, pain flooded her chest.

When she looked at Jorand, a stranger peered back at her through his damnably beautiful eyes.

"Brenna?"

How could his voice sound so unchanged, as if nothing had happened? As if the whole world hadn't just collapsed around her?

She scrambled upright and bolted from the circle of light cast by their campfire. Her feet flew toward the boat. In the moonlight, she groped for the knot tethering the coracle to an overhanging hawthorn. Bile rose in the back of her throat, but she forced herself to breathe slowly and evenly. The last thing she wanted to do was disgrace herself further by being sick. She heard Jorand thrashing through the undergrowth after her, but didn't look up till he grasped her elbow.

"Brenna, say something."

"And what would ye have me say?" She jerked her arm away, taking refuge in anger to avoid feeling pain, and turned her attention back to the double-clove hitch. The knot firmly resisted her fumbling efforts. "Pleased to make your acquaintance, Thorkill, Master of Dublin. Oh, by the by, I'm your son-in-law's new bed warmer."

"It's not like that."

If only she could shoot lightning from her eyes. She'd reduce him to a smoldering pile in an instant.

"Suppose ye be after telling me how it is then?" Brenna finally worked the tether free and flung it into the boat, satisfied by the resounding thud of the heavy rope on the hull.

"I never intended for this to happen," he said. "You know I didn't remember anything of my past."

"Aye, well, seems to me quite a bit slipped your mind." She put a shoulder to the prow and shoved. The boat didn't budge.

"You knew this was a possibility from the first. Don't you remember? Before we wed, you're the one who insisted we only handfast, just in case."

Damn the man. Why does he have to be right?

Brenna turned and pressed her back to the pointed prow, hoping to gain some purchase, but Jorand had pulled more than half the length of the coracle onto the spongy bank. She groaned with the effort but only managed to move the sturdy boat a few finger-lengths.

"Brenna." His voice was ragged. "Look at me."

She drew a deep breath and let herself meet his gaze. The pain she read on his face lanced her heart afresh.

"I never wanted to hurt you, I swear it."

Too late.

He reached for her, but she shrank back. His pained

expression told her he was hurt by her withdrawal. Her natural impulse was to try to ease his suffering, but she couldn't bring herself to give him comfort, even though it broke her heart to deny him a small kindness.

"What ye say is true, I grant ye. I went into this marriage hoping ye had no past, yet knowing in me heart ye might. Seems a good many things slipped me mind as well." She trembled, unable to control the shakes threatening to take her. Suddenly a new thought struck her. "When did it all come back to ye then? I suppose the sight of this Thorkill brought the remembrance of his daughter to your mind."

"No." A deep cleft formed between his brows. "I won't lie to you, Brenna. It was the night you clouted me on the head. That's when my memory came back entire."

"But that was weeks ago. We've come ever so many leagues since then. Ye let me make plans, the things we said and did together, it was all—" Her mind rolled over the events of the recent past in a new light. His furious lovemaking had delighted her, leaving her soul stripped bare and vulnerable but unafraid. Now a tight knot formed in her belly.

"Ye used me," she whispered, hardly daring to voice the sickening truth.

"No, princess, never that." He moved to embrace her but she shoved him away. "What passed between us was real, for both of us. Didn't you think it strange that I changed my mind and suddenly didn't want to come to Dublin? It was because I love you, Brenna."

Love. How she'd longed to hear him declare it. Now it rang false as a minstrel's play in her ear, even though the voicing of it made something inside her leap up in hopeless joy. She reined in her surging heart. Why had he waited till now when the word meant less than nothing?

"No, no, no!" she chanted, falling against him and pounding her fists on his chest. "Ye have no right to tell me that. Not now."

He caught her wrists and held her arms spread-eagle. "I do have the right." His eyes blazed at her, fierce as a goshawk with a mouse in its sights. "I love you, I tell you. I'm your husband, whether you like it or no."

"That's easily remedied," she countered, yanking herself free and re-attacking the coracle with fresh vehemence. "I release ye from your vows with me blessing. Go back to your Norse cow then. Ye needn't be bothered with the likes of me one moment longer."

"No, Brenna. Our agreement was for a year and a day." His voice was a low rumble, but she shivered at the core of hardness she heard in the tone. What right did he have to be angry? "I'll not settle for anything less."

"Ye'll settle for a great deal less if ye want to live out the rest of the term." Brenna knew she shouldn't bait him. It wasn't unheard of for a husband to murder his wife for a scolding tongue, but she was past caring if he killed her.

In fact, it might be a mercy.

She ducked under his arm when he moved to capture her. "Don't ye be daring to touch me. Not while ye have another woman who calls herself your wife."

She bit her lip as she shoved against the boat again. When it wouldn't give ground, she sank to her knees in despair.

He raked a hand through his hair in frustration. "What are you doing? Even if you could get her under sail, where do you think you'd go?"

Home. Home to Donegal. She was suddenly overcome with the need to see her family, to be surrounded by the people she was sure loved her. She'd learned a fair bit about sailing during their sojourn. Still, however much she might wish it, she knew it would be impossible for her to navigate solo over the greenish-gray waters encircling the isle.

"Why, by all that's holy, did ye not tell me sooner?" she whispered.

"For fear of this." All trace of anger drained from him and he knelt down beside her, close but not touching. "Brenna, I've faced battle. I've escaped from a walled city with an army at my heels. Before I washed up on your beach, I spent a night adrift in the open sea. But I've never been more afraid than when my memory returned and I remembered Solveig. That's when I realized I might lose you."

Her heart strained toward him, but she pulled it back. No honey-tongued words could salvage the wreck of their marriage.

"Ye cannot lose what ye never really had. How is it possible for ye to have me, when I don't have ye? Not all of ye at any rate." She worried her lower lip and let a single tear course down her cheek unheeded. "Merciful Christ, what's to become of us?"

"Check your bearings and remember where we are. This is a delicate situation, all right," he admitted.

Brenna tossed a look back up to their camp, where the four invaders had settled to empty her stewpot. Evidently, they had no interest in Jorand's domestic affairs.

"Fortunately, among my people, it's not uncommon for a man to have more than one wife," she heard Jorand saying.

She wished he'd slapped her instead.

Her vision tunneled and she had to remind herself to breathe.

"I cannot live with that." She strained to hold back the flood of tears pressing against her eyes. Once started, she feared she'd never stop. "If ever ye cared for me, even a wee bit, ye'll not ask it of me."

Since he was able to broach the possibility of keeping both of them, it was obvious Jorand wouldn't give up Solveig for her. And why should he? Solveig was the chieftain's daughter, obviously someone of importance in his world. His dalliance with an Irish girl would be tolerated and given no more importance than if he'd acquired a body slave.

Misere, Jesu Christe. Christ, have mercy.

How was it she was still alive? Her chest continued to rise and fall, each breath a searing blast from a kiln. But deep inside, she was hollow as a gourd. For the first time in her life, Brenna understood why some folk did away with themselves in despair. She wished she could just sink into the dark earth. It would be silent and cool and still, and she wouldn't have to feel anymore. If Father Michael hadn't pounded the reality of mortal sin and the terrors of hell into her head, she'd step into the black waters of the Liffey and let herself float to the sea and oblivion.

"Take me home," she begged. "For the love of God, take me back to me father's keep."

"You want to leave without getting what we came for? Have you forgotten the child? I still mean to get that book back for you, and if I have to kill Kolgrim to do it, so much the better."

He ground a fist into his other palm and Brenna imagined for a moment those strong fingers laced around Kolgrim's neck, squeezing the life out of the man who'd ruined and ultimately killed her sister. Her chest constricted painfully. Even the thought of retribution for Sinead wasn't worth the indignity of sharing her husband with another woman.

"Brenna, I swear to you, I'll still help you find your sister's bairn. Do you not think you can bear me company long enough to do that?"

The child. A soft throb started inside her. The last good thing she could do for Sinead. She could love her sister's child. A sweet ache longed to be assuaged by a pair of chubby arms around her neck. *Aye.* She'd come so far. To turn back now for the sake of her own heartache seemed the height of selfishness. She'd never have a better opportunity to learn what became of Sinead's bairn. She could bear much for the sake of the child, even the indignity of seeing Jorand with his first love. With the woman he might still love.

In answer, she rose to her feet and trudged back to the camp, leaving him to tie up the coracle again lest the rising tide pull it back into the Liffey during the night.

The other Northmen had made themselves at home around Brenna's fire and were fighting for the last dollops of stew in the supper pot. As she walked across camp, she felt their eyes on her, alien and probing, but she held her head high and carried herself with the remembered dignity of a daughter of the house of Ui Niall. Her Donegal pride was in tatters, but it was all she had left.

Brenna crawled into the lean-to and curled up in Jorand's cloak, giving her back to the fire. The boisterous conversation that had died when she emerged from the brush started afresh, raucous and crude to her ears. In a few moments, she recognized Jorand's voice joining them in that savage, strangely modulated tongue.

Somehow she had forgotten what he was. In the months leading up to their marriage, she'd been fascinated by him, as deceived and entranced as if he were a faerie king come to charm her into the hills with him. Since their wedding, his nearness and the treachery of her own body had led her into the delusion that Jorand was, in truth, Keefe Murphy, her own handsome sea warrior.

Now, hearing him in his true element, surrounded by his rough countrymen, knowing he had a Norse wife he had no reason to leave, Brenna finally had to face the truth.

Jorand was just a Northman, after all.

Chapter Twenty-six

Jorand's boat rode low in the water, the added weight of Thorkill and his band dragging it down. As she huddled miserably in the prow, Brenna was doused from time to time with a fine spray. Since there were men enough to man the oars, she was no longer needed to tend the steering.

No longer needed. She resigned herself to it. Jorand had wed her so he could leave Donegal and return to Dublin. His fine talk of love notwithstanding, she'd been a means to an end. Now she was only so much ballast weighing down his craft.

"Dublin is ahead, on the left," Jorand called up to her. Her gaze jerked back toward him, surprised to hear him speaking to her in her own tongue. The bewildering sounds of Norse he'd been speaking with his comrades formed a protective barrier between Brenna and her nominal husband. She resisted his efforts to breach her defenses and turned away without a response.

The village of Dublin loomed before her, surrounded by a fortified earthen dike topped with wattle-and-daub walls. She saw countless thatched hip roofs, sloping steeply above the ramparts. She understood the need for protection, but why, on God's earth, would that many people want to live packed tightly together like so much cord wood?

Jorand told her Dublin meant "black pool" and she could certainly see how it had acquired the name. The coracle nosed into the deep harbor created by the confluence of the Poddle River and the Liffey. The water was the color of peat and the paddles of the oars all but disappeared into the murk with each stroke.

Dozens of dragonships lined the wharf, like winged monsters at rest, quiescent now, but capable of rousing and spilling death and destruction over the whole of the island. With their lithe necks and elegant lines, the ships were at once beautiful and terrifying. Brenna shuddered and stepped lightly on to the waiting dock, careful to tread softly, lest her Irish footsteps wake the longships to wrath.

Thorkill and his crew strode away, leaving Jorand to tie up his craft alone. One by one, the other Northmen on the wharf recognized her husband and shouted greetings to him, a few of them coming to clasp forearms and pound him on the back. Obviously, Jorand was well thought of in this den of thieves and rapists. Other than a couple of inquiring looks, Brenna was ignored by one and all, for which she thanked the saints and angels alike.

"Come, Brenna," Jorand said, taking her elbow to guide her up the graveled path to the main part of town.

It was the first time he'd touched her since she learned of Solveig's existence, and though she stiffened, she allowed it. His hand might be hateful to her, but in this world his touch was the only familiarity she had. She resisted the urge to cling to him for comfort.

Last night, she'd lain awake listening to the frightful sounds of Northmen in conversation, waiting to see if Jorand would join her in the lean-to. He finally did, but was careful not to brush her with so much as an arm hair as he stretched out beside her. If he'd reached for her, she'd have rejoiced to rebuff him, she told herself.

But another, darker part of her heart damned her for a liar. The way her traitorous body still clamored for him, she knew her own senses would conspire against her if he tried to take her with tenderness.

Spineless wanton.

The knowledge filled her with shame and self-loathing.

As they crested the rise, her gaze swept over the town. All the rectangular houses were laid out, cheek by jowl, along straight narrow streets, which were covered with wooden planks to keep the paths from turning into muddy ruts. Each home had its own fenced yard and carefully tended garden, groaning with fall produce.

They passed by a smith's shop, tanners' sheds, and workers of amber, the glowing orange jewel prized by Northmen and Irish alike. The marketplace bustled with the same frenetic energy of one of Donegal's fairs, but with far more exotic wares for the offering. Brenna saw bolts of flowing fabric that shimmered like water and realized it could only be the silk Jorand told her of.

You're soft as silk, you know.

She heard his remembered words as clearly as if they hovered in the air above her head. Skin on skin, water rippling around them, his first heart-stopping penetration. Her belly clenched, the desire in her memory still hot enough to stir a response. She glanced sideways at Jorand to see if the cloth had triggered a similar remembrance. He stared straight ahead, his face like stone.

Brenna shivered. No, there was no tenderness in the man now. She forced her attention back to the merchants' stalls.

There were heavy soapstone kettles, fine lace, ornately carved caribou horns—some of them as long as she was tall—and countless kegs of ale. Strange spices pricked at her nostrils, along with the yeasty smell of brewing, and the less welcome stench of too many privies and midden heaps in close proximity.

"I've learned a few things you might find interesting," Jorand said.

"Kolgrim is here?" she asked with hope. Perhaps their stay in this Norse hell would be mercifully brief.

"No, he's gone North for a bit, but is due back within the week." Jorand nodded in acknowledgment of a neighbor's wave. "Thorkill is safekeeping the Codex here in Dublin for Kolgrim while he's raiding."

"Then perhaps we can petition your ... father-in-law for its rightful return." She nearly choked on the words.

"I've already tried that. Thorkill does not see it as you do. The book is Kolgrim's so long as he can hold it. But there is another way."

Brenna cast a speculative glance at Jorand. There was a hardness around his eyes that she'd never seen before.

"You see," he went on, "Kolgrim and I had a disagreement the last time we were together. He's the reason I ended up in the sea and on your beach. There's a score to settle between us, so I have legitimate cause to challenge him in the *Holmgang*."

There's the small matter of me sister's lost maidenhead, as well. The spitefull words rose unbidden to the tip of her tongue, but she bit them back.

"I'm not forgetting what Kolgrim did to Sinead either," he said as though he'd heard her secret thought. "But that's not likely to be considered valid reason for a challenge. If I'm to regain the Codex for you, the law has to be fulfilled."

"For an unprincipled pack of thieves, ye seem to set much store by your precious law."

He stiffened at her insult, but kept his voice even. "Whatever you may think, we are a people of law. If some of them seem strange, remember that the Irish way of doing things is just as incomprehensible to us."

Brenna felt a tingle at the nape of her neck and recognized the pressure of eyes on her. She pulled her hood up to shield her face from the prying gazes. All around her the singsong Norse voices reminded her of a gaggle of geese. A new question popped into her mind.

"All I hear about me is Norse. How is it ye alone speak me language?"

"It's rather a long story." Jorand's voice dropped low. "When Thorkill first led sixty longboats up the Liffey, he only wanted a safe base for the winter, a place to launch raids without having to cross the sea to do it. Once he got the lay of the land, his plans changed."

Jorand put an arm around her shoulders and drew her closer. Since he lowered his voice, she leaned in to hear him, skittering two steps to his one to match his long stride.

"Thorkill needed information. To get that, he had to be able to question the inhabitants. I've always been quick with new tongues, so we captured one of your priests, a young man from a monastery in Kerry, and made him teach Kolgrim and me to speak and understand Gaelic."

He slowed his pace and, seeing a thick log by the side of the path, turned aside and sat down. Brenna perched uneasily beside him.

"I hope Father Armaugh is still alive," Jorand said, dragging a hand over his face. "He was when I left."

Was that compassion? A small corner of Brenna's heart warmed to him, but she quickly snuffed it out. "And once ye learned Gaelic, what was it ye were to do for Thorkill?"

"When I first came here I was to build him more ships. Most of the vessels you saw in the harbor are my work." The ghost of a smile played about his lips, a remnant of his satisfaction with a job well done. "After I married Solveig, I became Thorkill's eyes and ears," he admitted. "Kolgrim and I would scout out likely places for raids, looking for deep harbors and undefended shores. We'd capture and question people about defense plans, about the local rulers, how many men they could raise in battle and the like."

Brenna trembled beside him. The truths in her world kept getting worse. Her husband was not only a Northman, he was a filthy spy. Connor McNaught was right, after all. Her father should have drowned Jorand in a bog when he had the chance.

"Thorkill may have originally come to your island to raid, but now he means to reign," Jorand said.

"Oh, no," she said. For the first time since she learned her husband had another wife, Brenna was able to lay aside her own burden and be swept up in concern for someone else. "But that means he'll make war on me father, on the Ulaid, the Connacht, all the clans. Hundreds, maybe thousands of people will die."

"Brenna, I'm putting my life in your hands by telling you this, and given the way you feel about me right now, it's probably not very wise."

She pressed her lips together in a hard line, not trusting herself to speak.

"I mean to stop Thorkill if I can," Jorand said softly. "I owe you and Brian of Donegal that much." He stood and extended a hand to her. "Come, princess. It's not far now."

She rose to her feet, ignored his offered hand and started trudging up the planked street beside him. She shouldn't trust to hope that Jorand meant what he said. He surely couldn't mean to betray his own people to save hers. "What's not far?"

"My home."

"Your wife's home, ye mean."

"*Ja*, Solveig is there," he said, his voice sounding unspeakably weary. "She'll be expecting me. Her father went to give her the news straightaway. Seems Kolgrim gave out that I was dead, so seeing me without warning would have been a shock to her."

"Not as much as seeing me, I'll warrant."

He grimaced. "Well, I expect you've the right of it."

"So she knows of me as well."

"Thorkill is a brave man, but he's no fool," Jorand said, with a frown. "He's left the telling of that tale to me, I'll wager. But a second wife is not uncommon. Solveig will get over it."

Brenna knew *she* never would. A thousand questions clamored to be asked. What on earth was she to do till Kolgrim came back and they recovered the Skellig Michael Codex? Did Jorand mean for her to stay in the same house as his other wife, the three of them in an unholy trinity, all living under the same roof? He was daft if he thought she'd hold still for it. Then her aching heart wondered if Solveig was pretty. And did he love his Norse wife still?

She found she couldn't voice any of her questions. It was all she could do to put one foot before the other and stay upright. When he pushed open the gate to a neat yard surrounding a sturdy-looking longhouse, and shepherded her through the opening, she pulled back from him.

"Perhaps, I'll be waiting here," she said, not ready to meet her rival.

His look of relief made her stomach churn uneasily.

"*Ja*, that might be best."

She could be mistaken, but she thought Jorand looked a little pale himself. She settled herself on a stump and waved him away. He squared his shoulders and strode toward the open doorway with the heavy tread of a condemned man.

Serves him right, she thought crossly. *The very least the man might expect is a wee bit of discomfort.*

Then she heard the excited sound of a woman's voice and her heart sank to her toes. Solveig was happy to see him. Was he holding her in his arms? Kissing her now? At least she was spared the indignity of having to watch Jorand's homecoming, but she wasn't sure her own vivid imagination wasn't worse than fact.

For the first time in weeks, Brenna thought of her mother. Faced with unspeakable loss, Una had withdrawn from the world. Now Brenna understood and was tempted to follow her mother into that dark place. But she couldn't deny her heart. Even though the pain was heavy as a millstone on her chest, she still loved Jorand. She was angry and hurt and determined she wouldn't continue to be a wife to him, but she couldn't dismiss her feelings for him, either.

Strange that he seemed able to flick off what he felt for her, as if his emotions were nothing more than the buzz of a pestering fly.

No more sounds came from the dark interior and Brenna slumped down, seeing in her mind's eye a tangle of arms and legs, Jorand's strong body joined to this other woman. Would he do the same heart-stopping things to her that he'd done to Brenna? She doubled over and was promptly sick behind the neatly stacked woodpile.

Brenna wiped her mouth on a corner of her cloak and stood up shakily. If not for her vow to find Sinead's child and the need to recover the Codex to do it, she'd run screaming out of Dublin so fast, Jorand would never be able to catch her.

Her ears pricked to a new sound coming from the house.

Voices. Jorand's low and even, the woman's louder and increasing strident. This growling and caterwauling certainly didn't sound like lovemaking, unless the Norse truly were different. Brenna strained to understand. She caught the meaning of only one word in ten, but it was enough to convince her of one thing.

Solveig was not taking Jorand's news gracefully.

She jumped when she heard the unmistakable crash of crockery against the wattle-and-daub walls.

When a small keg of ale sailed through the open door and landed with a splintering thud on the gravel path, she allowed herself a small smile.

If they had met under different circumstances, she thought perhaps she would have liked Solveig.

Chapter Twenty-seven

Eventually the angry voices ceased and Brenna stood, breathless, wondering what to do next. Iron-gray clouds had been boiling overhead since they tied up at the Dublin wharf. When the sky began to weep large drops, she gave up and skittered to the open doorway. No matter what scene she might be stumbling upon in the longhouse, she wasn't fool enough to stand about in the rain, catching her death.

There were no windows in the house, the only light coming from the smoky central fire and the hazy ambient daylight fighting to make its way through the smokehole in the high spine of the roof. It took a moment for Brenna's eyes to adjust, and even so, she dared not look much farther than her next step.

Underfoot, the floor was not the packed earth she expected but solid planks instead, a neat display of joinery that was swept meticulously clean. Each side of the long, narrow house was lined with a low bench, just the right height for seating or, Brenna noticed the pile of furs in one spot, bedding. A standing loom leaned against the wall near the open doorway to take advantage of the additional light. A swath of cloth with wide stripes hung suspended between the solid top beam and the dangling loom stones, a work in progress. The garish colors didn't strike her fancy, but the fabric was even and smooth. The lady of the house was a skillful weaver.

Brenna took a deep breath and stepped farther into the longhouse. All the small hairs on her body stood at attention, as though she had ventured into a she-wolf's lair. On the other side of the small fire, she made out a hazy form, no, two figures.

The truth will set ye free, Father Michael had often admonished her. She collapsed on the nearest bench and forced herself to look at her truth.

Jorand was seated, a woman beside him. One of his arms was around her while she leaned into his chest. Brenna saw the other woman's shoulders shudder and realized Solveig was weeping.

How could she not?

Brian Ui Niall had told Brenna that frequently a buck he was stalking would turn and look him in the eye just before he loosed an arrow. Some mysterious inner warning told his quarry it was being hunted. Jorand must have possessed the same elusive sense, for he raised his head and looked directly at Brenna.

His face had a hunted expression, a mixture of panic and resignation in the set of his mouth and the furrow on his brow. Regret. Sorrow. Hopelessness. She read them all in his deep-set blue eyes. If hell had a gallery, her husband could have posed for a work entitled *Lost Soul.*

Brenna realized suddenly that Jorand had two first

wives. When he'd married them, as far as he knew, each was his one and only. If he'd shared himself with Solveig with the same abandon he'd given Brenna, his heart must be torn in two.

It was so unfair. None of them had looked for this unsolvable conundrum. How could this have happened to the three of them? She even spared a moment to pity the woman in her husband's arms.

As if Solveig also sensed an intruder's presence, she raised her head and looked toward Brenna. The Norse woman's eyes glinted at her in the dimness with a predatory flash.

After that scathing look, Brenna decided to keep her sympathy to herself. And resolved to only eat from the same trencher as Jorand for as long as she bided in Solveig's house.

A hard steel core fashioned itself around Brenna's spine. Somehow, she would find a way to quit this ill-omened longhouse and leave Jorand to sort out his domestic entanglements on his own. She wouldn't beg. She wouldn't plead.

But if in the end, he didn't choose her, Brenna knew her heart would never recover.

Jorand expected this would be difficult, but he was wrong. It was impossible.

"Look at her, cowering and sniveling. I'll not have an Irish slut sullying my house." Solveig pulled away from him.

"My hands built this place. Seems to me it's my house." He kept his voice even, but it was an effort. Solveig hadn't asked for any of this, he reminded himself, but she wasn't making it any easier, either. "Brenna will stay here. She has no place else to go.

And you'll keep a civil tongue in your head when you speak to her."

"Why should I?" Solveig stood and glared at the tiny Irish woman. "It's plain she doesn't understand what I'm saying. Perhaps you can make yourself useful, Irish. My pisspot needs emptying, and I think maybe it's one job you're qualified to do." When Brenna's expression didn't change from one of wary puzzlement, Solveig turned to smirk at him. "You see?"

Brenna rose to her feet and stared back at Solveig. The way her smooth brows knit together told Jorand that even though she did not understand the exact words, she knew she'd been insulted. Brenna's gray eyes flashed a warning. She might be over-matched for height and weight, but if matters progressed to a brawl, his silver would be on Brenna.

Jorand had been in battle numerous times and sometimes the only prudent course of action was swift retreat, in order to regroup and fight again on a more advantageous day. This looked to be one of those times, but he didn't dare leave the two of them alone. From the expressions of hatred on both women's faces, he feared he might go from husband of two to grieving widower all around in short order.

"Hello the house!" a familiar voice called from the yard.

"Armaugh," Jorand said. He strode to the door and bid the priest come in, clutching Armaugh's spindly arm with the fervor of a drowning man latching on to a life rope. "I was hoping you were still with us."

"*Ja.*" Father Armaugh shed his cloak and gave it a shake, sending droplets of water hissing into the fire. He continued in fluid Norse with only a hint of an accent. "I came to Dublin in bonds, but now I stay a bond servant to Christ. A few have converted to the true Faith, so they have. We've a small church here now, just outside the walls."

"Thorkill allows it?"

"As you know, I did him a service, teaching you and Kolgrim the fair tongue. Thorkill is a hard man, but he has a sense of justice. He's not stopped any from converting. He cares not what other allegiances his men take so long as they honor their oath to him first." Armaugh lifted his narrow shoulders in a self-deprecating shrug. The gesture made him look like an earnest young crane bobbing for minnows in the shallows. "In truth, I've had more success with women than men. And speaking of that, I was told you brought an Irish girl here with you."

Jorand made the introductions. If Armaugh was shocked to learn Brenna was Jorand's second wife, his sharp features didn't show it.

"The peace of Christ be with ye, lass," he intoned in Gaelic, his bony finger making the sign of the cross in the air before her.

Brenna dropped to her knees.

"Bless me, Father, for I have sinned," she recited, clearly relieved to see the little priest and hear her own language. "It has been so long since I've been shriven. Is there somewhere ye might hear me confession?"

"Aye, come with me, my child. Ye'll have the comfort of the confessional." The priest extended a hand to her and helped her rise. She pulled her hood up against the rain, and followed Armaugh to the door.

When she turned at the last to cast Jorand a backward glance, one corner of her mouth curled up in a sad half-smile. Jorand knew it was a farewell. She'd not be coming back to his house. Not willingly.

"Typical Irish," Solveig muttered, as she watched her rival leave.

The last traces of Brenna's heather-fresh scent dissipated in the airless stuffiness of the longhouse. Jorand tried to focus his attention on Solveig, resisting the urge to chase his fleeing Irish wife.

"My father always says he kills more Irishmen from behind than he does face to face." Solveig closed the door, as if she'd read his thoughts and decided to make it more difficult for him to follow Brenna. "They're sorry fighters. All the Irish know how to do is run away."

Jorand knew Brenna wasn't running from the fight. She was running from him.

"You've shamed me, you know," Solveig went on, her stubborn chin jutted upward. "By rights, I should have had a say in this."

"I'm sorry I've hurt you," he said truthfully.

"Pah! I'm no mewling Christian to be shocked by your needs. I'm my father's daughter and I know what men are. There was no reason for you to skulk around behind my back. Honestly, husband, if you wanted a second wife, why did you not come tell me? You should have waited till you got home and we'd choose one together. One we could both live with."

"That's not how it happened," he said with frustration. "I told you. I was injured and didn't remember anything."

Solveig's smile stretched unpleasantly across her usually pretty face. "Did Irish believe that? If she did, she's even more insipid than she looks."

"Her name is Brenna, not Irish. And you know nothing about her."

"I know that little Irish whore has no knowledge of our ways and doesn't understand a thing I say to her," Solveig said with vehemence, hands fisted at her slender waist. "At least I would have picked someone who'd be useful for more than occasionally warming your bed when I'm indisposed."

She paced away from him, then wheeled back, cocking her head in question. "Is she good at warming your bed?"

"Solveig, that's enough." He clamped his lips together. Bedding Brenna was definitely not something he was prepared to discuss with her.

"It's all right. You can tell me everything. I want to hear about it." Solveig floated toward him, pale eyes gleaming, a feline hardness sparking in their icy depths. "Is she soft and willing? Does she lay there like a lump, or does she know what she wants? And how to get it?"

She reached out a long-fingered hand and slid it up under his shirt, raking his chest with her nails. His skin shivered under her touch.

"Does she please you as much as I do?" She kissed him, her lips hard on his, demanding a response. Jorand felt her nipples, pebble hard, as she melded herself against him.

"No, of course not," Solveig answered her own question. "She doesn't know you like I do." Her hands fluttered over his groin.

It wasn't a seduction. It was an assault. She did know his body. Solveig had always known where to touch, when to caress and when to hurt, how to drive him to a *berserkr* frenzy of lust. He fought to maintain control, but his body roused to her anyway.

A throaty chuckle escaped her lips. She slid a hand down his trews and grazed his erection, sending a painful ache along the hardened shaft.

"It's been a long time. Still, it's nice to know some things haven't changed," she all but purred.

Jorand yanked her hand out of his breeches, grasped her by the shoulders and held her at arms length. *Ja,* she was still beautiful, still made his blood run hot, but in her eyes all he saw was lust and triumph. She'd help him, he knew, if he wanted power or land or command of a host of men. His success would increase her stature. Lovemaking with Solveig had always been a mirror of their marriage, rough and fiery, sating their body's appetites, but ultimately selfish. Both of them used the other for their own ends.

When Brenna was in his arms, he reveled in the feel of her, the little sounds she made when she lost herself in him, but mostly he loved looking into her soft gray eyes and seeing the way she trusted him. It made him want to be as fine a man as she thought him.

Solveig saw him as he was. Brenna saw the man he could be.

Which did he want?

"You're wrong, Solveig," he said quietly as he turned and strode to the door. A walk in the cold rain was just what he needed. "Some things have changed."

CHAPTER TWENTY-EIGHT

"Come out of there, ye wee foul reminder of original sin," Brenna said, as she yanked the stubborn root of a cankerwort. She grunted with effort and suddenly the plant released its hold on the earth, sending her reeling backward to land on her bottom with a thud.

She scrambled to her feet, beating dust off the back of her skirt with one hand, and surveyed the rows of turnips with satisfaction. Only thriving plants now swayed in the breeze, the promise of a good harvest with not a single foxtail or thistle left to be sifted out. She shoved her hair back out of her eyes, leaving a grimy smudge of dirt on her forehead, and picked up the watering bucket.

After Father Armaugh gave her absolution for her sins, he let Brenna claim sanctuary in his tiny church. She didn't have to return to Solveig's house to suffer watching Jorand reunite with his first wife. Despite Jorand's protest, the priest allowed Brenna to stay in the church with him. Then Armaugh did the next best thing for her.

He put her to work.

From before matins till well after vespers, Brenna scrubbed the stone flooring of the nave, polished the altar, trimmed the candles in the apse behind the chancel and swept the walkways to and from the church door. After she'd made the small house of worship sparkle like a jewel, she tackled the overgrown garden with the vehemence of Samson slaying the Philistines. Only her choice of weapon differed—a hoe instead of the jawbone of an ass.

The labor was blessedly numbing. Throughout the day, she managed to keep thoughts of Jorand at bay. But at night, until she sank into exhausted sleep, visions of her husband with Solveig danced salaciously before her eyes.

Her dreams were no comfort either.

Jorand had come to the church a few times, looking for her. She huddled behind the sturdy oak door, listening at the crack.

"If ye wish to worship, ye are always welcome in the House of God, my son," Father Armaugh had told him. "But if ye are after troubling Brenna, then I'll ask ye kindly to be taking your leave. She has no wish to see ye. The lass is at peace and I'll not be having ye disturb her."

Part of her wanted Jorand to batter down the door and disturb her anyway. But if he intended to take her back to Solveig's home, it was just as well he left each time without her.

"*Ave amicus!*" An unfamiliar voice called out to her over the churchyard fence, interrupting her thoughts. *Hail, friend,* the voice had said.

Brenna looked up from her watering to see a fresh-faced Norse woman about her own age with a wreath of coppery curls circling her head like a fiery halo. The woman leaned on the fence separating them and smiled. It was an easy, open expression. Her wide mouth was creased with tiny lines at the corners, lips that were accustomed to smiling. There was no trace of guile in the woman's face.

Brenna's own mouth turned up in response.

"Hello, friend," Brenna answered back in the crisp liturgical Latin Father Michael had taught her. "I'm called Brenna of Donegal. Who are you?"

"Oh, you do know Latin. I'm so glad!" The girl's smile widened further. "He said you were educated. I was afraid we wouldn't be able to speak with each other."

"Who said I was educated?"

"Jorand, of course." The young woman sauntered down to the gate and let herself into the churchyard. "He told me all about you. My name is Rika Magnusdottir."

"Rika," Brenna repeated, the Latin leeching away her usual lilting accent. "He has told me of you as well. You're his friend Bjorn's wife, yes?"

"That's right." She took the empty bucket from Brenna's hand and linked elbows with her. "Jorand has talked so much about you, I feel I know you already."

So Jorand still thought of her often enough to warrant a mention to his friends. The small candle of hope kindled in her chest, but she pinched off the wick before it could burst into full flame. Her carefully constructed peace depended upon maintaining no expectation beyond the passing of each day. She couldn't bear to hope.

"I thought you and your husband were confined to

your fjord," Brenna said. She immediately regretted her words. The woman might take offense at the reminder of her husband's brush with Norse justice.

"So we were," Rika acknowledged with a nod and no trace of resentment. "But Bjorn's three years of punishment are ended and he had an itch to travel once more. We came to trade in Dublin and to see Jorand as well. We'd never met his wife, you see, and then to learn once we reached Dublin that he had two." Rika's face crumpled into a grimace. "It was a complete shock, given what I know of Jorand. A bit of a surprise for him and Solveig, too, for us to show up suddenly on their threshold. Still in all, Solveig has been a gracious hostess."

Brenna had nothing to say.

"But after Jorand told us of you, I wanted to meet you, too," Rika rattled on quickly. "In fact, we barely missed you when we arrived earlier in the week. Though I gather it was just as well to let the three of you have a moment to yourselves before houseguests descended."

Rika was looking at her intently, as if she willed Brenna to read more into her words. Bjorn and Rika had arrived on the heels of the same rainstorm she escaped into on Father Armaugh's skinny arm. So Jorand and his first wife weren't the only residents of the little wattle-and-daub longhouse. She'd been torturing herself with images of her husband and Solveig together. Perhaps her imagination wasn't the truth of what was actually happening. The weight on Brenna's heart eased a bit.

"Let's go have a seat somewhere and get to know each other better, shall we?" Rika suggested. "Does the priest keep any mead on hand?"

"Mead, no," Brenna said, her lip curving again impishly. Brother Armaugh had left for the market before Rika arrived. Since he did most of his evangelizing while buying provisions, she knew he'd be gone most of the afternoon. "But I do know where he stores the wine."

"In vino veritas," Rika quoted. "Shall we see if we can discover a little truth together?"

Brenna couldn't have said why she felt so instantly comfortable with Rika. Perhaps it was the other woman's frank friendliness, so different from the mistrustful glares she'd received from the other women of Dublin, even some of the ones who came to worship in Armaugh's church. Or maybe it was because Rika's glorious red hair reminded her of Moira, her dear sister and trusted confidant. But Brenna suspected she felt an instant connection with Rika because they were linked to the same man whom they both cared for in vastly different ways—Jorand.

She led Rika into the small stone church and was surprised when the Norse woman genuflected and crossed herself.

"You are Christian?"

"Ja," Rika said simply. Brenna noticed for the first time that a silver cross dangled from one of Rika's two brooches. "Our own Father Dominic drives a hard bargain. I had no choice but to convert. At first, it was just so he would marry Bjorn and me, but now ..." she glanced shyly at Brenna, "now, it's personal."

"Jorand had to take the sign of the cross before me da would see us wed as well," Brenna confided. It felt good to talk about Jorand.

"Did he? Oh, I'm so glad. When we saw him last, Jorand still followed Thor. He was adamant against the Kristr. He must love you well."

"Or loved what marrying me gained him." *His freedom to leave Donegal*, Brenna reminded herself.

The two women tiptoed through the nave to the sacristy, a cell off the chancel where the sacred vessels and vestments were stored. Brenna found a bottle of as-yet-unconsecrated wine and two obviously unholy drinking horns, then went back out through the church.

They settled themselves in a shady alcove in the yard and poured out the wine.

"What shall we drink to?" Rika asked as the ruby-colored liquid splashed into her horn. "I know. How about men?"

Brenna shrugged noncommittally and filled her own drinking vessel.

"To men, then," Rika went on. "May they never know as much about women as they think they do."

For the first time since she learned of Solveig's existence, a giggle escaped Brenna's lips. She touched the rim of her horn to Rika's, then let the wine slide down her throat, cool and smooth. The vintage had a definite bite and an aftertaste of the oak cask it had been aged in.

"My thanks," Rika said as she tipped back her horn. "I was that dry."

"Weeding is thirsty work as well."

"Jorand told us what happened," Rika said, her expression suddenly serious. "His loss of memory, the way you found him, everything. He told us the harm Kolgrim did as well."

Brenna felt a flash of warmth in her cheeks. The

shame of her sister's rape and the story of the lost child weren't topics she was prepared to discuss with a stranger, even one as pleasant as Rika. How could Jorand spread her secrets like they were so many barley seeds to be broadcast about?

"Did he?"

"But don't worry. Jorand will get the Skellig Michael Codex back for you. I can certainly see why you'd want to return such a treasure to your old abbey."

From Rika's omission, Brenna deduced that Jorand hadn't told her everything after all. Perhaps she could still trust him on some counts.

"You said we'd uncover some truth together." Brenna took another careful sip of her wine. "What truth did you have in mind?"

Rika's emerald eyes rolled up and to the right as though she was casting about for the right words. She sighed. "The main truth I want you to know is that Jorand is miserable."

'Tis a misery of his own making. Brenna wasn't being fair and she knew it. It was hard to get past her own despair long enough to pity his.

"What makes you think he's miserable?" Brenna asked.

"Bjorn has known him most of his life," Rika said, picking up the wine jug and refilling her drinking horn. "He's never seen him like this. He says Jorand's only half paying attention when he speaks to him. He's not eating enough and drinking far too much."

Brenna studied the horn in her own hands. She recognized the temptation to tumble into a wine bowl and not come out. The thought had crossed her mind on several sleepless nights.

"He'll mend," Brenna said. "He has Solveig after all."

"Yes, but he doesn't love Solveig."

Brenna clenched the horn hard enough to turn her knuckles white. "And yet, he's still sleeping in her house," Brenna said with bitterness. "Ye may claim what ye wish about how he feels. His actions speak much louder."

"No, they don't. He's in an untenable position. You may not fully understand the politics of Jorand's situation. Solveig is Thorkill's daughter. Jorand is oath-bound to Thorkill. He can't just cast the man's daughter aside without reason."

"Guess I'm not reason enough."

"Among my people, an oath is seldom given, and honor demands it be kept, even at great personal cost. Jorand has two more oaths to consider," Rika explained. "One to Solveig and one to you. He doesn't know how to honor them both."

"I thought having multiple wives was a fairly unremarkable practice among Northmen."

"It is," Rika said with a sigh. "Though it's becoming less common. When he married Solveig, it was a love match, or he thought it was, at least. Now, Jorand is confused."

"Is Solveig changed?"

"No," Rika said. "Jorand's the one who's changed. He's said as much to Bjorn."

Brenna allowed herself a sad little smile. "Mine was an arranged marriage. Jorand and I were no love match."

"Maybe not at first," Rika conceded. "But it doesn't

take second sight to divine that your marriage bloomed into one, else you and he wouldn't be in such sorry straits now. You haven't seen him and Solveig together or you'd not worry over which of you his heart craves."

Brenna let the horn slip from her fingers and buried her face in her hands. "I can't bear to see them together. That's why I'm here."

"I guessed as much."

Brenna felt Rika's hand on her head, stroking her softly as if she were a child needing comfort. "What am I to do?"

"Well, for a start, I'd suggest a bath," Rika said, squinting at the smudge on Brenna's forehead. "Then, you need to dress in your best and come with me to Thorkill's hall. There's a feast tonight. You need to be there."

"Why?" Brenna swiped her nose on her sleeve.

Rika stood and held out her hand to Brenna. "Because Kolgrim has returned."

Chapter Twenty-nine

"If this isn't heaven, don't tell me different," Brenna said as she slid under the surface of the warm soapy water. A little liquid surged over the sides and splatted on the plank floor. For weeks, she'd been making do with quick dips in chilly streams or a slapdash wash with a basin and cloth. This round tub of fragrant delight was beyond luxurious. It was even worth the trepidation she felt about being in Solveig's house again. She emerged with a sputter and a sigh, taking in the fresh scent of the soap. "Sweet St. Brigid! I needed this."

"Once I told you Solveig had already left for the *jarlhof*, I knew the promise of a bath would lure you here. No woman in her right mind can resist a steaming tub." Smiling, Rika finished hemming the slate blue tunic and tied off the knot. She bit off the thread with her teeth, then shook out the garment, holding it up for Brenna's approval. "Here you go. Barring the difference in our heights, we're of a size, I think. This should do nicely."

" 'Tis very fine." Brenna ran a bit of the soft woolen tunic through her fingers. "I thank ye, Rika. 'Tis lovely."

Since Brenna's own clothing was threadbare from travel and filthy from her labors in the garden, Rika had graciously offered her a spare kyrtle and tunic to wear to the feast. Jorand's friend was kind as well as perceptive. She realized Brenna felt awkward enough in Dublin without looking a pauper to boot. Brenna was sure Jorand would have bought whatever she wanted from the merchants, but she couldn't bring herself to even talk with him, let alone ask him for anything.

He wasn't hers to ask.

"You'll be lovely in it, too," Rika promised as she handed Brenna a thick cloth to dry herself. "I love this shade of blue, but it never really suited me. It'll be fine on you with those silver-gray eyes of yours."

Brenna stood and enjoyed the myriad of tiny rivulets streaming down her body. She ran her hands over herself, swiping off a few clinging trails of soap. Was it her imagination or were her breasts a little swollen? They were certainly tender when her fingers brushed past her nipples. Perhaps it was just the dimness of the longhouse, but the areolas around each stiff peak seemed darker as well. How often had she felt nausea in the last few weeks? An unthinkable thought swirled in her mind, but she pushed it away.

No. She couldn't be bearing. If her breasts were sensitive, it was only the joy of a hot bath. As for being sick, they'd been traveling for ages and she was still no sailor. And making the acquaintance of the other woman who also claimed a girl's husband, well, that was enough to give anyone an uneasy stomach.

Brenna rubbed herself vigorously with the towel, reveling in the pink glow of cleanliness. Then she pulled the tunic and a dove-gray kyrtle over her head. Rika provided her with a set of matching silver brooches for the tabs to hold the kyrtle at her shoulders. They were cunningly designed, a pair of fanciful horned animals so entwined it was hard for her eye to determine which leg went with which beast.

"The twists and turns in these brooches put me in mind of the serpentine interlace I used to work on me manuscripts." Brenna traced the pattern with her finger. "What a conundrum!"

Rika smiled in agreement. "I imagine that's how Jorand feels right now. It's a hard knot he's in and no mistake."

"If he hadn't felt the need to wed the daughter of every headman he meets, he'd not be finding himself in this snarl," Brenna snapped. A tickle of guilt washed over her. She knew she shouldn't blame him. Jorand hadn't intended for any of this to happen, but he wasn't stepping lively to extricate himself from the puzzle, either. "Seems to me he has no dilemma. Did he not tell you I released him from his vow to me?"

"No," Rika said, "but even if you did, he wouldn't accept it. His honor binds him to you no matter what. You see, he can't dismiss his oath, even if you release him from it."

"And he's oath-bound to Solveig as well," Brenna said.

"Divorce is not unheard of among our people, especially if both agree to part. It's more that Jorand is oath-bound to Thorkill. Men frequently put more store in a pledge of fealty to another man since often their life depends upon the faith and the sword arm of the other," Rika admitted, the line between her brows deepening with the injustice of the double standard of honor. "And Jorand may well be confused by Solveig. He's a man." Rika shrugged, the gesture lightly dismissing the brawnier half of the human race. "And sometimes men are the last to know what they are feeling. But he's heart-bound to you, I see it plainly. And I suspect you still care more than a little for him."

Brenna bit her lip. "Aye, much more than a little." She dropped the Latin and lapsed into Gaelic, but Rika seemed to understand her intent if not her words.

"I thought so," she nodded thoughtfully. "You need to decide if what you and Jorand have together is more real than what he and Solveig had."

What passed between her and the big Northman in the months gone by was real enough. It was only her present that seemed a waking phantom.

"Let's see what we can do with your hair, shall we?" Rika suggested, picking up a horn comb. Brenna surrendered to the skillful fingers of her new friend as Rika tamed her willful curls into a long plait. As a finishing touch, Rika placed a lace kerchief on her crown.

"Among my people, married women cover their heads," she explained. "As a sign of the honor due them by their husband."

Brenna started to protest, but Rika led her to Solveig's polished silver mirror. Dressed in borrowed finery, a stranger peered back at her. Only the gray eyes seemed familiar. She'd always been told she had her father's eyes, and Brian Ui Niall's eyes didn't belong to a Norsewoman.

"I'll wear me hair as I always do," Brenna said, removing the fine lace and undoing the thong corralling her tresses. "I thank you for all you've done, but this is not for me."

She couldn't wear a symbol of her husband's honor when she didn't feel he'd shown her any of late. She ran a hand through the long braid, leaned forward, and shook her hair out. Even damp, it curled in wayward ringlets over her shoulders and down her back.

Rika looked at her approvingly. "You should always be who you are. It's a wise woman who knows that, my friend."

Even though the moon was full, the sky was so overcast with clouds, there was no light beyond the few guttering torches on poles to illuminate Brenna and Rika's way to Thorkill's *jarlhof.* Far larger than any other structure in Dublin, the headman's domicile was both home and meeting hall in the same fashion as Brian Ui Niall's keep. But where Brenna's home was a cylindrical stone tower, Thorkill's *jarlhof* was a massive wooden structure with jutting dragonheads on either end of the ridgepole. Fanciful carved beasts leered down at Brenna from points where the support beams of the roof met the outer walls.

Brenna's heart fluttered as she and Rika entered the wide open doorway. She squinted at the brightness of the blazing torchlight inside after the darkness in the street.

The feast was well under way. The aroma of

roasted meat and bread and alcohol competed half-heartedly with the smell of too many bodies, not all of them as clean as hers, crammed into one place. There were both men and women in the hall, eating, laughing, and swilling mead, and all of them so big. Even seated, the Norse seemed to dwarf her. She felt very much like a mouse sneaking into a byre full of cats. Cats intent on feeding, at that.

Her belly clenched as she followed Rika through the throng. Part of her was desperate to see Jorand again, but another part remembered that *he* would be there as well, the nightmare from her past she now knew as Kolgrim.

She took comfort knowing that Kolgrim was unlikely to recognize her from that ill-fated day. Sinead had made sure he'd only caught a glimpse of her before she ordered Brenna to run. Besides, Kolgrim had probably defiled so many Irish virgins, he wouldn't even remember Sinead if she were here.

Her body stiffened when she saw him. Kolgrim was seated on Thorkill's right, leaning in to talk with the master of Dublin. Then he knocked back a long horn brimming with mead. The golden substance trickled from the corners of his mouth and dribbled down his russet beard. He put down the empty horn and swiped his greasy lips with the back of his hand. His eyes met hers for a brief flicker and her breath caught in her throat. When his gaze moved on, she exhaled slowly.

Solveig was seated in the place of honor on her father's left side. Clad in a snowy white kyrtle and tunic, with her golden hair dressed in an elaborate series of plaits, she looked pure enough to have stepped from a folio of the Gospels. Her skin was pale as parchment and her eyebrows so blond as to be invisible at a distance, giving her the supremely calm look of the Madonna Herself. Everything about her was pallid, except for her very red mouth. She was quite beautiful, Brenna realized with a pang.

But when Brenna saw Jorand, the rest of the room, including the fiend named Kolgrim and the lesser demon Solveig, dissolved into nothing. Her husband sat still as stone, a deep frown chiseled between his brows. But stern-visaged or no, his face was like a woodcut of such pure line and balance, it hurt Brenna's heart to look at him. Even so, she drank in the sight of him as thirstily as a shipwrecked victim craves sweet water.

When he turned his head and saw her, a smile lit his features. He stood to welcome her. It was all Brenna could do not to run to him, arms outstretched.

Aye, what we had was real, she thought. But the menace she felt in Thorkill's hall was real as well and she forced herself to walk sedately at Rika's side.

"Bjorn, this is Brenna." Her new friend motioned to the dark-haired man seated near Jorand. Bjorn smiled at her briefly, but his attention immediately turned to the glorious redhead who was his wife.

Brenna took her place at her husband's side. Jorand settled beside her and placed a possessive hand on her thigh.

"Thank you for coming," Jorand said softly. "I feared you wouldn't."

"Rika told me ye were planning to challenge Kolgrim in the Holmgang," she answered, trying not to be distracted by the heat of his palm. "Since I'm the reason ye are trying to win back the Codex, I wanted to be here to support ye. Surely Thorkill will hear me testimony as well?"

"Testimony?"

"Aye. Ye've made a big stramash about your law and all," she said. "I only hope your Holmgang court sees justice done."

"Whatever she's saying about the Holmgang, tell her that, as head wife, mine is the right of first choice among the spoils." Solveig leaned across Jorand to glare at Brenna.

"She doesn't know anything about that," Jorand said, impatient with Solveig's greed. "She doesn't even realize the Holmgang is a physical challenge, not a trial. Don't worry, woman. You'll get your full due."

"I should hope so. I deserve something for the heartache you've put me through. First, I'm told you're washed overboard and grieve for you as a wife should. Then I find you've turned Irish for more than half a year. And now you flaunt your little concubine before the whole of Dublin," Solveig said, eyes narrowed at him. Then she lowered her voice. "But since you're intent on challenging your old captain, they do say Kolgrim has a stash of hack silver big as a two-year-old child hidden under the floor of his longhouse."

Jorand studied Solveig's flawless face and saw her clearly for the first time. Looking back, he realized he'd been enthralled by her beauty and more than a little dazzled by her father's power. Now he understood the emptiness of both. He was a fool to let his cock and his ambition lead him into marriage with such a shallow creature. He shuddered to realize that if he hadn't met Brenna, Solveig might have always been enough for him.

Solveig hadn't changed. He had.

A small hand on his arm made him turn. *Brenna.* Her name had once more become his talisman, a whispered prayer to keep him sane. When things had become too trying with Solveig the past week, Brenna echoed in his mind. He caught himself chanting it under his breath more than once.

"When will it start?" Brenna asked.

"Soon enough," he said, covering her hand with his own and not allowing her to escape. Even though Brenna was no stranger to hard labor, her smooth palm was still so soft. He inhaled deeply, taking in the fresh, clean scent of her. Her eyes were clear when she looked at him, the soul he loved glistening in their moist depths. The possibility that he could lose her completely this very night flitted across his mind, but he shoved it away. No profit in thinking the worst.

As if in response to Brenna's question, Thorkill stood and bellowed for quiet.

Brenna listened in tense puzzlement, trying to decipher what Thorkill was saying. As if she sensed Brenna's dilemma, Rika leaned in to whisper an interpretation. "He's calling all to witness the accusation."

Brenna nodded. That much made sense.

Jorand rose and began speaking. Even though he sounded strange in Norse instead of the heavily accented Gaelic he used when he spoke to her, she let his sonorous voice roll over her. She wished she could wrap herself in the rich deep sound, go to sleep and, please God, never wake.

"Jorand says Kolgrim attacked him during a storm and knocked him overboard to drown," Rika whispered. "That normally wouldn't be considered so bad, but Kolgrim struck from behind with no warning."

Kolgrim leaped to his feet, his face a snarling mask. Brenna flinched.

"Kolgrim is demanding the Holmgang," Rika explained. "Jorand wanted to call Kolgrim out this afternoon when he first arrived back, but Thorkill forbade it. Kolgrim had to be told Jorand was not dead as he first supposed. No warrior will stand to fight a ghost, after all. Jorand was under orders not to challenge until after the feast."

"So this exchange of insults is Thorkill's idea of entertainment for his guests?" Brenna asked under her breath.

"I'm a well-known skald in my own land," Rika said with a trace of annoyance. "I've not been asked to recite all week. Thorkill is not interested in sagas or poetry that don't tout his own exploits. Alas, I know of none worth retelling."

Kolgrim lunged at Jorand, but Thorkill interposed his own formidable body between them and pushed the combatants apart. Then he spoke at length in stentorian tones. When he finished, everyone stood and pushed toward the open doorway.

Jorand shot Brenna a parting look, then strode away with purpose.

"What now?" she asked.

"The Holmgang begins," Rika said, a grim tightness about her lips.

"But I thought this was the Holmgang court."

Rika cocked her head at her. "He didn't tell you.

The Holmgang isn't a court trial. It is trial by combat, winner take all."

Brenna felt suddenly light-headed.

Solveig brushed past her, pausing long enough to toss a string of stinging invective toward her. She looked Brenna up and down, the expression on her face plainly saying Brenna had been weighed in the balance and found sadly wanting. The beautiful Norse woman made a noise that sounded suspiciously like a snort and stalked away.

"I'm almost afraid to ask," Brenna skittered after Rika as they pushed through the throng toward the doorway. "What did she say to me?"

" 'Pray to your God, Irish,' " Rika repeated verbatim, her prodigious memory able to grasp and retell the spoken word with exactitude. " 'May our husband be victorious. If not, we belong to Kolgrim from this night.' "

"No," Brenna protested. "Not even Northmen could be so barbarous. Surely a man isn't allowed to take another's wife."

Rika put an arm around Brenna's shoulders and hurried her along. "It is allowed ... but he must kill the husband first."

Chapter Thirty

... he must kill the husband first.

The words echoed in Brenna's mind. She hoisted her skirt and dodged in and out among the crowd, trying to work her way out of the *jarlhof* to find Jorand. She had to stop this insanity.

"Jorand!" she cried out, unable to see him over the sea of taller bodies.

Rika caught up to her and grabbed her shoulders, turning her around. "What are you doing?"

"I'm going to stop this," Brenna said. "It's my fault Jorand is in danger and the Codex is not worth it."

"You can't stop it. It's already begun." Rika gave her a shake. "He fights for his honor. Do you want to shame him?"

That made her pause. Jorand wouldn't thank her for behaving in a way that brought him disgrace. But she never imagined getting back the Codex would involve such high stakes. As much as she wanted her sister's child in her arms, the possibility that Jorand could die trying to bring her dream to reality had never entered her mind. She fought to bring herself under control, to still her trembling.

"That's better," Rika said. "Come. Bjorn will be his second. He will have saved us space. As Jorand's wife, you are expected to watch."

The two women pushed through the throng, out of the *jarlhof* and into the night. Clouds had blocked the moon's light earlier. Now they mushroomed into a full-blown thunderstorm. Lightning split the sky, illuminating the bustling throng with flashes that made people's movement appear macabre and disjointed.

Rain started to fall, a rustle on the thatched roofs at first, then a steady dripping that soon plastered Brenna's borrowed clothing to her form and impeded her progress. The wooden planks on the path grew slippery underfoot. A long roll of thunder rumbled over her. A flicker of hope surged up in her breast. Perhaps the combat would be halted due to the gathering storm.

Brenna elbowed her way through the tight knot of spectators gathered around a roped-off area about twelve long paces square. Someone was pegging a cloak to the ground in the center of the square. The reek of burning pitch invaded Brenna's nostrils as several men arrived with fresh torches to replace the old ones, already sputtering in the rain. Rather than dampening the spirits of the crowd, the foul weather seemed to add excitement.

A jagged bolt shredded the clouds and the resounding boom that followed made Brenna jump. "Won't they stop because of the storm?" she shouted to Rika.

"Thor favors a good fight," Rika said with a glance at the sky. New Christian or not, the Norse woman seemed to have a healthy respect for her old gods still. "The Thunderer has come. That makes this holmgang even more propitious."

Brenna heard several people bickering amongst themselves and she saw small bags of coin change hands. The Northmen laid bets on the outcome.

In one corner of the roped area, Jorand and Bjorn were heads down in earnest conversation, deep in discussion of fighting strategy, Brenna supposed. Kolgrim was in the opposite corner, taking practice cuts with a sword as long as his arm. Lightning flashed and his wickedly sharp-looking sword seemed to glow blue for a moment.

Solveig joined Brenna at the rope, looking down on her with disdain. Brenna saw she was holding a sword, swathed in a bloodred cloth. When Jorand approached them, Solveig presented the sword to him, hilt first.

The crowd quieted. Solveig said something to him, her voice ringing clear, without the slightest hint of a quiver.

"Victory and honor," Rika whispered, prompting Brenna to offer the correct words of encouragement to her husband. Jorand turned from Solveig to look at Brenna, his face stony and unreadable. Moira had told her Jorand looked like a different man when he slew the raiders on the beach. Hard and vicious. Clearly, he had already passed into a state that would allow him to hack into living flesh without hesitation.

"Live," she pleaded in Gaelic. "Just live."

Thorkill took his position across the square from Brenna and gave an almost imperceptible nod.

At this signal, Kolgrim opened his mouth wide and made a noise like a bull standing at stud. Jorand answered with a full-throated roar of his own. The two men flung themselves toward the center of the square and met with a resounding clang of steel on steel. Sparks flew as the blades grated along their sharp edges. Jorand and Kolgrim grappled with each other for the space of several heartbeats. After this test of strength and will, which neither of them won decisively, the combatants separated and began circling, searching for weakness.

Both Jorand and Kolgrim were tall men with long reaches and the small roped-off area designated for their fight meant they would surely connect with every blow. Each man was armed with only a lethal broadsword and a round wooden shield.

Kolgrim was barrel-chested, carrying a stone or two more in brawn than Jorand. Kolgrim raised his beefy arm to deliver a slashing stroke, throwing his whole weight behind the blow.

"Sweet Jesu!" Brenna clamped a hand over her mouth to keep from crying out again. The last thing she wanted to do was distract Jorand at a critical moment.

Kolgrim may have had extra weight, but Jorand was favored with the agility of youth. He managed to dodge Kolgrim's blade, deflect it with his shield, and deliver a counter stroke aimed at Kolgrim's sword arm. The older man was quicker than Brenna anticipated, jumping back out of the deadly arc of Jorand's sword.

Kolgrim bared his teeth at Jorand in a death's-head grin.

"Thought I killed you once, boy," Kolgrim said as he sidestepped, looking for an advantage.

"You thought wrong," Jorand countered, mirroring his opponent's movements. He stepped carefully, his footing slick with rain. "You relied on the sea to kill me. You were either too lazy or too cowardly to finish the job."

Kolgrim's eyes narrowed at the insult. "I see now I was too easy on you. It's a mistake I won't make twice. I only sent you into the coils of Jormungand last time. And here you are, back again like a boil on my ass. This go-around, I'll see you to Hel for certain."

Kolgrim's sword dipped slightly, leaving him open to a swift attack. Jorand lunged, his blade snaking toward Kolgrim's chest, but Kolgrim lurched to protect himself with the small shield. The point of Jorand's sword wedged in the wood and he couldn't wrench it free.

Kolgrim followed up his advantage, raining a hailstorm of blows on Jorand. He barely managed to cover his exposed shoulder with the shield in time to avoid a slash that would have cleaved him from the base of his neck to his breastbone.

"My crew thought they'd seen your shade on that beach, you know. That's the only reason you were able to kill those few." He hammered Jorand but was clearly frustrated when Jorand met every blow with his sturdy shield until he finally pulled his sword free. "You're no fighter. You've always been just a shipwright."

Jorand skewered Kolgrim's shield. He yanked back on his blade and pulled Kolgrim's shield from his grasp. Kolgrim's eyes widened with the shock of finding himself without a defense.

"I'm fighter enough to beat you," Jorand said, as he took a step back and pried the splintered circle of wood from the point of his blade. According to the law of Holmgang, when either combatant lost a shield, the fighting was stopped long enough to let him re-arm with one of two spares. A man was allowed three shields in the square, but only one sword.

"No, my old shipmate," Kolgrim promised as he slid a heavy fist through the straps of his new shield. "You may not realize it yet, but you're on your way to Niflheim. Nothing but ice and mist for the dead cursed to the ninth circle of Hel. There's no coming back from there."

"You talk too much," Jorand said, and launched a series of feints and cuts. When a flash from the heavens lit the combat, his sword glittered like molten silver. A roar of approval boiled up from the crowd and the sky answered it with a thunderous boom.

Jorand realized the two of them were evenly matched for strength. Each time his steel slammed into Kolgrim's, the force of the impact shot up through the sword, jarring his joints all the way to his shoulders. There was no give to the man. It was like hacking away at stone.

"Don't... worry about... your wives, son," Kolgrim grunted in short pants between blows. "Once they've had a taste of me, they'll forget all about you."

Brenna. No, he couldn't think about her now. The only way to keep her safe was to win.

"Besides, the Irish vixen looks a bit familiar. Think maybe I know that one already. Mayhap I opened her up for you. Tight little bitch, isn't she?"

The bellow of rage pouring out Jorand's throat didn't sound human, even to his own ears. He swung his arm over his head and brought it down with all the force he could muster, again and again, as though he was pounding a stubborn post into the ground. Safe behind his shield, Kolgrim was jarred and battered, but untouched. All Jorand succeeded in doing was wearing himself out.

Suddenly Kolgrim went on the offensive, slicing and hacking. He had no finesse, but tremendous power. Jorand backed and dodged but there was no place to run from the relentless attack. His shield splintered with a sickening cracking sound. It dangled in pieces from his arm and yet Kolgrim didn't stop.

"Hold!" Thorkill bellowed above the noise of the crowd and the storm.

Kolgrim changed direction in midstroke, but not before he'd managed to run the tip of his sword down the length of Jorand's shield arm. Blood welled along the shallow cut and oozed toward his fingers.

A chorus of hissing seethed from the crowd at this breach of Holmgang protocol, but Kolgrim just spat on the ground and scowled back at them.

Furious with the course of the combat, Jorand stalked back to his corner to let Bjorn refit him with a fresh shield.

"He's a hard nut to crack," Jorand said, sucking in air between the words.

"*Ja*," his friend said. "He's got your measure. Don't let him rattle you with words. His sword is menace enough."

Jorand shook his head, trying to quell the ringing in his ears. "The man's strong as a bull. I think I've met my match."

It was a testament to their friendship that Bjorn didn't disagree and rush to reassure Jorand. "He's a little bigger than you and he's fast, which is the very devil of it," Bjorn said, eyeing Kolgrim appraisingly.

Jorand lowered his voice. "If he wins, steal Brenna away and take her home. Don't let her go to Kolgrim. Your word on it."

"I promise." Bjorn clapped a hand on Jorand's shoulder and nodded grimly. "But don't let him win."

Jorand turned back to face Kolgrim without taking time to glance at Brenna. He couldn't stand to see her, tight-lipped and terrified. It was bad enough he could feel her fear across the square as strongly as if he held her trembling body in his arms. He supposed she had a right. His opponent was the source of all the evil that had befallen her and her family, and if Jorand lost, she'd be Kolgrim's chattel, to be used and tormented at his whim.

Jorand would only be dead.

All around her, Brenna heard the crowd of Northmen growling out what sounded like both encouragement and imprecations at the fighters. Rain pounded out of the sky and she swiped the moisture out of her eyes so she could see.

The two men collided in the center of the square again, blades slicing shimmering arcs through the downpour. Their swords struck and rasped against each other. The whine of metal on metal hurt her ears.

Both men appeared to be tiring, but it seemed to Brenna that Jorand had to back away from the blur of blades more often than Kolgrim. Once Jorand's foot left the pegged-down cloak and a roar of disapproval went up from the onlookers.

"He gives ground," Rika explained. "If both feet leave the cloak, he flees. It's cowardice to run from a fight."

Brenna wished they could both run away, far, far away from Dublin and never look back.

Jorand leaped toward the center of the cloak, trying to keep his steps from the muddy edge, pivoting to meet Kolgrim's assault as the other man circled him like a corbie hovering over a battlefield.

Brenna had to remind herself to breathe as the battle wore on. Both men lost another shield. Jorand managed to land a blow on Kolgrim's thigh, opening a gash that reddened his leggings, but didn't stop his sword from singing its deadly song.

Kolgrim's blade sliced across Jorand's chest. Brenna's vision tunneled for a moment, thinking him killed, but Jorand kept flailing away, even as the red stain spread across the front of his slashed shirt.

Kolgrim seemed to sense Jorand was flagging. He dropped his shield and, grasping his broadsword with both hands, raised it above his head to deliver a deathblow. Jorand ducked and plowed into his enemy, using Kolgrim's own weight and momentum to lift him off his feet and flip him onto his back. Jorand stomped on Kolgrim's sword arm and wrenched the blade out of his hands.

Brenna heard a loud crunch as the long bone in Kolgrim's arm snapped under Jorand's booted foot. A thrill of horror coursed through her as her husband raised his sword to bring it down on his fallen foe's unprotected neck.

"Hold!" Thorkill ordered. Rika continued to offer a whispered translation for Brenna, but since the headman knocked down the rope and entered the Holmgang square, his intent seemed clear. "The contest is ended."

"This combat is to the death," Jorand argued,

blood in his eyes making them glint feral in the darkness like a wolf over a downed ram.

"I am *jarl* and I say it is ended. Unless, of course, you wish to challenge me over the matter here and now?" The master of Dublin was even larger than Kolgrim and rested to boot. Brenna breathed a sigh of relief when Jorand let his sword clatter to the ground.

Thorkill lifted Jorand's arm in triumph, and the crowd gave the measure half-hearted approval. Beyond the disappointment over lost wagers, Brenna sensed only heart's blood would truly appease them, but Thorkill's will was not to be gainsaid.

Solveig stepped forward and demanded Kolgrim forfeit all his property since Jorand had won.

Thorkill reached down and yanked his injured lieutenant to his feet. "Since the fight was stopped, there is no clear winner. Kolgrim might have rallied, but Dublin is the victor, for I have need of both my lieutenants." He raised a hand to forestall Solveig's argument. "Still, Jorand deserves to be compensated. One possession among all that belongs to Kolgrim. Choose. Even if it be his dragonship, it shall be yours."

"This is most unusual," Rika whispered to Brenna. "Jorand is Thorkill's son-in-law, yet he seems to be protecting Kolgrim for some reason. Or perhaps . . ." Rika bit her lip.

"Perhaps he's upset with Jorand for taking another wife?" Brenna suggested. Rika shrugged.

"The silver," Solveig hissed. "Demand the silver."

Jorand looked at his Norse wife for a moment, then met Brenna's steady gaze.

"When Kolgrim went viking up the Shannon, he pilfered a book from Clonmacnoise Abbey," Jorand said. "I'll have that."

Kolgrim cradled his broken arm, tight-lipped with pain. "As if you could read it. Have you been gone from us so long you've crossed over to the White Christ?" He spat on the ground with disgust.

"If it has no value, why did you take it?" Jorand crowded close to Kolgrim.

"Enough," Thorkill shouted to be heard over the wind and rain. He stepped between them, a hand on each chest. "The book is in the *jarlhof*. Come. But first, bury your enmity here in the *holmhring*. I have need of both of you yet."

Thorkill turned and marched through the crowd, like a dragonship under full sail, expecting his followers to fall into his wake. Brenna trailed Jorand, thanking the saints and angels he was still alive. She scarcely believed they'd succeeded in regaining the Codex as well.

Inside the *jarlhof,* Thorkill dismissed the rest of the populace and called for a large trunk to be brought from his chamber.

"I can't believe it," Solveig muttered. "You have your pick of all a man owns and you choose a worthless book."

"Wait till you see it before you complain, daughter," Thorkill admonished. He unlocked the trunk, drew out a parcel, wrapped in oilskin, and handed it to Jorand. "It's yours."

When Jorand unwrapped the package, it was as though a living rainbow glowed in his hands. Precious stones gleamed in riotous color, sending shards of light dancing along the smoke-blackened beams of the *jarlhof*. The front and back of the binding were encrusted with jewels.

"I promised I'd see the Codex safe in your hands,"

Jorand said in Gaelic as he crossed the room to deliver the incredible treasure to Brenna. "I always keep my promise."

"So I see," Brenna said, lifting trembling hands to receive the unspeakably beautiful book. She'd been able to look at it only once before and knew as ornate as the cover was, the artwork inside was far beyond anything she'd ever imagined. "I thank ye . . . husband."

Solveig snatched the Codex from her hands, growling a string of Norse at her. Jorand started to grab it back, but Thorkill stopped him with a hand to the chest.

"Never get between your women in a fight," the master of Dublin advised.

"No," Jorand said as he shoved past Thorkill and reached for the Codex. "I won it for Brenna. Give it back."

Solveig picked up a long knife someone had left on one of the tables and waved it toward him threateningly. "Unless you wish a large wound, husband, I advise you to stay where you are. I will decide how the spoils are divided between your two wives."

She opened the book and slashed the binding. The folios of illuminated manuscript fluttered to the floor like so many oak leaves in autumn. Then she put down the knife and swayed back toward Jorand, her chin jutting toward.

"I find I can no longer be the wife of a man who can't even kill his opponent in the *holmhring*," Solveig said evenly. "We both know I have grounds for divorce. You have become like one of those eunuchs from Miklagard since you took that little Irish to bed. No man would willingly avoid my couch if there wasn't something seriously wrong with his manhood." She delivered a ringing slap across Jorand's face and her lips turned up into a malicious smile. "Now we're even. You have grounds as well. Expect witnesses and a declamation tomorrow morning."

Bejeweled cover clutched to her chest, Solveig turned and strode from the hall with the dignity of retreating royalty. She stopped under the lintel and turned back to face her husband.

"Know this as well, Jorand," she said with a sly smile."Being a widow had its rewards. When I was yours, my bed was never cold. Men lined up to console me and I accepted their comfort without a backward glance. You will be easy to replace."

She turned with a flourish of her ermine-trimmed cape and slipped into the night.

Mutely, Brenna knelt to pick up the scattered pages, but her heart sang inside her chest. Jorand was about to be freed from his Norse wife. Then she jerked back the reins on her joy.

He hadn't been the one to make that choice.

"I'm sorry," Jorand said as he stooped to help her retrieve the damaged treasure.

" 'Tis not your fault," she said, carefully arranging the delicate parchment in the correct order. She forced herself to concentrate on the Codex to avoid thinking about what Jorand's divorce from Solveig might mean. Gold filigree on the pages caught the torchlight and gleamed as she inspected a *Chi-Rho* page devoted to the adoration of a symbol for Christ. She knew the creation of that one page had consumed months of the illuminator's life.

"But she took the most valuable part," Jorand said, his mouth hard as he glared after Solveig.

"Sometimes, what's inside is more valuable than

the outside. The Almighty has caused the earth to yield thousands of gemstones. But the artist who worked this manuscript is no more. His like will not come again on earth till the last trumpet shall sound." Brenna laid a reverent hand on the stack of loose pages, an astounding collection of artwork and the Word of God. "I'll not begrudge Solveig a rock or two when she's left me the true treasure."

She bit her lip. Did he think she meant he was the treasure? Her heart certainly seemed to think so.

"I imagine the abbot will see things differently."

"Mayhap," she conceded, then let her gaze drift down from his tired face to the bloody gash on his chest. No matter what the morrow held, she was so thankful he was alive. "Ye'll be needing a bit of tending, I'm thinking. Come ye back to the church with me and I'll bind your wounds."

That offer brought a smile to his lips. He put an arm around her shoulders and started to lead her out of the *jarlhof*.

"Stay a while," Thorkill commanded. "Let your woman go, but I have need of you yet this night, Jorand."

Jorand motioned for Bjorn and Rika to see Brenna to Father Armaugh's little church. Then he joined Thorkill by the fire.

Kolgrim was seated there as well, his arm stuck out at an unnatural angle. He raised a horn to his lips and drained it in one long drink, obviously trying to dull the pain of the splintered limb. When he lowered the drinking horn, Jorand saw that Kolgrim was white as the chalk cliffs on the Isle of the Angles.

His enemy was in agony. *Good*.

Chapter Thirty-one

"Not that I care, but what's urgent enough to keep Kolgrim from the bonesetter?" Jorand asked.

Sweat beaded on Kolgrim's forehead and his jaw ticked with the effort of ignoring the pain of his broken bone. Jorand's own wounds throbbed, but they were minor compared to Kolgrim's obvious suffering.

"Kolgrim's got news, and he wouldn't tell all during the feast. Said it wouldn't do to speak it in the hearing of so many ears." Thorkill's brows met over his long, thin nose. "Now, what was important enough for me to interfere in the *holmhring?*"

"You mean to rule this island," Kolgrim said, breathing heavily between his words.

Thorkill nodded gruffly.

"I ask you, can it be done by the sword alone?"

"You think we can't outfight these miserable little Irishmen?" Thorkill demanded.

"Not that," Kolgrim said. "Of course we can defeat them. I mean, once the battles are done, can you hold Erin?"

Thorkill frowned.

"I think I know what he's getting at," Jorand said, surprised Kolgrim would be so far-thinking. "We can take the island by force, raze the monasteries and burn their farmsteads. We can kill their chieftains, but for each one we put down, another will take his place. The Irish outnumber us by a long stretch. We'll be fighting forever to hold this rock."

"Exactly." Kolgrim's wary eyes flickered with grudging respect at Jorand. "Unless you win the hearts of the Irish, you'll not hold Erin more than a short spate of winters."

"Win their hearts? Bah!" Thorkill paced like a caged bear. "Even if I wanted to, how would I go about doing that?"

"My tongue is fair cleaving to the roof of my mouth," Kolgrim said, holding out his empty horn for more mead. Thorkill filled it and Kolgrim knocked it back. "Jorand here has shown you the way,"

What did he mean by that? In the week since his return to Dublin, Jorand had given Thorkill nothing of strategic importance. He meant it when he told Brenna he intended to stop Thorkill.

Perhaps Kolgrim's pain was making him stupid. Jorand knew the splintered bone shifted each time Kolgrim moved. If it wasn't set properly, and soon, his enemy could lose the use of the arm. The thought caused a smile to flicker across Jorand's lips.

Kolgrim stifled a groan as he waited for the alcohol to dull the throbbing. "The Irish hold as much store in lineage as they do in might when it comes to their rulers. Join your blood to one of theirs. Take an Irish queen for yourself."

Thorkill's eyes shifted back and forth as he rolled

the idea around in his mind. "So you think an Irish wife will make the natives willing to follow me?"

"Not an Irish wife. An Irish queen," Kolgrim said. "Join yourself to the right house and this island will fall into your hand like a ripe plum. And I know exactly the one for you to take. Moira, Queen of the Ulaid."

Jorand schooled his features into a blank mask to hide his shock. He reached for his own horn and took a long gulp, not trusting his voice to speak.

"She's beautiful, as people of this island count beauty. Fair of face and form," Kolgrim went on. "I've seen her from a distance with my own eyes and in this case, the rumors don't do her justice. She's only worn the crown for four months, but already the people of Ulaid think the sun rises and sets on her tight little arse. And I've got it on good authority that this Moira's not only a queen, she's the daughter of another king, Brian Ui Niall of Donegal. You've already got Dublin as your stronghold in the south. Take Moira of Ulaid as your queen and you'll control the northern clans as well."

Thorkill tugged thoughtfully at his beard. "Back in the Northlands, fostering was useful for binding allies. Raise a man's son in your home and you've got them both for life. And fosterlings make admirable hostages if the bond is broken. If the Irish aren't disposed to follow willingly," Thorkill mused, "I'd think a queen of Erin with a blade hanging over her head would serve the same purpose as a fosterling."

Jorand watched helplessly as the leader of Dublin fell under Kolgrim's spell. Thorkill was a ruthless warrior, but he depended on his lieutenants for strategy. In the past, Jorand had offered advice and counsel alongside Kolgrim. With a pang, he realized there had been a time when he'd have lent his support whole-heartedly to Kolgrim's plan. Now the idea of Brenna's sister being abducted and forced into a union with Thorkill left a bitter taste in his mouth.

"Ulaid is far to the North. We'd need to take most of the ships and men to launch an assault on their stronghold," Jorand said, wondering whether Ulaid had a stone tower like Donegal with successive levels and ladders designed to outlast the most determined siege. "Besides, I've seen an Irish keep from the inside. If they're well-provisioned, Ulaid can hole up and wait for the rest of the clans to rally to his defense."

"Fearghus of Ulaid helps us with that. He's just buried his father and come into his kingship, so his defenses aren't what they should be," Kolgrim reported. "And he's an arrogant braggart from all reports, so the likelihood of reinforcements from surrounding clans is slim."

"Still, a raid of this sort would take too many men from Dublin," Jorand argued. "What kind of victory would it be if you gained an Irish queen in the north while you lost your stronghold in the south?"

"By Loki's hairy toes! You sound like an old woman, Jorand." Kolgrim turned his gaze back to Thorkill. "If you listen to my plan, it won't take that many men. Your smallest dragonship will do it." Kolgrim shifted his weight on his seat in obvious discomfort. "If we but wait till the next full moon, Moira of the Ulaid will nearly come to us."

"We aren't likely to catch a queen roaming unescorted." Jorand snorted. "Even the Irish have better sense than that."

"In that, you'd be wrong," Kolgrim said. "Every fall before the foul season hits, the queen of Ulaid must make a pilgrimage to a monastery on St. Patrick's island, an undefended bit of rock sticking up out of the Irish Sea."

"Surely the queen will have heavy protection," Jorand said.

"Not at all. Once she sets sail, all she'll have with her are a couple of spineless priests to sail the Irish excuse for a ship and a complement of twelve virgins to pray with her. Something to do with prayers for all the souls of the clan and seeing them safe through the winter."

Kolgrim's coarse laughter turned into a coughing fit that wasn't abated till he hacked up a huge glob of phlegm and spat it on the packed earth floor.

"The man I squeezed the information from said the queen was to pray for a son as well since she's been wed several months and is still as flat-bellied as a child herself." Kolgrim swilled another gulp of mead. "That's a prayer a Northman could answer quicker than one of those thin-wicked Irishmen."

"By the gods, I'll give it my best effort!" Thorkill roared with laughter. "You're right, Kolgrim. I could do with a change of women. We'll take a few of the virgins as well."

Jorand had sworn an oath of fealty to Thorkill shortly after he came to Dublin. Perhaps he'd been swayed by the force of Thorkill's personality, or the way he'd carved the thriving town out of hostile territory. Probably it was the siren song of Solveig's icy beauty. But whatever the reason, Jorand had sworn.

In all his life, it was the only decision he'd ever regretted.

He used to believe that a man was entitled to whatever wealth his sword arm could bring him. Now, he realized that just because he *could* take something, that didn't mean he *should*. It was an odd notion, one he was still getting his mind around, but the principle was glaringly true in this case. Thorkill couldn't be allowed to take Moira, even if it meant Jorand must break faith with his own kind.

Still, if he was going to be damned as an oath-breaker, at least it was for a good cause. Yet all would be for naught if he didn't get Brenna out of harm's way first.

"You should sleep on a decision like this. An Irish wife may be more trouble than she's worth," Jorand said.

Thorkill lifted a wiry brow at him in question.

"I've had no joy of mine since we arrived in Dublin." Jorand shrugged eloquently. "Willful, disobedient, and full of all sorts of strange ideas."

Thorkill nodded sagely. "I heard your little Irish bit had taken up residence with the priest. You're too soft with your women," his father-in-law accused. "She's begging you to show her who's in charge. Cuff her across the face a time or two and she'll come to heel. Truth to tell, I've even had a few who grew to like a beating now and then."

"No, she's tried my patience for the last time. I'm through with her." Jorand laid his horn on the table and stood up. "Now is as good a time as any to give up women in general. In fact, once Solveig and I have finished our business in the morning, I plan to take Brenna back to that abbey Kolgrim sacked."

"Well, I can't say Dublin will be sorry to see her go. Even though you and Solveig have divorced, your place with me is still secure. Only be sure you're back by the next full moon," Thorkill said. "And you—" He pointed at Kolgrim. "Get to the bonesetter now. I'll want you both with me when we round up Queen Moira and her twelve virgins."

He punched Jorand in the shoulder. "I'll give you first pick after me. Maybe you'll be ready to try another woman by then."

Jorand's brain worked furiously, trying to puzzle a way to both whisk Brenna to safety and keep Moira from being taken.

"*Ja,* a successful raid together. That's all the two of you need to bury this feud once and for all." Thorkill slapped both of their shoulders soundly. "Almost makes me wish it was a boatload of those damned Irishmen guarding the queen instead of a gaggle of girls. It'd be a little better sport at least." He snorted. "But only a little."

Kolgrim made his way out of the *jarlhof,* cradling his wounded arm. Jorand followed him into the night.

The rain had stopped, but the full moon was still obscured by thick clouds. Only a sliver of light, curved as an Arab's blade, managed to slice its way through the scuds. Twenty-eight days till the next full moon. He only had twenty-eight days to see Brenna to safety and figure out some way to thwart Kolgrim's plans for Moira. With a sigh, he trudged toward his home.

Jorand heard footsteps behind him and whirled, drawing his long knife in a fluid motion.

"Be easy, friend. It's only me." Bjorn's voice came to him from the shadows. "Thought I'd watch your back in case Kolgrim has allies who decide to try and finish what he couldn't."

Jorand relaxed his defensive stance and breathed easier as Bjorn came alongside him, falling into step with him as he had so often in the past. "You saw Brenna back to the church?"

"*Ja,*" Bjorn said, scratching his head. "Though you didn't warn me how much trouble she'd be. She didn't want to go at first. Kept insisting on waiting to tend your wounds. I had to threaten to carry her before she agreed to go peacefully." Bjorn shook his head in disbelief. "The woman is as stubborn as a rock."

Jorand smiled and nodded. "That's my princess. I'd say she let you off easy. She skewered me with a pike the first time I laid eyes on her."

"No wonder you're so smitten." Bjorn chuckled, then his tone turned serious. "I know you didn't intend to wed twice, but you've got a hornet's nest for yourself here and no mistake. Slighting the *jarl*'s daughter is a game for fools We've been in some tight spots together over the years. For once, friend, you're in more trouble than I can help you out of."

Jorand sighed. Bjorn didn't know the half of it. Not only was he saddled with the unpleasant prospect of untangling his domestic arrangements, he was determined to keep Thorkill from seizing Moira—and all of Erin with her.

"Thorkill still needs my services for the time being and at least there's an end in sight to my woman troubles. You can be a witness at my divorce tomorrow," Jorand said, then stopped dead as an idea struck him. Something Thorkill had mentioned triggered a plan in his mind. It was a dicey job at best, but it might work. How was he to set all the elements in motion and see Brenna back to Clonmacnoise? "If you're willing, there is something you can do to help me with another matter as well."

"Anything. You know that."

"Good." Jorand put a hand on his friend's shoulder. "After Brenna and I leave in the morning, I need you to kidnap the priest."

Chapter Thirty-two

"We should reach Clonmacnoise by midday tomorrow," Jorand said, fingering their route on the leather map.

Brenna slanted a glance at him. It was the sixth time he'd consulted the chart since they made camp. He was definitely avoiding her.

"That's good then." Brenna banked their small fire for the night and sat down, pulling her knees up to her chin, and wrapping her arms around her shins. Autumn chilled the night, sending a crisp breeze ruffling over her, a harbinger of frost soon to come.

The morning after the Holmgang, she had watched while Jorand and Solveig dissolved their marriage. Then another man escorted everyone from the house Jorand had built and closed the door behind them. The man stayed inside with Solveig, and Brenna decided the beautiful Norse woman had wasted no time in replacing her first husband.

After a warm good-bye to Rika, Brenna left Dublin with a lighter heart, but no real peace about her relationship with Jorand. If only he'd been the one to end it with Solveig. Brenna wasn't prepared to be his second choice and if he wasn't willing to broach the subject, she wasn't about to. Much as she loved him, she still wouldn't beg.

After studying the map, Jorand had insisted on a different route from the one they'd taken to reach Dublin. They sailed up the Liffey instead of back down and out to sea. In little more than a week of sailing, they covered an amazing distance in the little ship, owing much both to fair winds and Jorand's ability to tack and reef the craft to take advantage of the smallest breath of air.

When they reached the headwaters of the Liffey, Jorand had tied up the boat and traded with some locals for a pair of sturdy horses to take them overland for the relatively short march to Clonmacnoise.

Brenna had reassembled the tattered remains of the Skellig-Michael Codex and bundled the precious folios in thick oilskin. The jewels might be lost, but the artistry remained. She hoped it would be enough to satisfy the abbot. If not, she didn't know how they'd make Father Ambrose keep his end of the bargain.

She looked across the fire at Jorand, flickers of light licking at his features. A shiver quaked under her ribs. She recognized the faint shimmer as hope, but it was quickly overpowered by a stronger, sinking sensation.

Loving this Northman was like falling into a well, she decided. A sudden drop, a disappearing circle of light, and the sure knowledge she'd never claw her way out again.

She'd been thrilled when he came to tell her they

were leaving Dublin, but his manner had been so stern and silent since then, her joy was quickly dashed. They walked on tiptoe around each other during the past few days, neither speaking to the other beyond the few phrases necessary to smooth travel. So she huddled behind distant courtesy, a wholly inadequate shield for her heart.

"When we find the child, I'm thinking you'll want to return to Donegal as soon as possible?" His voice interrupted her thoughts and she looked up at him. His eyes were hooded under half-closed lids, his expression blank as a new sheet of parchment.

"Aye, 'tis best. I mean to compensate the child's foster parents, of course." She patted the leather pouch she kept hidden under her kyrtle, filled with the small amount of silver she'd scraped together in Donegal. It might not be much, but it was all the portable wealth she possessed in the world. "Still, they may take it hard to lose the bairn. With the abbot's blessing on the matter, they'll have little to say, but 'twould be best to be off before they think things over and come to a different view."

Jorand plucked a foxtail and studied it with absorption. "That Murtaugh," he said with seeming indifference. "He struck me as a capable fellow."

"For all his age, he's a handy man in a pinch, is Murtaugh."

"Do you think he'd make the trip?"

"To Donegal?"

Jorand nodded.

"The boat will be crowded enough with us and an infant on board, let alone another adult. Why—" Suddenly his unspoken reason hit her with the force of a blow. Her innards twirled in a slow spiral. Her voice sounded distant to her own ears, as though someone else was speaking. "*Ye* don't mean to make the trip, do ye?"

He closed his eyes for a moment, squeezing them tightly together as if shutting out bright sunlight. The fine lines around them, reminders of rough living on the sea, had become more deeply etched since they left Dublin. He looked thin and worn as an old cloak. Then those startling blue eyes opened and she read the answer to her question in their crystal depths.

God in Heaven! He means to leave me.

"I see," Brenna whispered. Her eyes were dry. She wished she could cry. If only the tears would start, she'd feel the relief of them. But instead she felt dead as the lichen-covered rock at her back. "I do see."

"No, you don't, princess." He smiled wearily and moved closer to her. "It's not what you think."

Fire danced through her veins. Anger? Aye, that was safe. "We've not said more than a handful of words to each other all week. How would ye be knowing what I think?"

"Because everything that goes on in your head shows on your lovely face." He reached across and cupped her cheek, his thumb tracing the curve of the fine bone. His hand was warm, and she found herself leaning into his touch.

The heat she'd mistaken for anger a moment ago flared into a darker flame. She despised herself for rousing to this man who intended to leave her. She didn't trust herself to speak.

"Even if you had it in you to lie, you don't have the face for it. Your soul, your thoughts, your feelings all shine out of you so strong, you're incapable of hiding what's rolling around inside you. But this time you're wrong, Brenna." He leaned forward and planted a gentle kiss on her forehead. "I'm not leaving you."

"Ye mean to send me alone back to me father. If that's not leaving, what might ye be calling it?"

"A temporary separation. At least I hope that's what it is." Jorand dropped his hand back into his lap and Brenna felt instantly colder, deprived of his touch. "I've tried to think of another way, any other way I can do what I must in the next few weeks, but I can't." He stared at the smoldering remains of their fire as if a solution might be lurking in the smoky depths. He shook his head slowly. "You'll have to trust me."

Brenna swallowed hard. He'd said the same words the first time he took her body, the first time he swept her to that incomprehensible place where she lost herself in him. She had little choice . It was either trust him or stop breathing. "Where are ye bound?"

"Back to Dublin for a start," he said. "I have some unfinished business there."

"Unfinished business? Is that what Northmen call it?" she asked, unable to keep the bitterness from her voice as she edged away from him. "That business wouldn't be called Solveig, would it?"

"Solveig and I are well and truly done," he said.

"And now ye settle for your poor second, me?"

Jorand's brown knit together. "Is that what you think? Never, Brenna. You're not second to anyone." He dragged a hand over his face. "I know I've been distant, but it's because something is about to happen and I'm not sure I've thought through all the possibilities."

"What is about to happen?"

"Brenna, I don't know how to explain it to you, but this is something I have to do. Do you remember when I told you of Thorkill's ambitions?"

"Aye. He means to rule the whole of Erin, ye said."

"I promised you I'd stop him if I could. What I must do touches on that. Thorkill is about to move and so will I." His words were guarded but his grim expression told her he was determined on his course. "Otherwise, you and I will never have peace together."

Together. Oh, Mother of Mercy, aye, together. She could meet any future so long as it included him.

He cast her a searching look. "If you'll still have me after what I've put you through."

"Of course I'll have you," she said, her chin quivering and her Donegal pride be damned."I was so afraid you'd choose Solveig."

"When my memory came back, it was a confusing jumble, but the part that was hardest was remembering how I'd felt about Solveig. I confess I was afraid I'd be torn between the two of you."

"You weren't?"

He shook his head. "No. Once I saw her, it just wasn't real. I mean . . . it seemed as if *I* wasn't real. As if my life with her had happened to someone else and I'd somehow stepped into his skin. So now there are two men trapped in here." He thumped his chest hard with the heel of his palm. "Jorand the Northman and Keefe Murphy the wandering stranger."

"What is it ye must do?" Even though relief flooded through her, she felt unaccountably shy, as if he were still the stranger she found on the beach instead of the man she'd come to know and love. She ventured to place a hand on his arm and he covered it with his. Warmth spread up to her shoulder and across her chest. "Can ye speak more plainly?"

He frowned, clearly torn about how much to tell her. "No, you'll be safer if you know nothing of what I've planned."

Jorand turned from the fire and fixed her with a steady look. She scarcely dared breathe as his gaze left her face, traveled down the exposed whiteness of her neck, and lingered on her breasts before returning to meet her eyes.

Could he feel her heart, she wondered, fluttering like a snared bird against her ribs? Did he know the heat of his gaze had warmed her more than the smoky fire ever could?

"I've missed you so, princess," he said, raw hunger plain on his face.

"And I you," she acknowledged. His rumbling voice sent shivers over her skin.

When he reached a hand to touch her, his fingertips skimming across her collarbone, her breasts ached for him as well. A tiny sigh escaped her lips, the breath catching in her throat as his hand dipped lower.

"And I've missed the blissful look on your face when I pleasure you." His blue eyes darkened to indigo as he watched for her response. "I do love you, Brenna, and if you don't let me love you right now, I think I'll die."

"Don't die." She let her cloak slip from her shoulders and slid into his waiting arms. "Promise me you won't."

"I promise." His mouth covered hers to seal his pledge.

* * *

Her lips were soft and yielding. He tried to hold back, not to let the raging need overpower his ability to control it. She'd barely allowed him to touch her since they'd come to Dublin.

Then she moaned softly into his mouth and the beast sprang free. He answered her, bruising her lips with his, crushing her to him so he could feel her breasts pressed against his chest. His lips left hers and devoured her cheeks, her eyes, down the softness of her neck.

She didn't pull away.

Instead, her blessed fingers twined through his hair, pulling his head down. He sucked the skin at the base of her throat, tasting her sweet saltiness. Even in the dim firelight, he saw he was leaving love marks on her, but he couldn't seem to stop.

She didn't seem to want him to.

Even as his hands and mouth invaded, Brenna met him at every turn with encouragement—feverish whispers, an arched back pressing a soft breast into his hand. He felt a stiff nipple rise under the cloth of her tunic. He tried to unfasten the brooches at her shoulders, but couldn't get his clumsy fingers around the delicate catches. He heard the fabric ripping and gave it a stout tug, baring her to the waist.

She gasped, but didn't cry out.

Her breasts shone pale as moonstones, unbearably soft mounds of flesh, each topped with a sensitive tip, deep rose in color and quivering for his touch. He laid his head between them and decided, promise or no, he might just die, after all.

Her hands fluttered over his shoulders, a pair of butterflies teasing along his spine. He found a nipple and took it into his mouth, his tongue swirling ever-frenzied patterns around the sensitive flesh. She squirmed beneath him, murmuring his name.

It made him feel like a god.

Jorand fumbled with his trews, his patience quickly waning. Brenna's eyes drank him in as he bared himself to her, a soft smile on her angel mouth. She gave a low groan when his hand slid up under her hem.

Oh, the feel of her, all slick with need.

She opened herself to him, a warm, wet haven that molded around him to fit more perfectly than the finest knife-sheath. He slid into her up to the hilt, straining to be accepted in total, all his faults laid bare, just as he was.

She grasped his buttocks and pulled him closer yet.

Heat. Friction. Each stroke took him closer to the edge. Long past the point of being able to stop, he opened his eyes and looked down at her.

Her face was alight with passion, her skin glistening in the moonlight. She was close to the edge. He felt the start of her release in the mounting tension of her body.

"Come with me, love," she breathed as waves of delight rolled over her, arching her back to meet him.

He cried out as his seed burst forth inside her, his frame racked with spasms. He let his weight settle down on her, content to bury his nose in her hair and breathe her in.

He meant to say something, to tell her how he loved her, but by the time he rolled off her, Brenna was already breathing with the relaxed rhythm of deep sleep.

Jorand brushed a wayward strand of hair from her forehead. When he touched her cheek, the corner of her mouth lifted in a fleeting smile, but she didn't stir.

He didn't mind. He drank in the sight of her, relaxed with spent passion, the starlight playing over the hollows of her cheekbones. He longed to kiss her again, but didn't want to wake her. He closed his eyes, imprinting this vision of her on his memory, just in case this was the last time he'd see her thus.

He settled beside her and drew her into the circle of his arms. Then he passed silently from this waking dream into a deep dreamless sleep.

Chapter Thirty-three

"I hoped we'd be there before now." Jorand reined in his mount and dropped back on the trail to ride alongside her.

"Aye, but ye weren't counting on me having mending to do, I'll wager," Brenna countered, a wicked grin lifting the corners of her mouth as a wave of remembered passion surged over her. In the early morning light, she'd stitched up the front of her tunic and kyrtle. She was a dab hand with a needle, but the repair still meant getting a much later start for the last leg of their journey.

"I'd say I'm sorry about your clothes, but you'd know I'm not." He leaned over and kissed her, his mouth warm and firm. Her lips tingled when he pulled away.

"Well, and if it comes to that, I'm not feeling a bit sorry meself," she admitted. Blood sang joyously in her veins. Jorand was hers. Hers alone. And they were within a pinch of finding her sister's lost bairn.

If she were any happier, she'd sprout wings and fly the rest of the way.

Brenna and Jorand topped the last hill and looked down the velvety green slopes rushing to the river Shannon. The clans who lived near Clonmacnoise had been busy in the weeks since the raid. The wooden skeleton of a new chapel rose in the center of the desecrated abbey. The pounding of hammers and the steady thrum of two-man saws rent the air. Clonmacnoise had been washed clean of the reek of smoldering fires, and now the smell of newly hewn wood and cut thatch greeted the travelers.

Brenna and Jorand skirted round the abbey and wound their way to Murtaugh's little croft. The old man was seated on a stump outside his doorway, pipe in hand, soaking up the last remnants of the day's sun.

"Murtaugh, we're back!" Brenna called out as she dismounted and tied up the piebald cob she was riding.

"So ye be." He peered at her from under his scraggly brows, his sharp-eyed gaze raking Jorand as well. "I see ye still have the Northman in tow. If he saw ye safe to Dublin and back, I expect he might be worth the keeping."

Brenna noticed Jorand's lip twitched with suppressed amusement. She let Murtaugh's backhanded compliment pass without comment. "Where will we be finding the abbot?"

Murtaugh jerked his head toward the open cottage door.

Brenna spied Father Ambrose huddled over a makeshift desk inside Murtaugh's one-room croft. The sexton had evidently been evicted and Father

Ambrose had transformed the gardener's home into his private chambers until new ones were prepared for him in the rebuilt abbey.

Father Ambrose looked up when she stepped over the threshold. He'd dropped a stone or two in weight. His formerly pudgy cheeks now hung in flaccid jowls, making him look like an aging hunting dog. But his eyes were clear, and he no longer had the haunted look he'd worn when she'd last seen him. Father Ambrose didn't cross himself when Jorand followed her into the cottage, though he might have surreptitiously made the sign against evil with his left hand for a moment.

"Well, child." He laid aside the stylus he was writing with and fixed her with a hopeful look. "Were ye able to retrieve it?"

"Aye, Father." Brenna placed the oilskin packet on the desk as carefully as if it contained Germanic glass. "We brought most of it."

"What do ye mean—most of it?" A deep cleft formed between his brows as he tore open the package and rifled through the loose folios with a lack of delicacy that made Brenna want to jerk the Codex back from him. "Ah! The fiends! They've kept the jewels, then."

"Aye," Brenna said. "But we have the most important part still intact. The Word of God is surely the true treasure of the Skellig-Michael Codex, and it is restored to ye entire. We must be thankful for God's mercy."

"His mercy might spare the part that would pay for rebuilding Clonmacnoise," the abbot muttered under his breath.

Brenna knew the Codex had been an important

draw for pilgrims from the whole of the island and a valuable focus for donations as well. A look passed over the abbot's face, hard as flint and, had it been anyone but Father Ambrose, Brenna would have said she recognized the gleam of thwarted avarice. Then Father Ambrose seemed to remember he was not alone and quickly recovered himself. "Ye have the right of it. Thank ye, Brenna, and ye too, Northman. Go now in God's peace."

He gathered up the Codex and stashed it on one of the shelves that had lately held the sexton's vines and seedlings.When he turned around, he seemed startled to see Brenna and Jorand still there. Father Ambrose sketched a hasty blessing.

"Off ye go then." He waggled his fingers in a gesture of dismissal.

"Father, have ye forgotten your promise? We brought ye back the Codex." Brenna couldn't have been more stunned if he'd slapped her. "Ye must tell me where to find Sinead's bairn."

The abbot harrumphed loudly and made a great show of blowing his nose. "Our agreement was conditional on the return of the Skellig Michael Gospels. Ye must admit, the Codex is somewhat less than it once was."

Jorand closed the distance to the abbot in a few strides, snatching up Father Ambrose by his cowled cassock and slamming him against the back wall of Murtaugh's little house. Dust jarred loose from the rafters and rained a spatter of mud chips and old thatch on them. "You'll tell her what she wants to know and quickly. Or perhaps you'd like to be less than you once were as well."

Father Ambrose blanched, and his eyes rolled uncertainly. Brenna put a restraining hand on Jorand's arm. In response to the commotion, Murtaugh had slipped into the cottage behind them. The abbot had reneged on his promise, so she didn't have much sympathy for him, but Brenna didn't want to see Jorand do the sexton any damage should Murtaugh decide to rush to Father Ambrose's aid. But Murtaugh just looked on, sucking on his pipe with an air of expectancy on his wizened face.

"There's no need for ye to do him harm, husband," she said, her voice mild as milk. "I'm sure the abbot will see the wisdom of keeping to his part of the bargain."

Jorand lowered the priest till his feet touched the dirt floor once more. He stepped back a pace to give Father Ambrose room to breathe, but Jorand's eyes still glinted with the promise of mayhem if his wishes were ignored.

" 'Tis not that, not at all." Sweat popped out on Father Ambrose's broad forehead, and he mopped his brow with a grimy kerchief. "I'd hoped to spare ye more grief, my child."

"Where is me sister's bairn?"

"The babe is dead," he said flatly.

"You lie. I'll not believe it." Brenna balled her hands into fists, longing to lunge at the abbot herself. White-hot anger flared inside her. If he were anyone else, she'd have scratched his eyes out. "The bairn can't be dead."

Father Ambrose just looked at her, a mixture of pity and suffering benevolence on his face.

"How could you send us in search of the Codex if the child were not still alive?" she demanded.

The abbot's gaze flicked to Jorand. "You had a

Northman with you. I saw the slimmest of chances that the abbey could recover one of its lost treasures. I regret that I had to trick you into doing the right thing, but I'd do it again for the good of the Clonmacnoise."

No. Brenna opened her mouth, but no sound came out. She felt as though someone had kicked her in the ribs and knocked all the breath from her lungs. Not trusting her wobbling knees to support her any longer, she sank down on the three-legged stool by the abbot's desk.

"... never any real chance at life, given its sire, so we might well consider its passing a blessing. In times like these, we must call to mind ..."

The abbot droned on about God's mercy and the inscrutability of His perfect will, but Brenna heard none of it. Only the echo of the child's birth cry, a lusty wail half remembered, like something from a feverish dream, resounded in her ears.

A weight settled on her shoulder—Jorand's hand, she realized. She knew he was trying to console her, but like Rachel in Ramah, she would not be comforted, for the child was not.

"Was it a boy or a girl?" she asked, neither knowing nor caring that she interrupted Father Ambrose as he was working into the moral of his sermonette.

"There's no need to trouble yourself any furth—" the abbot began.

"Sinead bore a lad," Murtaugh said. "A bonnie wee manikin with a tuft of red on his little head."

"Enough." Father Ambrose scowled at the sexton.

"But how? How did he die?" she asked.

The abbot's eyes flared a warning at Murtaugh, then turned back to Brenna. "Let the past be, my child. No good will come from—"

"Where is he?" Brenna demanded. "Ye must at least tell me that. Where does he lie?"

The abbot's thick lips flattened into a hard line. "All the indigent poor are gathered to God in one place." He turned around as though he couldn't bear the sight of Brenna one moment longer. "Grieve, if ye must, at Potter's Field."

The graveyard of Clonmacnoise was a peaceful place, rows of headstones and standing crosses, some so covered with moss and weathered by rain and time, the inscriptions had faded to no more than dimples in the stone.

There were many fresh mounds, the loamy soil bare and dark against the green. Old Murtaugh had been busy with burials for those whose bodies had not been consigned to the flames. Mother Superior. Brother Bartolomeo. Sister Mary Patrick. Brenna ticked off the names as she passed their final resting places. Many of the cemetery's new occupants had been her friends, but she couldn't think on that now.

One grief at a time, she told herself as she trudged through the silent rows. If she let the enormity of the loss sink in, she'd be done for.

She stopped before Sinead's grave. Brenna had seen to it an ornate cross was erected for her sister before she left Clonmacnoise to return to Donegal. Grass covered the mound thickly now.

"Oh, Sinead," she said with a sob. "I'm so sorry."

She'd failed her sister, and there was no way to make amends. She had no flowers, nothing to leave at the graveside. Then she reached up and clasped the silver cross necklace that had belonged to their mother. She draped it over her sister's headstone.

"Ye were the first true bride among us," she said softly. "Mother sends this to ye."

She turned away and continued her mourning march. Her step slowed even further as she neared the far corner of the patch of consecrated ground.

Potter's Field.

It was a gaping mass grave, where the bodies of the poor and unknown were stitched into shrouds and dropped in. The pit reeked of the lye used to mask the miasma of putrefaction, but a hint of the sweet stench of corruption reached her nostrils. Brenna's knees buckled and she sank to the ground near the lip of the pit.

To end thus ... unnamed ... unloved ... unmourned. How could she have let Sinead's babe come to this? The lad may have had an ill-getting, but the blood of Sinead Ui Niall flowed in his veins as well. If only she'd defied the abbot and fought for the child when it was born....

"Sweet Jesus, forgive me," she whispered, praying as much to the little ghost that had hovered near her for the past year and the memory of her beloved sister as to Christ. Brenna wrapped her arms around herself to keep from flying in all directions. Her pulse throbbed in her ears and she swayed in time with the steady rhythm. Tears ran down her cheeks. Her breath came in a rasping sob as she gave vent to her grief in a banshee's wail.

She felt Jorand's strong arms around her. He knelt by her side, holding her as she cried. His breath slid hot and comforting across the back of her neck and she finally quieted in his embrace. He smelled of sun-warmed wool and stiff sea breezes. Vibrant. *Alive.*

She dissolved into fresh spasms of despair.

"Brenna, my love, be easy." He stroked her hair, pressing her to his chest. "There's naught you can do for the bairn now. You'll make yourself sick."

"I *am* sick. Sick at heart." She beat her fists against her thighs, and he caught up her wrists to keep her from hurting herself. "If only I'd fought to keep him . . ."

"What? You think you could have kept Death from claiming him?"

She met his steady gaze. That was exactly what she thought.

"My people believe a man's death is determined before he is even born, fixed by the Norns, the three weavers of human fate. Run from Death on the sea and he will find you in the forest," Jorand said with certainty. "Do Christians think they can cheat Death, then?"

"No," she said soberly. "No, we cannot cheat death." She swiped her cheeks. "But we live in hope. I must live in hope that in the resurrection, I will be allowed to hold the babe. And I will place him in Sinead's arms for the first time."

A pained expression flitted across Jorand's face, and she knew they were truly joined. He felt her grief.

"Brenna, let's leave this place," he said, closing his hands around both of hers in a doubled gesture of prayer. "Let me take you away from here. The world is bigger than you can imagine. We can forget the grief of this island and start fresh together somewhere else. We'll go to the Hebrides or the Faroes, or even back to Sognefjord. I'll give you children, Brenna, a whole houseful of them, I promise. Only say you'll come away with me."

She ran a knuckle over his cheek. What was it she recognized in his anxious eyes? Fear? Not in a Northman, surely. Then the truth stabbed her, a thin stiletto to the heart. "Ye fear I'll depart, like me mother, into the deep darkness over the loss of the bairn."

He looked down and then back at her with a swift nod.

"Ye must understand. A small piece of me heart will always be here. It cannot be otherwise. I owe as much to Sinead." She clutched at her chest, feeling the rhythm of her heartbeat under her breastbone. She was amazed it was so steady. Despite all she'd been through, she still breathed, still felt her regular heartbeat.

"But I'm not so fine a lady as me mother to be completely undone by loss. I have more of the Ui Niall stubbornness in me than Connacht sensibilities." As if to give lie to her words, tears coursed freely down her cheeks and stung the corners of her mouth. "The wee bairn who rests here will have a small piece of me. 'Tis fitting that he should. But the rest of me is yours till I die."

"Then you'll come away with me." Brenna felt relief roll from him in caressing waves.

"No, love, I cannot go," she said. "Not to any foreign land. I'm born of Erin and bound to her shores. But I will travel with ye to stop Thorkill from overrunning me island. We cannot let him have his way with the people of this land."

The look of shock on his strongly hewn features told her he'd all but forgotten about Thorkill. Now that she'd reminded him, a gritty air of resignation and determination settled over him once more.

"No, Brenna," he said. "You can't come on this

raid. It's too dangerous." He didn't need to add *especially this time,* but Brenna heard it hovering in the air anyway.

"Then I'll wait in Dublin for ye to return."

"In the same town as Solveig?" His brows shot up in surprise.

"I'll bide with Father Armaugh in his wee church till ye come for me. I doubt Solveig will be darkening the door of the Lord's house. I'll be safe enough there."

"No, that won't work. Armaugh is no longer in Dublin." He raised his hands as if to ward off her questions. "Don't ask how I know, but trust me for it. He's long gone."

"Then if Murtaugh will travel with me, I must hie meself to Donegal before winter comes," Brenna said, placing one hand over her abdomen. "Ye'll come to me there?"

"*Ja,* my princess," he promised, sealing the oath with a kiss. "If I've breath in my body, I'll be in Donegal before our handfast year is over. You said I may have you till you die, and I mean to claim you at your word."

Chapter Thirty-four

Rain pelted them steadily, the drizzling mist dripping off the horse's tack, off the trees whose low-hung branches thrashed her as they plodded past, off Murtaugh's disreputable old hat and off Brenna's chin. The sky had wept for her for the last two days, ever since she parted from Jorand, heading north over the moors and through the glens to Donegal.

Murtaugh had insisted they come this way, following the Shannon upriver, instead of cutting across country as she had when she'd made the trip to and from Clonmacnoise as a novice. She didn't recognize any of the landmarks. Brenna was certain the old man was taking her the long way around, and the journey was a long weary way without his adding anything to it. She raised a sodden sleeve to her nose to catch a sneeze. Brenna decided irritably she'd never be warm or dry again.

"Not far now," Murtaugh called up to her in encouragement, his croaking voice reminding her of an ancient bullfrog. When she'd been ill again that morning, he strapped most of their provisions onto his own bent back, cooking pots dangling from his waist, and insisted she ride. Watching him slog through the mud ahead of her, she felt ashamed of her grumbling self-pity.

"The husbandman I bought a beef from last season has a wee house in the next glen but one," Murtaugh said, waving a gnarled hand toward the unseen refuge. "We'll bide there till the weather clears."

Brenna nodded mutely. *There! There it is again. Or did I just imagine it?*

A brief flutter, light as a butterfly coming to rest on a thistle, stirred deep in her belly.

She hadn't breathed a word of her suspicions to Jorand. She was too afraid voicing them would make it not true. Even if she was right in her surmise, he didn't need the burden of knowing he might become a father when he was about to go into danger. He could not afford any distractions in battle.

Without Jorand, she felt adrift, alone with her thoughts and had more than enough time to examine her grief.

She'd brought the Codex back only to have her hopes dashed by the news of the child's death. Now she had no way to atone for the grief she'd caused her sister. She'd won the love of her husband only to have him yanked by ill-chance into a struggle over the fate of the whole of Erin.

Brenna closed her eyes, letting her mount pick his own way after Murtaugh. She prayed feverishly for Jorand's safety. It was all she could do.

Her head lolled forward and she nodded to sleep in the saddle. Nightmarish images of Jorand fighting Kolgrim in the *holmhring,* flashes of lightning reducing both of them to stark skeletal figures, Solveig's bloodred mouth curved in a taunting smile, and the pit of Potter's Field all jumbled together in disjointed visions.

With gratitude, she jerked to wakefulness at Murtaugh's loud "Hello, the house!"

She saw a tidy cottage, ringed by the forest. The remains of a fruitful garden stood nearby. The produce was all gathered in against the coming winter, empty brown stalks rattling against a small cattle byre.

"Murtaugh? Heaven bless me, is that ye?" The crofter in the clearing stopped chopping wood in midswing and strode toward them in welcome. He was a man of middle years, still strong, but with thinning hair slicked back above a plain, honest face. He clasped forearms with Murtaugh, then smiled up at Brenna. "No amount of foul weather will hurt this old devil, but an' ye forgive me for sayin' so, miss, ye look fair done in. Hie ye both inside, and me wife will get some good hot broth into ye."

As the two men bundled her beneath the low lintel, Brenna learned the farmer's name was Finian and his wife, a moderately stout young lady about ten years his junior, was called Grainne.

"Mary, Michael, and St. Bride, but ye're soaked clear through!" Grainne exclaimed after introductions were made. "Come ye with me and we'll see ye set to rights."

The main room of the cottage held the fire pit ringed with Grainne's cooking utensils, a sturdy table and stools, and cupboards lining one wall. Woven strands of onions and garlic hung from the rafters. Brenna noticed a set of stone stairs along one wall disappearing down into a *souterraine* beneath the cottage, full of pumpkins and other assorted gourds, no doubt.

Gratefully, Brenna trailed her hostess behind a cloth partition in the small house. The couple's bed stood behind the curtain, a thick straw tick with a number of woolen coverlets. Brenna could've happily tumbled into it and not come out for a week. She tried not to let her longing show when she looked at the bed.

"Here ye be, Brenna," Grainne was saying as she pulled an old tunic from the trunk at the foot. "A mite big for ye, I'd expect, but dry enough forbye."

"'Tis heaven to be out of me damp things," she said as she peeled off her soggy tunic. Brenna swam in the borrowed clothing, but the fabric was soft and warm against her skin. "I thank ye."

From the dark corner of the curtained space, she heard a soft sound. She strained her eyes to see in the dimness as the noise grew in intensity and finally launched into a full blown wail.

"I'm sorry. I've waked your child," Brenna said.

"Ach! Don't fash yourself. His little Highness was needin' to be woke or he'll be keeping me up all night." Grainne scooped up the child in her capable arms and he quieted immediately. "Murtaugh'll be wanting to see the bairn anyway, him being the lad's godfather, ye see."

They rejoined the men in the warm main room and this time Brenna's nose pricked to the savory aroma coming from the kettle suspended over the central fire. A few raindrops dribbled in through the smokehole in the little cottage's roof and hissed on the heated stones ringing the blaze. Thankfully, most of the smoke seemed to be drifting out the same opening.

Grainne plopped the child onto Murtaugh's lap,

and a small hand flailed up to grasp Murtaugh's scraggy beard.

"Ho there Rory, me wee red king!" The boy promptly grabbed his godfather's nose and pulled himself up to a wobbly standing position on the old man's bony knees. "Walking now, is it?"

"Aye," Finian said with pride. "Set him down and let him try a step or two. He started that a day or so ago."

Brenna watched in fascination as the child bobbled from one set of adult legs to the next, venturing halting, unassisted steps between each safe haven as he worked his way around the fire pit toward her. A lead weight gathered in her chest even as she smiled at the boy's antics. She counted back the months in her mind. Had he lived, she figured Sinead's child would have been of an age with Grainne and Finian's little Rory.

"Hello." She leaned toward him when his dimpled hand lighted on her knees. He gabbled a string of nonsense sounds in answer.

Grainne laughed. "A talker, that one. No doubt, he has the makings of a great bard."

The great bard evidently had enough of walking on his own and lifted both his chubby arms to Brenna to be picked up. She plucked him up without any more encouragement, realizing that her arms ached to do so.

Rory gave her a one-toothed grin and then tried to jam his whole fist into his mouth. Brenna studied the boy closely. His hair curled over his head in a profusion of red, gold, and roan. The barest hint of auburn brows drew together in consternation as it became apparent to him he couldn't gnaw his own hand without feeling pain.

The boy's face was snub-nosed in the manner of all bairns, the jaw and cheeks too puffed with baby fat for Brenna to tell what manner of man he'd make. But the lad's eyes drew her rapt attention. Behind a fringe of ruddy lashes, her sister's eyes, gray with silver flecks, stared back at her.

Sinead bore a boy. A bonny wee manikin with a tuft of red on his little head.

She glanced across the fire at Murtaugh, the question burning in her gaze. His thin lips drew downward even as he shrugged an assent. Rory began to struggle in her arms, fussing in frustration over the inadequacy of his fist.

"He'll be hungry again. Are ye not, me fine wee fiend?" Grainne lifted him from Brenna's lap and settled the boy on her own. She drew out an ample breast, blue with bulging veins, and gave the boy suck. His eyes closed in ecstasy, auburn lashes quivering against his cheeks.

Grainne sighed, the placid contentment of nursing mothers stealing over her. She hummed softly under her breath.

"He's a beautiful child," Brenna said, fighting to keep from reaching out to fondle the curls glinting copper in the firelight.

"Aye, he's a good-hearted lad, too," Grainne said with pride. "Though Finian and me can scarce take the credit. Rory is me angel sent straight from heaven."

"Grainne," Finian's voice held a note of warning.

"Sure and the truth never did harm," Grainne countered. "Brenna here is friend to Murtaugh. That's good enough for me."

"What did ye mean when ye say Rory is your angel?"

"Murtaugh can tell ye that tale as well as me, I'd expect," she answered, but being the sort who enjoyed the sound of her own voice, Grainne went on. "Me own bairn died in his crib not a month after his birth. He was a goodly boy too, but a mite puny and, truth to tell, not near as bonny as wee Rory."

Finian harrumphed loudly. Untroubled by her husband's interruption, Grainne babbled on. "I was fair wild with grief, ye see. Wouldn't let Finian even bury the boy. But I prayed, aye, and prayed mightily.

"But the Almighty had somewhat different in mind than I asked for," Grainne conceded as she shifted the boy to her other breast. "And the next night, who should come bearing a newborn babe in his arms but our own Murtaugh."

Rory's pudgy hand patted Grainne's swollen breast. "And me still heavy with milk," she added as though that cinched the matter. "Murtaugh had visited us the month before. He knew I'd born a child and had milk enough for two." Her voice had a slight catch. "Of course, I only needed milk for one by then. I came to me senses and let Finian bury our dear little Dermot under yon hawthorn. So ye see why I say Rory is me angel."

A dull ache in her chest, Brenna had to admit the child at Grainne's breast did have a cherubic look about him. Who'd have thought a brute like Kolgrim could father such a sweet boy?

And what, by all that's holy, am I to do about it now?

The next morning, a thin sun broke through the clouds but gave no added warmth to the earth. A chill wind, an early breath of winter, swirled Brenna's skirt and slid its icy fingers down her neck as she stepped out of the cottage. She hadn't slept well on her pallet by the fire, dreaming fitfully of a red-haired lad and her flaxen-haired man, but now the brisk air jolted her fully awake.

Finian appeared from the trees, coming up a path from the river bearing a yoke with two buckets of water, sloshing full.

"Good morrow," Brenna said with false cheer, her decision made and nothing to be gained in delay. Her gaze swept around the small farmstead. A swaybacked gelding leaned, one hoof crooked up in repose, against the cattle byre. "I notice ye have a spare mount there."

"Not exactly a spare," Finian said as he set the buckets down. "I use old Reuben for spring planting. He's all we have now."

"And probably not much use over the winter but to eat up your extra grain and fill a stable with muck, aye?"

"Ye've the right of it, there, miss."

"Would ye lend him to me then? 'Tis a long way to Donegal and we've only the one horse between us, Murtaugh and me." Brenna reached for the leather pouch and held it out to him, giving it a shake. The bag emitted a satisfying jingle. "This should do for his hire. Murtaugh will be coming back by the time ye have need of him and can see him back to ye safe before spring."

Finian hefted the pouch and looked inside. His brows shot up in surprise.

"Ach! Beggin' your pardon, but 'tis plain ye've no eye for horseflesh. 'Tis not a fair trade," he said. "This would buy a dozen the likes of old Reuben. I cannot take your coin under false pretense."

Honest and fair. She already knew Grainne would protect Rory like a she-wolf would her pup. She was satisfied Finian had the character she wanted instilled in her sister's son. Could she ask for more?

Aye, to have him meself.

She quickly stomped down the selfish desire. After seeing Rory with the couple, she knew she couldn't yank the child from the only parents he'd ever known. She couldn't do it to Grainne and Finian, who obviously adored Rory. And she wouldn't do it to Sinead's boy.

"Let's say the coin is for the lad, then," Brenna said evenly. "He needs to be taught his letters when he's of age. See to his education with the extra. It would please me greatly to hear that your Rory grew to be a man of learning. Will ye do that for me?"

"Aye, with a willing heart," Finian said, tugging his forelock in respect. "I'm after thankin' ye." He shook his head in wonderment. "Learning for me son. That's a bargain I can live with."

"There is a priest in Donegal, Father Michael, who'd be willing to advise ye on the lad's education. When the time comes, I'll have him arrange for a tutor to be sent to ye." Then Brenna's face brightened with another thought. "Me father is Brian Ui Niall of Donegal. He'd foster the boy when he's of age if ye like. Or mayhap ye and Grainne might wish to come to Donegal as well. Me father would see ye settled on a fine parcel if it came to that."

"Murtaugh told me ye were a princess, and I guess I hadn't believed it till now." Finian stowed the pouch of silver and hoisted his buckets once more.

"It wouldn't do for the likes of me to question me betters, but I do wonder at your interest in Rory."

Had he noticed that the lad's eyes were like hers?

She waved her hand dismissively. "He's a bonny child and of lively intelligence. Anyone can see that. If I wish to help him along in life, ye'll not deny me, will ye?"

"Not for worlds," Finian said. "Thank ye, I'm sure."

Brenna turned away to curry Reuben and to inspect her sorry end of the deal. She examined his hooves and determined Reuben was strong enough to bear Murtaugh's weight. The gelding was decidedly long in the tooth but still sound.

"That was well done, lass," the old man said as he joined her in the stable yard.

"Aye, well, I didn't want to think of your old legs walking the whole weary way to me father's keep."

"I meant about the lad."

"He belongs with Grainne and Finian. Ye saw to that." Brenna brushed Reuben's flank so hard small plumes of dust rose from his hide. "I don't see as I had much choice."

"Aye, ye did now," Murtaugh disagreed. "And for what it's worth, ye made the right one."

"Is that why ye brought me here? So it would be my choice? Or maybe ye've been feeling guilty over keeping the truth from me?"

"There is that," Murtaugh said. "I didna hold with the abbot's decision in the first place, but he meant it for the best. And as bitter as ye were at the time of the lad's birth, I cannot but think he might have been right. Dinna be surly toward the abbot on that account. But I couldna let ye think the boy dead."

"What if I wanted to take him now?" She put

down the curry comb and leveled her gaze at the old man. "Would ye help me?"

"*What if* is a bridge over a far river that leads to fairy land," Murtaugh admonished as he started to load their provisions on Reuben's bowed back. "Let's be off. We've a fair bit to go before we see Donegal's keep."

"About that," Brenna said. "Do ye know the way to Ulaid? To Conaill Murtheinne?"

"Aye," he said. "And it's a good bit closer than Donegal."

"Good," she said with a sudden longing in her chest, sharper than a blade. If anyone could help her fill the lonely time till Jorand rejoined her, it was Moira. She felt the strange little flutter in her belly again and smiled. "I'm needing to see me sister Moira. Queen Moira of the Ulaid."

As they plodded out of the little clearing, Brenna felt the peace of forgiveness descend on her heart. Sinead could rest easy now. Brenna had seen to her bairn and would continue to mark his progress to manhood. In time, perhaps Finian and Grainne might even bring the boy to Donegal.

Brenna's conscience pricked her. She'd never been able to tell her father that Sinead was dead. Once a girl took the veil she was all but dead to her former life, so perhaps Brian Ui Niall need not be burdened with the truth now. Mayhap it was a telling that could wait, Brenna decided, till she could present her father with a living grandson to lessen the pain of a dead daughter. When Rory came someday to Donegal, Brian Ui Niall would recognize Sinead's slate-gray eyes, and his own for that matter, in Grainne and Finian's cherished lad.

Chapter Thirty-five

Moonlight wavered in a jagged streak of silver across the Irish Sea. From their lookout in the sheltered cove, Jorand could see the Island of St. Patrick, a bare knob of rock rising from the frothing waves, with its shrine casting a dark silhouette against the star-dappled eastern horizon.

"We've been here two days," Thorkill grumbled. "Are you sure about the time?"

"*Ja,*" Kolgrim said. "The pig of an Irishman I questioned about it wouldn't have lied to me. I threatened to cut off his ballocks if he didn't tell me everything I wanted to know. A man will tell you anything to protect that bit of skin." He laughed unpleasantly at his own crude humor, then shrugged, wincing as he cradled his barely healed arm. It had not been well set and though he still had use of it, Kolgrim would always be in pain. "Of course, I cut 'em off anyway when he was done singing. Now he'll sing a pretty tune for the rest of his unnatural life."

"Quiet," Jorand ordered. "Sound travels over water, in case you've forgotten. Are you trying to give away our position?"

More than anything he wanted to shut Kolgrim up. Jorand was grateful to be away from Dublin again. He didn't feel at home among his own people anymore, and he feared Thorkill would sense it. But being trapped in a longship with Kolgrim was even worse. Listening to the man's lewd tales of rapine and cruelty made Jorand's gut curdle. How had he ever fallen in with this lot?

Before he left Dublin with Thorkill, Jorand arranged to award all his property to Solveig, including his boat, as settlement in the dissolution of their marriage. As he suspected, she wasn't long in replacing him. The knowledge didn't pain him in the slightest.

He was more concerned about the success of his current scheme. He wished fervently there'd been more time to plan, some way to know if Bjorn's part in his plot had borne fruit. The day after Jorand and Brenna left Dublin, Bjorn was to snatch Father Armaugh and sail him to Ulaid. Jorand figured the Irish would never believe a Northman who warned them of an impending raid, so the priest would have to do it. But would the Ulaid trust a priest who ministered to Northmen?

Through Armaugh, Jorand had given the Irish everything they needed to mount an assault on Thorkill's raiders, including their present location. He scanned the craggy mainland, looking for any sign of archers. From the sea, the Northmen were totally hidden, but from the cliff face, they were vulnerable as a naked babe. If Moira's husband and his men were there, the battle would be over before it began.

Would the Irish go along with Jorand's scheme? Or had they imprisoned or killed his friends and proceeded with the queen's yearly pilgrimage as planned?

Jorand found himself praying often, though not for himself. He promised Brenna he'd return to Donegal, but he realized now that was wishful thinking. He fully expected to die in the upcoming fight. It would be fitting for a traitor and oath-breaker. He deserved no less than death for his treachery. But he prayed for Brenna.

May she come safe to Donegal, and may she find happiness, even if it be without me.

And surprisingly enough, he found himself praying to her Christian God. He was sure the Norse gods would take a dim view of him since he was even now betraying Thorkill and the men who went viking with him. But Brenna's Christ was betrayed by one of his friends, and yet He forgave the betrayer.

If any god would listen to the prayers of a traitor, surely Brenna's would.

The waves lapping against the side of the longship and the cries of night birds were such a constant he failed to hear them anymore. Suddenly, his ears pricked to a new sound.

Feminine laughter. A silvery peal floated over the water.

Moira.

The distant outline of an ungainly Irish craft appeared around a spit of land, sail billowed in the fresh breeze. The flapping fabric glared white in the moonlight.

So they'd come just the same. The damned stiff-necked Irish had sent defenseless women into harm even after being warned of the danger.

Then he heard another voice, lower in pitch, but musical and soothing nonetheless. Though he couldn't make out her words, the timbre was unmistakable.

Brenna.

Panic curled in his belly like an adder poised to strike. What was she doing here? She should be safe in her father's keep by now.

"Put your backs to it, men," Thorkill roared. "The virgins are here. Let's not keep them waiting."

Jorand's mind whirled at this new development. He gripped an oar, wondering how to keep Brenna out of the coming melee.

Twelve oars lifted in unison and sliced the dark waves, setting the longship bounding toward the hapless Irish vessel. Thorkill ran up the broad sail, and the dragonship quickened its race over the choppy waves, like a living predator hastening to devour its prey.

"Row faster, damn you!" Thorkill bellowed.

A woman's scream pierced Jorand's ear. He couldn't tell whether it was Brenna or not.

Christ, how am I to save her?

The daughters of Erin had spotted the longship, but there was no way for the Irish coracle to outrun them, even if the monks hadn't foolishly lowered their sail. It was as if they wanted the Northmen to close the distance as quickly as possible.

Beside him on the opposite oar, Kolgrim grunted with the effort of each stroke. He suspected Kolgrim was already stiff with the need to dominate and destroy.

Jorand glanced back over his shoulder and caught a glimpse of Brenna standing in the prow of the Irish craft, a thin glint of metal in her hand. She was armed with a knife. And she'd positioned herself in front of her sister. Still protecting Moira, like when he'd first met her.

In spite of the gravity of the situation, a smile tugged at the corner of his mouth.

Trust my Brenna to be prepared to do a man hurt.

The longship pulled even with the Irish vessel and Thorkill tossed a grappling hook across the narrow distance. The wicked-looking hook snagged the side of the craft, which dipped dangerously into the waves, caught as surely as a harpooned whale. At Thorkill's bellowed order, the rowers stood their oars on end, preparing to ship them.

Jorand pivoted on his seat and sized up the situation. Just a few more arm-lengths. As soon as the longship was close enough, he'd leap across the waves and plant himself in front of Brenna and Moira at the prow to defend them against all comers.

Damn the Irish for a stubborn, ignorant race! Jorand thought, furious at Fearghus of Ulaid for sending the women to St. Patrick's after his warning, for not mounting the assault he'd recommended. He couldn't do anything to help the pious virgins on board the hide-covered coracle, but he'd sell his life dearly trying to protect his wife and her sister.

Then suddenly the virgins threw off their cloaks and Jorand's eyes widened at the image of bewhiskered warriors with arrows nocked on the string. A hail of fletched death buzzed around him. He was shocked by a dull thud, then a sharp sting to his side. A long shaft quivered in his bicep, pinioning the arm against his chest. He tried to move it and felt the burn of rending flesh as the arrowhead grated against a rib. At this close range, the force of the shot sent the arrow through his arm and then on through the hardened leather encasing his torso as well.

"No!" He heard Brenna wail. "Not him. He wasn't to be touched. Ye promised."

Beside Jorand, a *berserkr* scream tore loose from Kolgrim's throat and the man vaulted over him. Obviously unhurt by the first volley, Kolgrim launched himself at the Irish before they could raise another arrow.

Jorand stood in the swaying longship. The Irish surprise had been effective. More than half the raiders lay dead or grievously wounded. He felt like a goose on a spit himself. But no matter what, he had to fight. He'd defend Brenna with his last breath.

He ground his teeth together and reached over to snap off the shaft where it protruded from his left arm. He took as deep a breath as he could with the embedded point still poised to graze his lung and threw his skewered arm out, raking the arrow through his flesh. A flash of light burst in his brain as the arrowhead shifted and burrowed deeper, but at least his arm was free.

He looked over at Brenna, still frozen in place. Her face was silvery white in the moonlight. She screamed.

He gritted his teeth as he broke off the last ten finger-widths of the arrow's length where it entered his rib cage, leaving the point where it had lodged. Then he drew out his sword with a metallic rasp, roared his defiance, and leaped onto the Irish vessel.

Everything was a blur of flailing arms and an unnaturally slow dance of death as time expanded and contracted around him. He was acutely aware of a host of tiny details—the coppery scent of blood on the wind, the cold water lapping at his ankles as the

Irish boat groaned under the extra weight of the raiders, the piteous bleating of an Irishman who held his own entrails in his hands.

When faced with an Irish defender, Jorand tried to do no more than meet his blade as he hacked his way toward Brenna. He dipped and whirled, parrying their slashing blows, as he knocked them out of his way.

But suddenly Jorand found himself face to face with Thorkill. "Defend yourself," Jorand shouted as his blade flashed toward Solveig's father.

Thorkill's face registered shock, but reaction was swift. He bared his teeth and turned the full fury of his broadsword on Jorand. Between the hail of blows Jorand was barely able to parry, the master of Dublin growled out, "I will take this woman and this island. Why are you trying to stop me?"

"There'll be no taking tonight. I won't let you." He had no breath for words as Thorkill rained a storm of blows on him. Jorand met his blade at each stroke and managed to turn it, even though the force of the assault rattled up his forearms and jolted his shoulders.

Luck was with him in some sense, Jorand realized dimly. If not for the cramped confines of the Irish craft, Thorkill would have been able to swing his broadsword wider and with more power. As it was, Jorand was barely able to fend off the attack of the larger man.

Darkness gathered at the edges of Jorand's vision. He forced himself to draw a deep breath to keep the blackness at bay. He seemed to move in slow motion as he struggled to keep his footing. Behind him, he heard a man scream, not knowing or caring if it was a

Northman or one of the Irish defenders. The air was heavy with blood and bile and the stench of fear. A sliver of moonlight caught on Thorkill's upraised blade and Jorand saw his chance.

He buried his sword up to the hilt in his father-in-law's midsection.

Thorkill's eyes widened in surprise, then faded into an unseeing gaze. Jorand yanked at his sword, but couldn't free it from his foe's flesh.

"I knew it!" Kolgrim hissed from behind Thorkill. "A traitor at the last."

Jorand jumped sideways in time to dodge his enemy's slashing blow. He scrambled past Kolgrim toward the prow, the hide-bottom boat underfoot slick with water and blood. Fortunately, Kolgrim's broken arm made him slower.

"Brenna." He'd finally reached her, but he was unarmed with no way to defend her. He could only place his body between her and Kolgrim and pray he didn't live long enough to see her end. "I'm sorry, love."

"No need. I regret nothing, husband." Her lips trembled in a crooked smile and she handed him her dirk.

It wasn't much, but it was better than nothing.

"Thank Christ for small mercies," Jorand muttered as he grabbed the knife from her. Then he turned back to meet Kolgrim's steady advance.

Over Kolgrim's head, Jorand could see the fight was still in question with tight little knots of hand-to-hand struggle. Northmen disappeared under gang assaults by the wiry Irish. Men of Ulaid were hacked piecemeal by a two-handed broadsword when a Northman found room to wield his weapon. But Kolgrim alone threatened Brenna and her sister.

"Thorkill isn't here to stop me from killing you this time," Jorand said, blood pounding through his veins in the frenzy of battle lust.

"I'll finish you, Jorand. And then I'll do your woman." He snarled as he whipped his sword in a slashing horizontal stroke.

Jorand leaped back from the glittering blade, feeling Brenna's warmth behind him. He couldn't dodge one of Kolgrim's blows again without shoving the women into the dark sea.

Malice dripped in Kolgrim's tone. "She'll beg me for death before I let her go, by Odin's lost eye, I swear it."

Kolgrim's sword flashed at him. It was as long as his arm, making the little blade Jorand wielded of no use at all except as a buffer to catch and turn the other man's blow. At some point, Jorand knew he'd miscalculate and be struck down. Brenna would be defenseless.

Kolgrim's next slice broke Jorand's Irish dirk off at the haft. The length of the blade disappeared into the ankle-deep bloody water in the coracle's hull.

Kolgrim bared his teeth and tossed him a wolf's laugh. "You've broken your oath to Thorkill. You don't deserve a battle-death. Jormungand will rend your flesh before daylight. I'll let the sea finish its work."

Kolgrim's sword whistled toward Jorand and this time struck him. But it was the flat of the blade, not its edge that connected with his temple. Brenna's scream pierced his ear. The blow sent him over the edge of the bobbing coracle and into the dark Irish sea.

The cold water jolted him, nearly making him expel all the air in his lungs. Silence closed around him like a heavy blanket. Moonlight filtered down through the murky sea for only the height of a man. He clawed his way back to the surface.

When he breached and dragged in a lungful of salty air, the sight in the coracle made him wish Kolgrim had used the sharp edge of his blade instead of the flat.

Brenna was on her knees before his enemy. Head down, she pulled her *brat* from her shoulders in abject submission. Moira clutched the prow behind her.

God, no. Jorand was powerless to save her. The water sucked at him, trying to drag him down. He almost let it.

"Come to me, my little Irish slut," Kolgrim taunted. "I enjoy watching you beg, but as long as you're on your knees, you may as well make yourself useful." He grasped his own crotch and laughed raucously.

Brenna rose to her feet, the brat dripping in her hand. "Aye, I'll come to ye," Jorand heard her say. "And I'll be very useful."

Slowly Brenna walked toward Kolgrim. She stopped before him, disarming him with a tremulous smile. Jorand caught sight of a sudden flash of metal concealed in her *brat*.

Brenna hadn't knelt before Kolgrim, pleading for mercy, Jorand realized. She'd been searching for the knife. She'd found the dirk's broken blade where it dropped in the shallow bilge and wrapped it in her short cape to keep from cutting her own fingers on the sharp edges.

"I'll be useful to send ye to Hell." Brenna thrust the blade into Kolgrim's chest. Then she leaped back out of his reach.

Kolgrim gasped in shock, the whites of his eyes

showing all around. He staggered toward the women, but lost his balance, teetered for a moment, then fell headlong into the waves.

Jorand roared and plowed the water toward Kolgrim. If it was the last thing he did, he'd make sure of Kolgrim's end. He grabbed his enemy and the two men disappeared into the deep.

Locked in a death grip, Jorand and Kolgrim sank together into blackness so deep, neither could see the other's face.

Kolgrim turned and rolled, struggling to free himself. Jorand knew if his enemy could put enough distance between them, Kolgrim would be able to use his sword, if he still held it. Jorand found the end of the dirk sticking out between Kolgrim's ribs, and shoved the dagger in farther. The arrowhead in his own rib cage shifted and he felt his mind waver uncertainly.

An explosion of bubbles rushed past his face. Kolgrim exhaled, but still clung to Jorand, tight as a barnacle, his movements frantic. Jorand shoved the knife in once more, this time striking true. Kolgrim's flailing ceased.

Jorand let the body go, feeling it float away from him.

A bit of hoarded breath escaped his nostrils. The blackness disoriented him completely. He and Kolgrim had rolled and twisted so many times together, he had no clue which way led to the world of light and air and which way to the sea's depths.

He peeled out of his heavy boots, hoping natural buoyancy would bring him to the surface before his breath ran out. He had no sense of movement, either up or down. His ears ached, pounding in time with his quickening heartbeat.

He felt a tickle of bubbles sneak from the corners of his mouth and he tried to follow the direction of the precious drops of air as they tickled past his cheek. Little by little, his last breath leaked from him, and his lungs screamed for more.

He fought the urge to inhale.

There! Light ahead. It seemed to envelop him, wrapping him in warmth and shooting out of his toes and fingertips in rays of peace. The nagging pain in his ribs subsided and he felt strangely calm.

The last coherent thought swimming through his mind was that dying wasn't so bad after all.

CHAPTER THIRTY-SIX

Moira paced the small chamber but Brenna sat motionless, hugging her grief tight as a well-worn shawl. She watched wordlessly as Father Armaugh dipped his thumb in oil and smudged the sign of the cross on Jorand's still forehead. The priest removed his stole, kissed it reverently, and secreted the sign of his office in one of his capacious sleeves. He laid a thin hand on Brenna's shoulder.

"Your husband has had the blessing of Extreme Unction, my child. Be at peace," he said softly.

"Is there nothing more to be done?"

"There is but one thing ye can do." Armaugh sketched a benediction in the air before her. "Ye must leave Jorand in the arms of God."

The priest closed the door behind himself as he left Brenna to keep a silent vigil at her husband's side.

The battle between Thorkill's raiders and the Irish warriors disguised as virgins was over by the time Brenna saw Jorand's body rise in the moonlit waves beside the swaying ship. After Moira's guards managed to retrieve him, one of them thumped Jorand's back repeatedly, trying to drain the salty water from his lungs. Brenna felt a thready heartbeat beneath his breastbone and his chest rose and fell of its own accord, but his open eyes were unseeing. The rest of the fallen Norse were abandoned to the untender mercies of the sea, but at Moira's order, Jorand was bundled in a cloak and brought to the monastery on St. Patrick's island.

Even when Armaugh dug the arrow's tip from his side, Jorand didn't twitch a muscle.

Brenna took one of his hands and pressed it between hers. His fingers hung limp and cold as she clasped them. She traced the thin scar running across his palm, the token of their handfast. He'd wanted to remember her always. Brenna planted a soft kiss on the scar.

Father Armaugh had eased Jorand's eyelids closed, but they were tinged an unhealthy blue and a dark hollow lurked beneath each socket. Jorand's skin was pale and waxy. Brenna could see a tiny network of blue veins at his temple. Only the slight rise and fall of his chest betrayed the fact that he was a living man and not a prone statue carved of moonstone.

"Reminds me of when we first saw him washed up on Donegal's beach. Even now, Brennie," Moira said as she laid a hand on her sister's shoulder. "Even now, I think your Northman is the bonniest lad I've ever laid eyes on."

"Aye," Brenna said, not shifting her gaze from Jorand's motionless features. "And too late I learned he has a heart to match his fine face."

Moira pulled up a three-legged stool and plopped down beside her. "I wish it was that pox of a husband of mine lying there instead of Jorand. By Heaven, I do."

"Moira, ye can't mean it." Brenna looked at her sharply. "Something's wrong then. I did think it strange for Fearghus to send ye on to St. Patrick's, despite the danger, but I supposed it was so ye could still make your prayers for an heir. Has your husband mistreated ye, then?"

Moira's lips curved into a sad smile. "If ever Fearghus of Ulaid gets an heir by me, 'twill either be by a mortal sin on me soul or a miracle of immaculate conception. I've been married all these months and I'm yet a maid, sister. Fearghus is ... I have no idea what to even name him."

Moira stood and circled the room like a caged lynx. "Ye'd think I was a toothless crone the way he avoids me bed. But any child, boy or girl, under the age of ten isn't safe from his lechery."

Brenna pulled herself away from her own grief to feel a little of Moira's. "Leave him, then. No one would blame ye. Come home to Donegal with ..." She started to say *Jorand and me.* With a hollow ache, she realized she'd very likely be burying him on this tiny island. "Ye know Da would not hear of ye being treated so."

"I know he wouldn't. But do ye think I could break the peace me marriage guarantees between our clans?" Moira straightened her spine and blinked back her tears. "More Irishmen die fighting other Irishmen than die beating back Northmen. No, I'll not start a war over an empty bed. Why cover the land with widows and orphans? Anyway, as long as I'm there, at least I can protect the children at court as best as I may. Queen I am to the people of Ulaid, and a queen I'll be."

Brenna leaned over and hugged her little sister, realizing in their months of separation that Moira had changed. She was no longer a giddy girl with romantic notions of royalty and courtly love. Now she was a sad young woman, broken of heart, but not of spirit. Moira had indeed learned what it was to be a queen.

"I'm proud of ye, sister."

"Oh, Brennie, 'tis sorry I am to be burdening ye with me sorrow when ye've plenty of your own," Moira said. "I'll leave ye now, but remember I'll be close by should ye have need of me."

"I just don't know what to do." Brenna sank back down on the edge of Jorand's bed. "I've prayed till I can't see straight."

"Then don't pray. But let Jorand hear your voice," Moira said as she stepped softly to the door. "Mayhap his spirit will follow the sound of ye home."

The heavy oak door scuffed against the lintel and Moira was gone.

"Let him hear me voice," Brenna echoed. "Aye and what can I say to a man who's not here?"

The tiny weight in her belly fluttered for the first time in days. Even though she'd missed a couple of her courses, she'd been unsure, afraid only the difficulties of travel had thrown off her body's natural rhythm, afraid the slight quickening was only her imagination, afraid to hope. She felt the stirring again and finally knew for certain.

"Husband," she began softly. "I have something to tell ye. Even if ye are after leaving me, I'll have a bit of ye yet. Ye see, your child grows in me belly, Jorand,

and ..." Her voice broke at the thought of him never seeing the child of their love. "And I thank ye for the joy of the bairn. I'll make sure he knows of ye. He'll be a prince and a poet and a warrior. A son to make ye proud."

Another thought struck her and she rose to pace slowly, fingertips grazing tiny circles on her still flat belly. "Of course, the bairn may be a daughter, and if such be the case, I can only pray she takes her looks from her sire. I'll raise her to be a strong, fine woman. I know 'tis important to a man that his seed lives on and I want ye to know if ye—" Her breath caught in her throat and she bit her lip for a moment before she was able to continue. "Whatever happens, your line has not died on the earth."

Not an eyelash stirred on Jorand's still form.

Her throat constricted. Tears welled in her eyes. A sob fought its way free.

"Damn ye, Jorand. Do ye not care that ye leave me alone? Do ye not want to be here when your babe comes into the world?" She climbed into the bed with him and buried her face in his shoulder, shaking with grief. "Oh, ye wicked, wicked man! Do ye not know that my life will be a burden without ye? How can ye leave me when ye know that I love ye more than breathing?"

She sat up abruptly and cupped his face in her palms. "Open your eyes, ye *Finn-Gall* demon!"

His eyes rolled beneath their closed lids. Brenna gasped. A thin slit appeared in one of them and he peered up at her. He blinked twice, then winced at the light of the precious candle on the stand by his bed. Then he turned his gaze back to Brenna and she saw intelligence spark in their blue depths.

"Well, woman, when you ask that prettily, how can I refuse?" he asked in a voice hoarse from the sea.

"Oh, Jorand, ye've come back to me." She peppered his face with kisses then sat back abruptly and squinted at him. "Do ye know me then?"

"*Ja,* Brenna, I know you and I love you." he said, grasping her and pulling her down for a long kiss. "You don't think I'd forget my Irish princess, do you?" A serious expression erased his smile. "But I think you've got my name wrong."

"What?"

"Do you remember when I told you I was two men trapped in one skin?"

"Aye."

"I couldn't live with that, so I broke faith with Thorkill and the men of Dublin," Jorand said. "I've turned my back on my people for your sake, Brenna. That makes me an oath-breaker. Are you sure you still want me?"

She hugged him tight. "There'll never come a time when I don't want ye."

"Then Jorand the Northman is truly dead." He kissed her softly and pulled her in to snuggle next to him. "I guess you'd better call me Keefe."

"Aye, that I'll do." Her own handsome warrior home from the sea. His color was returning to normal and she felt his heart thumping solidly beneath her palm. "Welcome back to the land of the living then, Keefe Murphy. But I'll warn ye of one thing."

"What's that?"

She nipped at his earlobe. "If ye're after trying to die on me again, I'll never forgive ye."